BLACK DIAMOND

ALSO BY SUSANNAH SANDLIN

The Penton Legacy series

Redemption
Absolution
Omega
Storm Force (stand-alone spinoff)
Allegiance

The Collectors series

Lovely, Dark, and Deep
Deadly, Calm, and Cold

The Wilds of the Bayou Series

Wild Man's Curse

Written as Suzanne Johnson

Pirateship Down

The Sentinels of New Orleans series

Royal Street
River Road
Elysian Fields
Pirate's Alley
Belle Chasse

BLACK DIAMOND

A Wilds of the Bayou Novel

SUSANNAH SANDLIN

Montlake Romance

Text copyright © 2016 Suzanne Johnson
All rights reserved.

Published by Montlake Romance, Seattle

www.apub.com

Amazon, the Amazon logo, and Montlake Romance are trademarks of Amazon.com, Inc., or its affiliates.

ISBN-13: 9781503940413
ISBN-10: 1503940411

Cover design by Michael Rehder

Printed in the United States of America

PROLOGUE

Dave Grummond always thought that when he died—which should occur no time soon since he was only twenty-five—he would experience a visual reel of his life followed by a beckoning bright light. He was no saint, but he figured he had time to right his wrongs and settle his debts before Saint Peter welcomed him to his eternal resting place.

Instead, as sinew and muscle ripped from bone and consciousness faded, his last, fleeting thought was of the robot in that old movie *The Terminator*, specifically Schwarzenegger's glowing orange eyeballs. And there was no bright light that followed, just a black emptiness settling across his vision.

The day had started like most early March mornings in eastern Terrebonne Parish, Louisiana: damp and low forties, with a dense fog that shrouded the bayous and marsh. Within a couple of hours of sunrise, the chill would burn off and segue into an overcast day of about seventy-five degrees.

Not yet, though. He'd rolled out of bed at five thirty, sneaked out of the house without waking Rae, and stopped in the mudroom long enough to slip a dark-blue jacket over his lucky LSU sweatshirt and tug on heavy socks beneath his boots.

Saturdays needed rituals, and this was Dave's. He'd go out early and catch a mess of catfish or, if he was lucky and had the energy to take his twenty-foot vintage Carolina Skiff down the bayou, he'd show up by midafternoon with a cooler full of whatever finfish was in season. Then the gang would get together and have a fish fry or, if it was a bad fishing day, a big iron pot of rich gumbo filled with turtle meat or whatever was in the freezer. There was always good bounty to be had in the freezer.

Yesterday, however, he'd had business farther up in the parish, so he'd borrowed his brother's little fourteen-foot skiff, which he now maneuvered into the tangled, narrow waterways of Bayou Pointe-aux-Chenes, hoping to catch whatever he could find. Tonight, when all his buddies gathered, he'd pull out the engagement ring he'd bought on the installment plan for Rae. The last payment had laid waste to most of his Friday paycheck from the refinery, but he wanted to ask her tonight. He felt lucky.

Inside the left pocket of his jeans rested the tiny emerald-cut diamond ring nestled inside its velvet-lined box, the stone set in platinum. It was the most expensive thing he'd ever bought besides his boat.

He couldn't wait to see Rae's face fill with that look she gave him sometimes when she didn't think he was watching. That look was love, and anyone who said that was too sappy had never seen it.

Dave picked out an isolated branch of the mazelike bayou, sank some lines, and settled back to soak in the first warming rays of the morning sun. He'd fallen half asleep when a hard jolt against the right side of the boat almost tossed him off his seat.

"What the hell?" He slid fingers around the worn leather cushion of the single captain's chair behind the steering column, clenching his nails into the padding as the boat took another hit farther back, hard enough to turn the prow twenty or thirty degrees to the right and knock one of his three rods into the water.

Maybe he had drifted against a submerged cypress log; this wasn't an area he'd fished before. Then again, there was barely any current, so the boat shouldn't be moving this much.

A soft bump from underneath his feet again sent the vessel rocking gently from side to side. Dave jerked his gaze from one edge of the boat to the other, spotting nothing but a few bubbles. No way that had been a log.

Screw this. He could fish somewhere else; more than half the parish was bayou or lake or inlet. Nobody had to know he'd let himself get spooked by what was probably a damned turtle or even one of those hellacious gars that occasionally made their way this far south. Those fish could grow to ten feet long, could weigh three hundred pounds, and could easily pull a lone fisherman overboard. He wanted no part of a gar.

Leaning to the side, Dave reached forward and grasped the two remaining fishing rods, pulling them into the boat. He stood slowly, keeping an eye on the water, but froze at the sight of two round, hooded eyes rising above the bayou beside him, followed by a long, bony snout.

An alligator. He'd almost pissed himself over a damned stupid alligator. Probably a mama whose nest he'd accidentally approached.

Dave let out a whoosh of relieved breath, the air condensing in small puffs from his mouth. He needed to switch on the outboard and get his ass moving. When confronted with the size of an adult human, gators weren't aggressive animals unless you attacked first or disturbed a mother protecting her young. Lessons from Alligator 101—among the first things one learned growing up on the bayous of South Louisiana.

Dave had better things to do than fool with a mama gator.

A hard thrust to the side threw him off balance, and he fell toward the back of the boat. His right ear jammed hard into the underside of the outboard and stunned him for an instant, until the tickle of a dark streak of liquid on his cheek brought him around. He scraped a finger across his earlobe and it came away crimson.

"Damned gator. Son of a bitch! I'm leaving already." He staggered to his knees and reached for the key to turn on the motor, but was startled by the reappearance of the reptile, its head rising above the side of the boat a couple of feet from where Dave knelt. This was no mama alligator. It was a big bull, about twelve feet long judging by the length and girth of its head, and its jaw span was enormous. Dave had a close view since it chomped down on the side of the boat nearest to where he knelt, frozen in place. It clamped its teeth on the edge of the fiberglass and pulled the vessel downward.

Before he could counteract the sudden movement, he lost traction, propelled himself over the gator, and hit the bayou headfirst. Above him, through the churning cold water, he could sense the gator still wrestling with the edge of the boat.

Gators didn't get rabies, but this one was sure acting like it. He'd never heard of one behaving this way, unprovoked.

Limbs heavy with his waterlogged clothing and boots, he swiveled and floundered downstream. If he could get to the bank and crawl out, he'd buy some damned fish at the market and have a helluva story to tell tonight.

He glanced back when he felt the pressure of a nudge against his right calf. He wouldn't have thought it possible, but through the cold water and rising panic, he'd begun to sweat. The gator had left the boat behind and caught up with him, opening its wide jaws as it took another pass at Dave's leg.

No, you don't, damn it. He kicked the gator a glancing blow to the side of its snout and, seeing a heavy tree limb protruding from the bank in front of him, grabbed hold of it. He could pull himself ashore, hopefully sending the gator off to find a smaller, easier target that wouldn't kick it in the teeth.

With a growl and a lunge, the reptile used its powerful clawed feet to propel itself ahead of Dave and sink its teeth into his upper right arm. Dave tried to conjure up the alligator lore he'd heard his whole life. He thrust his legs at the gator's body, yelled when he could get his head above water, used his free left arm to punch at the animal's eyes.

Then it began to roll—the infamous alligator death roll. Dave struggled until he wasn't sure what was up or down. He wasn't sure when to take a breath or when to hold it. His face would meet cool air and by the time he'd sucked a half breath into his lungs, he'd roll underwater again.

Rae crossed his mind. Who'd take care of her, and how long would she have to wait, not knowing what had happened to him? How long until somebody found his body? What if they never found him? What if there was nothing left to find?

Then he saw his salvation—a quick glance, but enough to make him struggle harder. A boat had pulled up along the bayou opposite him, and someone was onboard.

"Help!" was all he managed on the next spin, and hope rose as the man held up a rifle, taking aim.

But no shot came, and Dave became vaguely aware in his graying vision that the man had put down his rifle and had begun puffing on a cigarette.

The scream when Dave's humerus pulled loose from its socket sounded as if it came from someone else, someone in a bayou far away. He and the pain became a single being. Its burn radiated to every bone and nerve ending until the alligator spun again and the sinew and muscle of Dave's right arm gave way. Then the world around him grew deep red as his blood mixed with the bayou mud and his screams became no more than harsh rasps.

The pain disappeared, which on some level Dave knew was a bad thing, and as he raised his head from the water to take a last, gasping breath, he looked into the smiling face of the man who wasn't going to save him. He looked just an instant, before a huge clawed foot swung toward his face—a foot whose bottom held a tiny, blinking orange light.

Then blackness.

CHAPTER 1

Mac saw the body first, which ticked off his partner. Not that finding bodies was ever a good thing, but Mac spotting it first told Jena she was still too much in her own head.

For the past few hours, Louisiana Department of Wildlife and Fisheries enforcement agents Jena Sinclair and McKenzie Griffin, aka Mac, had been motoring along the inlets, fishing camps, and launch areas that lined both sides of Bayou Pointe-aux-Chenes in eastern Terrebonne Parish. Other than issuing a couple of citations for fishing without a license and a few warnings to people without the proper number of life jackets, they hadn't come across much of interest.

Jena tossed a couple of ibuprofen into her mouth and washed the pills down with a sip from her bottle of water. She eased a hand into the left pocket of her uniform trousers and snagged another pill, this one only a quarter-inch long, pale green, and oval. She didn't slip the pill into her mouth until she was sure her partner was looking the other way. That, and the bandage around her left wrist, were things her partner didn't need to see. The vertical line of pink scars that marched along her left wrist had healed, but she covered them up anyway; they were nobody's business but hers.

The scars on her body, also still pink and fresh, were nobody's business either. The scars on her face, she could almost hide with makeup.

Besides, Mac wasn't her partner, not really, or at least she didn't think of him that way yet. He was the newest and youngest member of the six-person enforcement team covering Terrebonne Parish for the LDWF as part of Region 6. At twenty-five, Mac fancied himself a ladies' man, had moved here from some outpost of Northern Maine in search of adventure, and had earned his reputation as a motormouth. The guy liked to talk. She didn't know much more about him. But she was on "easy field duty," and that had earned her a stint partnering with Mac.

She took the ibuprofen for the aches caused by bouncing on the water in their sturdy, speedy patrol boat. The small dose of alprazolam, the antianxiety meds from which she had almost tapered off, had been prescribed for the residual pain from the toll taken on her psyche over the last six months. Two bullet wounds that had left her scarred inside and out, a horrible lapse in judgment that had almost gotten a civilian killed, and four months under the roof of her parents in New Orleans. All three had marked her.

Scars marked her face and body.

Scars marked her wrist.

Scars marked her soul.

She'd wanted to quit her job, feeling she'd failed her LDWF team, not to mention a whole division where women enforcement agents were seriously outnumbered—not only because of the physical demands but also, Jena suspected, because of the longstanding tradition of male game wardens. She had considered transferring to a quiet, isolated research lab and putting her wildlife forensics background to work. But the expensive—and wise—psychiatrist hired by her parents had urged her to get out of their house as soon as she could. He'd convinced her that she would never be at peace with what had happened until she returned to her job and the place she called home.

New Orleans was no longer that place. Her parents' home hadn't been that place in a long time. Not that they didn't love their kids, but warm and nurturing wasn't her parents' style.

Transferring to a forensics lab where she could dig around with dead things all day would have made her life easier, but her lieutenant in Terrebonne Parish had offered her a deal, even after she came clean about the suicide attempt. He'd had her tested and retested, and she had passed both times, making her officially *not* a risky head case. It had been a moment of weakness she deeply regretted, and her lieutenant, Warren Doucet, could see that. He was unwilling to let her go before she made a genuine attempt to rejoin the unit.

Come back to the Terrebonne Parish enforcement team and give it six months, Warren had proposed. Then, if she still wanted to transfer into forensics or research, he'd help clear the way. She'd agreed out of respect for him.

Riding on the water today, however, surrounded by the wide vistas of marsh grass punctuated by the few scrubby trees that so far had resisted hurricanes and saltwater intrusion from oil drilling, she realized Warren and the psychiatrist had both been right. This was what she loved—this flat patchwork of fragile land sinking slowly into the Gulf of Mexico. The job she did could help preserve it a few generations longer. Even if she couldn't save it, she could do her part with every littering citation, every water-related DUI, every poacher put out of business.

Jena wanted to stay with this team of agents, but she didn't ever want them to learn about her blackest day. The day where she'd given up, where she could see no happiness in her future, where an overly vigilant private nurse had found her bleeding out on one of her mother's immaculate white bathroom floor mats. She had begged the woman to let her die and was glad she'd been denied.

Rich parents could cover up a suicide attempt since the nurse had found her early and they could afford a shrink who made house calls. Money could hide anything. If she'd learned one overarching lesson growing up among the elite of uptown New Orleans, it was that when money talked, everyone else shut up.

"What're the pills?" Mac had been quiet for a while, but now he glanced over his shoulder from his post at the wheel of their water-patrol boat. His warm brown eyes—which still reflected every emotion that passed through his mind because he hadn't been field-hardened enough to turn them blank and inward—were cloaked by dark sunglasses. It left his face smooth and void of expression, just like that of any other law enforcement officer worth his training. Keeping the eyes neutral, especially with a partner, was a harder lesson to learn. "You still having pain from the gunshots?"

"Take off the sunglasses and I'll tell you." Jena cocked her head. "I can't talk to you with those pretty brown eyes covered up."

Jena had only been cleared from the purgatory of desk duty at regional headquarters in Thibodaux a week ago, and she didn't know Mac well enough to confide in him. Not yet. She trusted his training, which meant she felt confident that he'd have her back while they were on duty. Trusting him with her emotions and her mental and physical condition was another matter.

What she had learned in a few days, however, was that he could be distracted if his guard was down. Mac had already gotten a rep as the unit's playboy; he'd fall for flirtation every time, even when they both knew nothing would ever come of it.

Mac grinned and settled the glasses atop his LDWF baseball cap. "Can't resist my sex appeal, eh?"

He was so easy. "You sound like a Canadian, Mac, or somebody from Maine. Folks around here don't end sentences with 'eh.' Ever."

The jester's façade dropped a moment, giving her a glimpse of uncertainty that was quickly replaced by what appeared to be genuine concern. "I just want to make sure you're okay. The lieutenant told me he advised you not to go on patrol for another couple of weeks, even though he eventually agreed to it. And Gentry said he'd beat my ass till

I couldn't walk if I didn't keep an eye on you." He paused. "I'd like to say Gentry isn't capable of beating my ass, but we both know better."

"I'm okay—really. It was just ibuprofen." She smiled and, for the first time in months, it didn't feel forced. She was embarrassed, though. Not only had she been put on junior fishing-license patrol, but everyone was watching her like sharp-eyed cormorants looking for the slightest splash from a fish. First her division lieutenant and now her former partner, Gentry Broussard.

She had probably returned to work too soon, but given the circumstances, it had been the right thing to do. She hadn't asked to return to fieldwork until she knew she was ready, and the lieutenant had eventually acknowledged that. It didn't mean he wasn't watching, or that Gentry and the others weren't going to worry about her. She just had to make it work, even if it meant being treated like a china doll for a while, until something happened that would let her prove she was ready to be back.

For now, though, she wouldn't complain about pulling light duty with Mac because it was what the lieutenant was comfortable letting her do. She and her new partner had spent hour after hour this week checking fishing licenses and making sure no one was catching more red drum than the regulations allowed. They handed out life jackets when people forgot them, and issued DUIs and other citations to beer-swilling yahoos who thought it was okay to tear up private land with unlicensed ATVs.

Teenage boys found the combination of mud and big tires almost as irresistible as sex. Probably because it was not as scary and was a lot easier to get for a fifteen-year-old.

The rest of the enforcement agents, including her temporary replacement, an agent named EZ on loan from Lafourche Parish, had been pulled into an interdepartmental drug case headed by the US Drug Enforcement Administration. It was the biggest story to hit Terrebonne since the string of murders last fall, fueled by some new synthetic drug from China that seemed to be flowing into the parish with deadly results.

Diamant Noir, or Black Diamond, was one of those drugs sold legally over the counter as an energy booster until people began dying from it. The state had finally banned its sale, and its usage had waned—except in Terrebonne Parish the last two months. Now, it seemed to be everywhere.

And yet here she rode along the isolated Bayou Pointe-aux-Chenes beside Highway 665, waiting for someone to cruise by with an out-of-date registration decal.

She tamped down the pang of jealousy, reminding herself again that she didn't need too much stress in her life yet, not after last September. And September turned her mind to Celestine Savoie. Jena hadn't been the only one hurt by the choices she'd made during last fall's chaos. She hadn't seen Ceelie in a while and missed the friendship they'd formed. Jena liked the guys she worked with, but women needed friendships with other women. As soon as she got a chance, she needed some girl time.

In the meantime, she'd serve on fish patrol, and she'd darn well enjoy it.

Except nobody was fishing today, at least not here in the nooks and crannies of this bayou that ran near the western edge of the Pointe-aux-Chenes Wildlife Management Area, not far from the Lafourche Parish line. Wednesday had fallen dreary and gray, and rain clouds boiled up from the south.

Her quiet contemplation had even turned Motormouth Mac silent as he maneuvered the patrol boat around a turn and into a narrow branch of the bayou made gloomier by the overgrown marsh grass on either side. It swayed in the rising wind, reaching higher than Jena's head before the water tapered off to what looked like a dead end and a short row of houses a half mile or so ahead.

She stood up so she could see over the mounds of grass. Who the hell would want to live out here? Talk about isolated.

Mac glanced back at her. "See anything?"

"Only a few houses; this inlet dead-ends just ahead." Jena's height gave her an advantage at lookout duty. At almost six feet, with shoulder-length, dark-red hair, she had earned her LDWF nicknames: Stringbean, Stretch, Agent Amazon, Red.

Make that her former nicknames. She'd fallen out of the nickname league since she'd been shot and come back with her face splotched by irregular, fading scars from the glass of a shot-out truck window. Her life had become a world filled with pity and eggshells nobody wanted to step on. But she'd survive. If she'd learned nothing else from the last few months, it was that she was a survivor.

"Hey, Sinclair! Looks like somebody lost his pants." Mac, at least, was consistently cheerful. "Wonder what he was up to for that to hap—oh, shit."

He trailed off about the time she saw the muddy jeans snagged onto a branch near the bank to their left and realized there was a boot protruding from one of the legs. Or part of a boot. Or a foot turned in a direction a human foot had never been intended to turn.

She frowned. "Nobody ever found the Grummond guy that went missing on Saturday, did they?" For a couple of shifts, she and Mac had joined the search-and-rescue teams that had mostly covered areas way down the bayous and branches southwest of here, where his girl-friend said he usually fished. The man had disappeared without a trace. Nobody had looked this far north and east.

"No, but I got a bad feeling we just did. Looks like there might be a partially submerged boat trapped in some grass farther upstream that fits the description of his ride." Mac eased the patrol boat toward the jeans, then killed the engine so they could edge in as close as possible without destroying or dislodging any evidence.

Jena moved to the front of the boat ahead of Mac as he nudged the vessel against the nearest end of the log. The body was distended and swollen from three days in the water, but the cold water temperatures had helped preserve what hadn't been nibbled on and had kept the winter-lazy gators from feasting on the rest of him. It was definitely a young, dark-haired male in jeans and a jacket, which also fit the description of the missing Dave Grummond.

"I'll call it in." Jena reached for the radio transmitter on the collar of her dark-green uniform, then thought better of it and grabbed her mobile phone instead, walking the length of the boat and leaving Mac to watch over the body. No way to keep anything quiet using the radio.

"I need to talk to Warren," she told Stella after her first call to the lieutenant's mobile phone went to voice mail. Warren's recently retired aunt, a former dispatcher for the Terrebonne Parish Sheriff's Office, handled calls from the office in Warren's house most days, just to stay busy. The district office was farther north, in Thibodaux, so Warren's home office passed for unofficial parish headquarters. "I think we found the fisherman that went missing last weekend."

"You need an ambulance?" Stella's heavy parish accent made *ambulance* rhyme with *pants*. "Warren's in a meeting with Sheriff Brown. You want I should disturb 'em?"

Jena sighed and tried to avoid the dead man's open-eyed stare, visible from just under the waterline. "This man's beyond the need of EMS. Call it in to the sheriff's office, though, and the medical examiner. Let them decide who to send. They'll want to collect evidence and make the final call, but it looks like a gator attack to me."

Which was weird. Gators weren't prone to attack humans. Their first option was usually to swim away and avoid contact. But there had been four water deaths since January scattered around the eastern side of the parish, all attributed to alligators. This was the second here on Bayou Pointe-aux-Chenes, and there had been a couple less than a mile away in Lafourche Parish as well.

After giving Stella their location for the sheriff's office, Jena joined Mac at the front of the boat. He stood with his arms crossed, his gaze fixed on the body.

"This your first one?" she asked. Mac was only five years her junior, but right now he looked like a pale teenager. A wave of guilt washed over her at the realization that, upon finding a man's body, she felt more alive than at any time since returning to Terrebonne. Finding this poor guy's remains had finally jolted her out of her massive self-pity wallow.

It was a wake-up call. She was here to do a job, and that job wasn't about Jena Sinclair. The time for navel-gazing had passed.

"First time I've seen a body in the water like this," Mac said. "If it was an alligator, it must've been a big one. Bit the poor guy's arm completely off at the shoulder."

"Worse than bitten off," Jena reminded him. They'd all had basic training dealing with alligators, considering the state's gator population was estimated at about 1.5 million. "Twisted off."

Mac blinked. "Yeah, right. Gators bite down, lock their jaws, and then roll until whatever they've bitten down on rips off. That is a hell of a nasty way to die."

Jena leaned over to take a closer look, avoiding Dave Grummond's face. "I think his foot's gone too."

"Maybe half of it," Mac said. "Or maybe the whole thing is just turned the wrong way, under the water." He barely got the words out before he lunged toward the back of the boat and retched into one of the empty coolers they kept for confiscated fish. Jena wasn't surprised; he'd been turning greener by the second.

She gave him a wry smile when he returned to stand beside her, guzzling a bottle of water. He kept his back to the body. The smell was starting to churn her morning oatmeal around in her stomach as well. "Feel better? I wish I could tell you it got easier, but it doesn't."

Louisiana Wildlife and Fisheries took the lead for the state in water search and rescue, and Terrebonne Parish was almost half water. Sooner or later, it was inevitable that Mac would see something ugly.

"Hey, Sinclair." He turned to look at her, trying to give her a flirtatious grin but failing. Jena smiled at him; his pale-green skin told her another trip to the cooler might be pending. "Could you, like, you know, not mention to anybody what just happened?"

Her smile widened. "You mean like if anybody asks who barfed in our fish cooler?"

His face turned the color of the ugly dress her parents had bought for one of her Mardi Gras balls in New Orleans—her father was an officer in the Krewe of Rex, King of Carnival. The dress was a dark, sickly pink that clashed with her hair and had a lot of chiffon with sparkles in it. That particular bit of fashion-backward nastiness still hung in a closet in the room of her parents' uptown mansion, a few feet away from the bathroom where she'd so carefully arranged herself before making neat vertical slices in her wrist with a razor-edged utility knife, the closest sharp thing she could find.

What had she been thinking?

So she patted his arm. "Don't worry. We'll ditch the cooler and never mention it again. Remind me to tell you about the time I puked all over a crime scene when I was with NOPD."

Life had seemed so simple then.

CHAPTER 2

An hour later, Jena yawned while waiting for a red light to change. She was again driving her own LDWF truck, back in the community of Chauvin, and headed for home.

No, headed for her house.

No, headed for *the* house. It was hers, technically, but it wasn't home.

While she'd been stoned on painkillers and suffering the controlling attention of her parents and the New Orleans physicians paid well for her private care, her father—make that Jackson Sinclair Sr., senior partner of the most powerful law firm in New Orleans—had moved into action as soon as the psychiatrist told him Jena needed to get back to her life and her job. Dad had taken it upon himself to pay off the lease on her little apartment in Houma, buy a house in her name in Chauvin, and install her younger brother, Jackson, as a roommate-slash-babysitter. Of course, he filled her in on the plan after the fact.

Her cat, Boudreaux, had been hiding under her bed ever since, making only quiet nocturnal visits to the cat bowl and litter box.

Jena loved Chauvin, as she loved most of Terrebonne Parish, but she hated the house because it was garish and looked like nothing she'd ever buy for herself. She wanted to paint it red and put flamingo statues in the yard to liven it up and make it look as if real people lived here rather than nouveau-riche idiots.

She also loved Jackson, but she didn't want to live with him. He was a laid-back, computer-wiz pothead that her father hadn't yet given up on brainwashing. Dad considered Jena a lost cause, or at least that's how she interpreted the house. He had given in to the inevitable, but he still wouldn't have his daughter living in a cheap Houma efficiency apartment. The deed to a house was Dad's equivalent of a hug and a peck on the cheek, and she could appreciate that. She just wished he'd asked for her input instead of handing it to her as a done deal. Then again, at least she had a place to go that didn't require driving all the way back into Houma.

Turning off the parish highway into a broad drive lined by tupelos and live oaks, Jena ground her teeth, waiting for the white columns of the house to come into view. They stretched across a wide, raised verandah like freaking Tara in *Gone with the Wind*. What kind of person would build such a house in a hurricane-prone, flood-prone, working-class community like Chauvin, Louisiana, population about three thousand on a good day?

The short answer: some unlucky dude whose business had gone belly-up when the 2010 oil spill almost destroyed the state's fishing industry and a series of hurricanes had driven storm surge high into the parish, flooding people out. Dad had probably been able to pick it up for a song. Why her brother Jacks had been thrown into the deal, she wasn't sure.

Like most homes in the parish, the house was raised, with storage on the bottom level tucked behind twin stone staircases that rose to the verandah. Jackson Jr. had dubbed the house the White Rhino because it was more rampaging than a White Elephant. And it was definitely white—a pristine white that practically glowed in the dark even on a night like tonight, when fog was setting in early.

The frantic thump of some insult to music, recorded by a rapper whose name Jena didn't know, vibrated the first-floor windows. She felt in the pocket of her jacket to make sure the ibuprofen was close at hand.

Jackson had always marched slightly left of center, but this wasn't his normal taste in music, which meant he probably had company. The kid—although at twenty-four he was hardly a kid anymore—had a genius for computers but no ambition to do anything with his talent except design elaborate costumes for cosplayers, which he then gave away. He was more socially outgoing than his reserved older sister, a trait she envied, but his lack of interest in crafting a future for himself annoyed Jena almost as much as it did their parents, not that she'd ever admit it.

She fumbled with her keys, distracted by the bright lights coming from behind the house, lighting up the sky like a rotating spotlight at a Vegas show. The White Rhino sat in the middle of a large tract of solid land—itself a novelty in water-bound Chauvin—so Jackson must have turned on all the lights around the backyard aboveground pool, nestled inside a natural wood deck that encircled it. Jena would have to talk to him about his electrical excess. Jacks wasn't the one paying the utilities on this behemoth of a house, and neither was Dad. She made a good salary, but not that good.

She set her pack inside the front door, removed her department-issued SIG Sauer from its holster, and locked it inside the foyer desk drawer. She had just unfastened the buckle to release her heavy uniform utility belt when she glanced up, looked out the living room windows that stretched across the back of the house, and froze.

Whereas Jena was tall, slender, ivory skinned, and red haired like her mother, Jackson was shorter, well built but more compact, and dark haired like their father. And every inch of him was on display, upside down, as he walked on his hands across the top of the concrete wall at the back of the property, naked as the day he was born—a day Jena remembered well because she'd been allowed to skip school.

God, I'll never be able to unsee that. Jena marched across the living room, which opened poolside, and shut off the music. Its sudden absence filled the house with a heavy silence that itself was almost audible.

"Shit, what're you doing?" Startled, Jackson lost his balance in the middle of what might have been a naked cartwheel, although Jena was doing her best not to look. She did glance around long enough to watch him tumble headfirst into a row of carefully manicured crape myrtle trees that had already been trimmed back into short spikes to prepare them for spring blooms. "Ow!"

Served the little weasel right. Jena turned her back as he maneuvered himself out of the trees. When he rounded across the lawn and into her line of sight, he'd pulled on a pair of shorts. Bloody red scratches crossed his arms and chest where the tree branches had made their mark.

Too bad. Jena had to get Jacks under control or throw him out. He'd been either sitting on his ass or off somewhere "getting to know the locals" since he'd arrived. He had to get a job. Better yet, he could move back to New Orleans and live with Parents Dearest, who must've had an ulterior motive for sending him here. They'd never endorsed laziness from either of their kids. He needed to come clean or go home.

She took a few steps closer to tell him exactly that. "What the hell do you think . . ." A good look at Jackson's eyes stopped her tirade before she got wound up. His blue eyes looked black, with pupils the size of Mardi Gras doubloons. "What are you on?"

Not pot. He would have had to smoke enough marijuana to be unconscious before he could get that kind of physical reaction, and she didn't smell any. He sure as hell would not be doing naked cartwheels atop a brick privacy wall from a few tokes of marijuana.

She left him standing there, frowning and trying to focus, and went in search of her own answers. She strode through the living room and opened the bedroom door down the hallway of his wing of the house. A Category 5 hurricane might have blown through his bedroom and done less damage than the mess he'd made in the last month.

"C'mon, Jena." Jackson had finally found his tongue. "It's no worse than those generic Xanax you pop every day. At least I didn't drag a sharp art tool across my veins."

She rounded on him, concern morphing to fury. "Don't *ever* mention that in front of me again." She took a deep breath, bringing her anger under control. "Show me what you took."

Jackson shoved her out of the way hard enough to knock her off balance. She landed on the floor atop a pile of dirty clothes, papers, and graphic novels. He looked down at her for a few seconds, the war that raged inside him visible in his trembling lips and his clenched jaw. She could practically see it through his skin: the little brother she loved wanted to apologize and help her up; the tanked-up lunatic he'd suddenly become wanted her to suffer and maybe was considering even doling out more punishment. She froze in place, silent, waiting to see which Jacks would win the battle.

Instead, he turned and stalked out of the room. The front door slammed and, outside, a few seconds later, tires squealed. She supposed he was off to get acquainted with more locals and whatever they were selling.

Jena sat up slowly, her bones aching like an arthritic octogenarian. She undid the top three or four buttons on her uniform shirt and pulled it aside, wincing at even that small movement. The gunshot wound on the underside of her left breast had left a round, puckered scar, thanks to all the soft-tissue damage done by the bullet and the surgery to remove it. The scar might be redder than what passed for normal these days, but nothing was bleeding. The gunshot wound located lower on her abdomen, the one that had done the worst internal damage, was smaller, round, and not as red.

Nothing had been visibly worsened by the fall, but she'd need to take it easy—maybe take one of the hydrocodone pills she still had left in a bottle in a kitchen drawer so she'd be able to sleep.

No, scratch that. She was on duty tomorrow and didn't need a drug hangover. Besides, she hated the way they made her feel.

She rebuttoned her shirt and looked around for something to hold on to while she leveraged herself back to her feet. Under the corner of the heavy white-painted oak dresser her mother had purchased to furnish this bedroom, she spotted a small plastic sandwich bag, the type that had the built-in zipper closure. Jackson's pot stash, damn it.

She snatched it up before using the corner of the dresser to drag herself upright, then looked down at the sandwich bag. Her heartbeat grew more erratic as she realized the small plastic bag contained not marijuana but a few teaspoons of black powder. It could've been a coarsely ground black pepper, but Jena feared it wasn't nearly as innocuous. Or maybe she was wrong. She prayed she was wrong, because she'd seen a drug that looked like this in a briefing in Thibodaux only a few days ago.

Jena opened the bag and touched a cold, shaky finger to her tongue, then touched the powder, praying that whatever this stuff tasted like, it wasn't anise. Black licorice was the signature taste of Black Diamond. Law enforcement officers who'd encountered the drug called it BSC—batshit crazy—because that was the effect it seemed to have on most who took it.

Jackson drove her nuts, but Jena loved him. She didn't know what to do if he'd gotten his hands on Black Diamond except turn him in and hope she could keep him away from doing any more of this stuff. It was said to have a greater addiction rate than heroin and meth combined, similar to the "Devil's Drug," flakka, that had been plaguing South Florida.

Could Jena turn in her own brother? The right answer wasn't easy, but it was clear. She had to. In good conscience, she couldn't send him back to New Orleans and sweep the whole thing out of her life without trying to get through to him. And she sure couldn't let him stay here, where he obviously had access.

Then again, maybe it wasn't Black Diamond at all. Only one way to know.

Jena touched her finger to her tongue and immediately spit the contents back out into her hand. She might as well have bitten into a black jelly bean.

Now what?

She returned to the central part of the house and tucked the plastic bag into the locked drawer in the foyer, taking out her SIG Sauer. Deep inside, she didn't think Jackson would come back into the house and hurt her. But the gun was sleeping with her tonight anyway.

If she slept at all.

She walked into the spotless white-tiled kitchen with its pale-gray granite countertops and glass-paned white cabinets, and pulled a bottle of wine from the fridge. A wave of dizziness hit her, and she thought better of it. She'd taken the ibuprofen and alprazolam earlier, plus she'd just fallen. Who knows—could that tiny taste of the drug have had an effect on her?

No point in taking chances, and seeing Jacks's dilated pupils had convinced her: she didn't need drugs in this house. She no longer needed them, and Jacks sure didn't need to add painkillers to his drug cocktail. She grabbed a bottle of water instead, pulled one of the stools to the kitchen's large island, and sat. From the junk drawer, she removed the bottle containing the rest of her hydrocodone prescription, then took a knife and crushed each one. Finally, she poured the mound of ground powder into the trash. She didn't want to flush the drugs or wash them down the drain where they'd enter the water supply. While she was at it, she did the same to the remaining antianxiety meds.

She'd keep the ibuprofen.

Jena had to talk to someone about Jacks, and it had to be someone she trusted on a personal level. He might not be her partner at the moment, but senior agent Gentry Broussard was still number two on her speed-dial list, right behind her lieutenant. Gentry was honest and, because he'd made his own share of mistakes, nonjudgmental.

He answered on the second ring, and in the background, Jena could make out shouts of "two more Bud Lights" and "wings and sauce on table three."

Damn. It must be his night off. Since the DEA investigation had begun, and she'd spent that month on desk duty in Thibodaux, she'd lost track of everybody's schedules.

"Sinclair? Is that you?"

Jena shook her head, trying to clear the cobwebs and what-ifs spun from fatigue and fear. "Hey, Gentry, sorry, I forgot it was your night off. This can wait."

"I'm just hanging out with Ceelie and Mac. Tell me what's up."

Jena closed her eyes. *This isn't selling Jacks out. This is* for *Jacks.*

"I found some drugs in the house, in my brother's room. I think it might be Black Diamond."

During a brief pause, exuberant voices filled the line. Gentry's tone, when he finally spoke, was nowhere near exuberant. More like downright terse.

"Is he there now?"

Jena took a deep breath. "No, he just stormed out of here. He was acting crazy." BSC. Batshit crazy.

"I'm on my way."

CHAPTER 3

Cole Ryan stepped out the back door of his solid early-century wooden house at the end of a dirt road optimistically named Sugarcane Lane, taking in the thick, cool air of morning. He still wasn't sure Sugarcane Lane was an official name since the street sign had been painted by hand. The "lane," only a block long, sat behind the back edge of a couple of no-longer-viable sugarcane fields the size of football fields and at the dead end of an inlet off Bayou Pointe-aux-Chenes in eastern Terrebonne Parish.

He'd found the place almost five years ago, although it might as well have been a thousand. Big blocks of time like months and years had ceased to have much meaning in Cole's quiet days and quieter nights. Now, he was guided by the hours and days and seasons as revealed to him by nature.

The little one-bedroom house met his needs. It had been cheap. Nothing had been wrong with it that he couldn't fix himself. It was private. Only one other house on the lane was occupied, thanks to those who'd eventually been run to higher ground by frequent flooding or moved to greener pastures by the disappearing need for manual labor in sugarcane harvesting. He didn't know the couple who lived catty-cornered across the lane but figured them to be people who had their own pasts and their own secrets. They stayed in their place, and he stayed in his.

Cole was aware he'd become known as The Hermit by his female neighbor, who was likely both Catholic and highly superstitious—a common combination of beliefs in this land at the bottom of the United States. He'd never even seen her husband, only the hairball on legs she called a dog. She yelled at both in equal measure. The husband was Ron; the dog was Chewbacca.

Cole didn't figure there was much difference between a formal religion like Catholicism and superstition. At least not anymore. He'd given up on God about the time God gave up on him. They were even.

He took a deep breath of damp morning air and could tell it was going to be a hot one. Might hit eighty for a few days before a big front moved through and cooled things down again.

He wanted to get some fish in the cooler before noon, maybe enough to smoke and take out with him into the bayous for two or three weeks. The water and overgrown cane fields always made him claustrophobic by the time winter was done.

Cole pulled on the muddy boots he'd left sitting on the back stoop, and it was then that he saw the alligator. He had no issues with gators. They'd usually leave people alone unless some damned fool had been feeding them, in which case they'd keep coming back in search of an easy snack until they had to be caught and relocated or some gun-happy imbecile killed them.

He respected alligators. They weren't afraid to show their teeth when backed up against the wall, and they were survivors. Except maybe this one.

This guy—a big gator, maybe eleven or twelve feet long with a broad, thick head—wasn't moving. It lay at the water's edge, between Cole's house and the spot where he tied off his small hand-carved pirogue.

He sighed and went back into the house, pulling his shotgun off its rack inside the back door. Hopefully, he could just scare the damned thing away if it didn't run when it saw him. Cole liked gator meat as well as the next guy out here in the wilds, but the state had a one-month gator-hunting season and this wasn't it. The rest of the year, the once-endangered animals were off-limits. The last thing he wanted was a state wildlife agent sniffing around and getting in his business for something like killing a gator out of season.

He was off society's radar and had no intention of changing that.

Only this gator wasn't going to be frightened away; it was already dead. Cole nudged it with his boot a couple of times to make sure, then knelt beside it and slipped a hand on the softer flesh underneath its bony head. Judging by its body temperature, it hadn't been dead long.

He hadn't killed the thing, so he technically wasn't breaking any laws by keeping it—at least he didn't think so. He could freeze or cure the meat and sell the hide and bones to one of the local processors. He didn't really need the money, but no sense in throwing it away either. He respected what the gator's life could represent to whoever found it. No death should be meaningless, human or animal.

Looking around to make sure no fishermen were visible and his neighbor's yappy dog hadn't wandered too close, Cole wrapped strong hands around the gator's tail and pulled it slowly into the square cinder-block building behind the house—the workhouse, as Cole called the structure he'd erected himself four years ago. The reptile easily weighed three hundred pounds or more, so by the time Cole got it inside, he'd broken out in a clammy, cold sweat.

Scratch the fishing trip; taking care of the gator would have to be his first priority today. And maybe tomorrow. Fully dressing a gator this size would take a while.

He searched the body for a clue as to what killed it. Bull gators didn't crawl into the mud to die as they sensed death approaching, and they could live to a ripe old age of fifty. They grew about a foot a year their first decade before growth slowed, so it was hard to gauge this gator's age. Maybe as young as fifteen, maybe as old as forty. Often, weak gators got attacked and eaten by other gators. As a carnivorous species, they weren't too picky when it came to diet, and if another, weaker gator was hanging around at dinnertime? Oh well.

But this gator didn't look weak, nor could Cole find any indication that it had been shot. If he couldn't find a hook in its gullet, he'd have to scrap the whole idea. Eating bad meat out of season could not only bring him onto the wildlife agents' radar, but onto the medical establishment's. Health insurance wasn't as high on his list of priorities as staying healthy.

Since moving to Terrebonne Parish five years ago, Cole had lived his own life on his own terms. He lived it alone. That had been his choice regarding how to deal with the hand life had dealt him. No regrets.

There was only one way to know for sure about the gator. Cole relished the burn in his thigh and shoulder muscles, and the strain of his biceps, as he took hold of the massive head, dragged the alligator onto his wooden cutting table on wheels, and rolled the reptile onto its back. He worked hard to stay in shape and keep his body running like the machine it was. If only he could keep his head running like his body—a reliable, well-made bit of mastery—but he found his brain a much harder machine to master. Most days, it ran more like a rusty bicycle wheel with a warped rim.

The hard, bony plate of the gator's skull had hit the table with a resounding crack when he turned it over, and Cole waited a few moments before proceeding. The noise didn't seem to have aroused any attention from neighbor or dog.

From the shelf beneath the table, he pulled out a one-by-two-foot length of tanned leather and unrolled it to reveal a dozen steel knives of different sizes, weights, and edges, each attached to the leather by a hand-sewn strap.

Removing the largest serrated blade from the set, he ran it across a honing rod a few times and set to work. The gator had been dead even less time than Cole had originally thought; its guts steamed in the cool air when he reached in gloved hands to remove them and throw them into an old blue plastic bin sitting beside the table. He didn't look at them—bad enough just to smell them.

Damn, but this thing reeked.

Cole used the knife to expertly finish splaying open the belly of the gator, then stopped to examine what was left. The meat was pink and firm. Nothing looked diseased or smelled worse than any other gator did. They were all on the aromatic side.

Cole opened the commercial walk-in combo cooler-freezer at the back of the workhouse and cleared some space on the cooler floor. Other than the house and the land, this refrigeration-and-freezer unit was one of the biggest purchases he'd made since moving here, especially if you factored in the cost of running an electric line to the workhouse.

He rolled the worktable inside, left the gator, and locked the door behind him when he came back out. Next thing he had to do was dispose of the guts before the smell of decomposed food—whatever the hell that gator had eaten—attracted some of its family members in search of a snack. From a gator's point of view, the more rotten the meat, the better it tasted. But he hadn't found a treble hook in the gator's gullet to have caused its death. Unless he found one in the stomach, he couldn't risk eating the meat and would have to settle for selling the hide.

Only one way to find out how this big boy had died.

He grabbed the handle of the bin and dragged it down to the small dock, then slid it into his pirogue. By the time Cole dug out a pair of heavy rubber gloves and joined the gator guts in the boat, the pirogue sat low in the water. It was slow going as he used a heavy pole to propel himself up the branch toward Bayou Pointe-aux-Chenes and northward along the bank.

After about twenty minutes of poling, Cole tied off the boat to the trunk of a spindly husk of an oak tree that hung over the water, and used a handkerchief from his back pocket to wipe the sweat off his forehead and the back of his neck. The air around him had already grown hotter and, as always here, thick and humid.

From his other pocket, he pulled a makeshift headband-cum-scarf, unrolled it, and used it to tie back his long hair, some of the thick blond strands woven into braids. It almost reached his waist now. Then he wrapped the whole thing around his forehead, turban style, and tucked in the ends.

It would keep the worst of the sun off his face and let some air hit his neck. If anyone saw a blond-haired, blue-eyed man with a turban of braids, well, it would only add to his reputation as a crazy hermit and keep them away.

Cole kept himself clean, but he had no use for barbershops or people. He kept thinking he'd use one of his knives and cut his hair off one of these days, but so far, that day hadn't come. In a way, he guessed it had come to symbolize his determination to play by his own rules and stay in his own sandbox. Its length was his measure of the passage of time.

He pulled on a pair of fresh plastic gloves and hauled the noxious bin onto the bank, then dragged it inland ten or twenty yards until it was in thick marshland—real land, not the deceptively soft marsh grass beds or flotons that might as well be quicksand.

Returning to the boat, he procured a short shovel, traced his steps back to the area next to the bin, and dug until the burn in his shoulders and upper back became almost unbearable. Once the hole was deep enough, Cole buried the entire bin inside it. He was pretty sure that the bin had no usable life after hauling this foul-smelling shit, so no point in taking it home.

First, however, he needed to feel around in its stinky contents and determine if there was anything in the guts to make him think the gator wasn't edible. Hopefully, he'd find the treble hook and all would be safe.

He made sure his elbow-length rubber gloves were firmly on and had no holes, then eased his hands into the mass of blood and gore. He held them there for only a few seconds before jerking them back out, his traitorous mind filled with scenes of blood and horror, shiny glass shards like jewels in a sea of crimson blood spread across a tile floor.

Stop being a pussy, Coleman Ryan. It's an alligator, not her. Not them.

He clenched his jaw muscles and forced himself to put both hands into the gory mess and stopped again—not because of a flashback this time, but because he felt something out of place.

Against the protest of his nostrils, he leaned over to look at what he was feeling. When he'd removed the intestines and stomach from the animal, he'd scooped them out in one big handful, but now, he saw the stomach more clearly and it was distended in an odd shape. What in the hell had that gator eaten?

Damn it. Cole pulled a sharp, medium-length blade from the sheath hung onto his belt and tried to avoid inhaling while he slit open the stomach. What he saw sent him staggering a few feet away. He had to process it before he could look again, but processing it wasn't easy. He dropped to his knees and fought the urge to barf up his breakfast.

Other unrelated scenes flashed through his mind. Blood, so much blood. Pooled on a tile floor. Soaked into carpet. Covering two hands clutched together.

Back in the present, Ryan.

He wasn't squeamish, but he was careful to prepare when he knew there was a chance the flashbacks would hit him. The gator stomach had caught him unawares.

Taking a deep gulp of fresh air, Cole maneuvered part of the makeshift head wrap around so that it covered his nose and mouth, got to his feet, and reluctantly faced what he'd found.

It was a human arm, with a watch still attached to what was left of the wrist. The flesh had come about three-quarters off the bone, probably dissolved by the powerful acids in the gator's stomach. Shreds of a couple of layers of clothing surrounded it. Thanks to the clothing, as well as the cool water and sluggish nature of the gator's digestive system this time of year, the arm was better preserved than it would've been if the attack had happened during the summer or fall. Plus, gators didn't chew their food if they could swallow it whole, so the limb was still fairly intact.

Closing his eyes, Cole reached his gloved hand beneath the arm to make sure there were no other surprise snacks in the gator's system. He pulled out a mostly disintegrated frog, a bit of Styrofoam, and a zippered sandwich bag containing something that looked like black pepper, probably lost or thrown off some litterbug's boat.

Finally, however, he found his quarry: a three-pronged snare known as a treble hook, lodged firmly in the wall of the gator's upper stomach. So Mr. Gator had already been dying from the hook even as he swallowed his final meal of a tasty human arm. That meant he should be safe to cure and eat, although Cole's taste for gator had dulled in the last few minutes.

He sat back on his heels, pondering his next move. The right thing? That was an easy call. He'd drive his old red pickup up the highway toward Chauvin and phone the sheriff or the game wardens' office since he didn't own a phone and didn't plan to. He could be a responsible citizen, whatever the hell that meant these days. In return, he'd probably be blamed for killing the gator. God knew how the arm would figure into things.

Cole wanted none of that bullshit. It wasn't like the arm was of any use to whoever had lost it, although he hoped the poor son of a bitch had survived. At this point, turning it over to the cops wouldn't help anything. Wasn't like they could arrest the gator, so they might go after him instead.

Done deal.

Cole recovered the bin, set it in the hole, then looked down at the gloves, thinking. He wanted no fingerprints pulled from inside them just in case this whole cluster was ever found, so he threw them aside until the hole had been filled and tightly packed down with muddy soil. Then he took the gloves, walked about twenty feet east, and cleared a spot of leaves and loose dirt. Again he dug, but not so deep. With the gloves inside the hole, he retrieved a match from the boat and set them afire. The burning yellow rubber smelled almost as bad as the gator and sent up small puffs of black-tar-scented smoke. Once they were charred, he refilled the hole with mud and packed it down.

Now he just needed to get home and get the gator cut up, cured, and ready to freeze. The animal's death wouldn't be a total waste.

He couldn't say as much for the poor guy who'd lost his arm.

CHAPTER 4

Damn, but the last twenty-four hours had been spent in lunatic city. Mac Griffin turned his black department-issued pickup onto a dirt road south of Dulac, looking for the turnoff to the home of the senior nuisance-gator hunter of the parish. Mac had only been in Terrebonne—hell, he'd only been out of the fine state of Maine—for a little over a year, but he'd learned enough to know that Ray Naquin was well respected around these parts.

Like most Wildlife and Fisheries agents, Mac loved animals, so he respected any guy who caught gators that were spending too much time around humans and hauled them away in the back of his truck. The nuisance guys would relocate the animals to an isolated area so they could finish out long, happy lives eating things that didn't walk on two legs and possess opposable thumbs. Naquin would only kill the gators if they were already injured or had killed someone or, more likely, had become someone's pet when they were four inches long. Once they grew four feet long, a gator pet had become a danger because it had no fear of humans and was strong enough to tear off an arm or leg.

But Dave Grummond, or what was left of him when Mac and Jena had found the guy, wasn't the only person killed recently by gators.

Four attacks in two months was a downright epidemic—six attacks if you counted the two in Lafourche. Between rampaging gators and the Black Diamond drug spreading crazysauce through the parish drug culture—and beyond it, into the high schools and suburbs—Terrebonne law enforcement had its hands full. And nobody had a clue how to stop either problem.

Mac wanted to be on the drug task force, but he told himself that being on aggressive-gator duty was of equal importance to a greater number of people.

He reached the turnoff and found Ray's house, one of the few on Shrimpers Row that sat on high enough ground to have brick siding and not need to stand on stilts. Still, even his house had a couple of old waterlines that circled the brick like bathtub rings a few feet from the ground. Ray's house had taken water before, probably during Hurricane Gustav, which had pretty much dunked the whole parish. Even Houma had flooded.

Nobody was home, so Mac settled in to wait. He hadn't called ahead. One of the first lessons drilled into him by both senior agents in his unit—Gentry Broussard and Paul Billiot—had been that he'd learn more by showing up and listening instead of making an appointment ahead of time and running his mouth.

Personally, Mac thought *just showing up* raised his chances of getting his head blown off, but despite the motormouth reputation he had in the Terrebonne unit, he'd learned to keep his ears open and mouth shut when the situation called for it. He'd also found most people, even the ones carrying guns, turned surprisingly docile when approached by the wildlife agents.

It was the ones who turned hostile—maybe a quarter of them, all armed—that made wildlife agents' jobs so dangerous.

Finding Dave Grummond's body hadn't been the weirdest part of the evening either. He'd met Gentry and his fiancée, singer-songwriter Celestine Savoie, in a Houma club that Ceelie was scouting as a place for a regular gig. Mac had been pushing The Aquamarine as a good spot for her; it was one of his favorite clubs. The crowds weren't hard drinking or rowdy, and the place was developing a good reputation for up-and-coming artists. Ceelie's voice was smoky and sexy—not that he'd be sharing that opinion with her overprotective fiancé—plus she was a damned good songwriter.

The club had been a perfect pick, and both Ceelie and the manager had exchanged business cards and talked about possible nights for her to play. The call from Jena was what had thrown the night into weirdness. Jena's brother had gotten his hands on some Black Diamond, and she had called Gentry.

Mac might be Jena's partner now, but he got it. They didn't know each other that well yet, and she and Gentry were tight.

Despite his reputation as the unit's skirt chaser and class clown, however, Mac saw more than people thought. He could tell Jena was second-guessing herself and her decisions. She was a good agent, and everyone knew it—except her. He'd seen the self-doubt before they found the body yesterday, and he'd heard it in her voice when he and Gentry arrived at her freaking mansion outside Chauvin last night after dropping Ceelie off at home. Gentry had hoped Jackson would be back early enough so he could talk him down, but the kid hadn't shown up by two in the morning, and both he and Mac had early shifts. To Jena's credit, she didn't seem to mind that Gentry had brought him along.

Mac's new partner had been in pain, both physical and emotional. She didn't know whether to turn Jackson in so the DEA agents could pump him for information on where he got his hands on the drugs or whether to cover for him. Gentry finally took possession of what sure looked to be Black Diamond, placed the sandwich bag inside one of his own evidence bags to preserve any fingerprints, and promised to be present when Jackson was questioned.

"Covering for him isn't going to help anybody, especially Jackson," Gentry had told Jena.

She'd looked relieved once the decision was made, but her fingers shook when she handed over the drugs. Her face was so pale, the scars stood out more than usual.

Any further worries about Jena were interrupted by a spray of mud as a silver long-bed pickup skidded to a stop in the drive next to him. Ray Naquin might be respected, but Ray Naquin, Mac decided, was a smartass, based on nothing more than the way the man pulled into his own driveway. No, the opinion was based on more than that. Gentry said Ray had been hitting on Jena pretty hard before she got shot but hadn't been sniffing around since.

So he was an asshole, in addition to being a smartass.

Mac took his time before exiting the truck, letting the gator hunter wait for him as he flipped through a notebook and pretended to look at citations, then got out as if in slow motion. He'd already made note of the detached garage with the padlock, and assumed it held a boat since Ray didn't have one attached to his truck.

"How'd I rate a personal visit from one of you state boys?" Ray asked the question before Mac could bother to introduce himself. Which was okay. Mac knew Ray was a jerk and Ray knew he was a state wildlife agent.

Still, he'd follow protocol. He pulled out a business card from his uniform shirt pocket and held it toward the hunter. "Mac Griffin, Wildlife and Fisheries. My partner and I found the body of that missing fisherman yesterday, and looks like it was a gator attack. Since we've had several in the last couple of months, I thought I'd check in with you. If anybody knows about an uptick in aggressive gators, that'd be your area of expertise. I hear you're the best."

Ray nodded, a small smile and a friendlier expression replacing his former scowl now that he realized he was being sought for his advice and expertise and not because he'd done something wrong. Which made Mac wonder why he thought LDWF might be looking for him.

The hunter had light stubble, brown eyes, blond-streaked brown hair just over his collar, and tanned skin that would turn tough as leather by the time he was in his midforties. In the meantime, he had about ten more years to enjoy the tattooed, outdoorsy bad-boy look women seemed to like.

Mac envied the bad-boy vibe. He'd probably appreciate his own youthful looks when he reached forty and looked thirty, but since the department policy prohibiting facial hair had forced him to shave his beard and expose his baby face to the world, complete with the dimple in his chin, he looked about eighteen. When he'd been eighteen he looked fourteen. In other words, he couldn't win.

"Come on in." Ray gestured toward the house. "Want a beer? No, guess you can't do that since you're in uniform, or are you even old enough to drink? Want a Coke?"

Definitely an asshole.

"Coke's good." Mac followed Ray into a house that proved looks could be deceiving. The outside of the house and the lawn were well tended except for the water rings. Inside, the house had been cleaned sometime in the last decade. Maybe. It held the vague, soured odor of vinegar and bleach, probably an occupational hazard of someone who spent a lot of time cleaning off the stench of alligators and other swamp denizens.

Mac perched on the edge of a brown-plaid sofa, scanning the arsenal sitting around him: a shotgun on the table that Ray had brought in with him from his truck. A pistol lay on the counter, and a rifle was propped in the corner. A wooden gun rack with a glass front hung next to the fireplace and seemed awkward and oddly formal surrounded by the chaos of the room. The other tools of the gator hunter's trade sat on the Formica kitchen table: what looked like a twelve-pack of heavy-duty silver duct tape, a pile of zip ties, and a few knives.

"Here you go." Ray returned from the kitchen holding a bottle of Miller Light for himself and a can of Coke for Mac, and took a seat at the nearest edge of the matching sofa. It had been piled with papers, which Ray shoved out of the way. Mac had his own stack of overdue paperwork, so he recognized a backlog of official forms when he saw one. He and the asshole had at least one thing in common; they were paperwork procrastinators.

"So you're wantin' to know if I've seen more aggressive gators than usual?" Ray took a swig of beer and leaned back. "Not really. I mean, we've had a few attacks in the last month or two, but I think it's because the winter has been so mild. The gators are more active now than they usually are this time of year, and people aren't being as cautious as they should be."

The weather angle was something that Mac, at least, hadn't considered, and it made a lot of sense. "You see any pattern in where these gator attacks have been?"

The four attacks that Wildlife and Fisheries had handled directly had been near the eastern edge of the parish, like yesterday off Pointe-aux-Chenes. But Ray saw gators whose paperwork would go straight to division headquarters in Thibodaux or even to Baton Rouge and not to the Terrebonne unit unless there was a problem that might involve law enforcement.

"Have you had to put down any gators for aggression that haven't actually attacked anyone yet? Any aggression calls we might not know about?" The state had more than sixty licensed nuisance hunters but only two worked in lower Terrebonne, one of whom was semiretired. So Ray was the man to ask.

Ray sipped his beer and propped his feet on a coffee table piled high with hunting magazines. "None that I can think of, but, man, you wouldn't believe the calls I get, 'specially as people hear about more gator attacks around the parish. It's just gonna get worse since you found the Grummond guy's body, especially if it's confirmed he died as a result of a gator attack."

He set his beer bottle on the floor beside the sofa. "I mean, some lady's poodle disappeared and she was abso-fuckin-lutely sure it had to be a gator even though she hadn't seen one. One guy spotted some bubbles in the bayou near his favorite swimming hole and I spent two friggin' days chasin' after air bubbles that turned out to be a turtle."

Mac smiled. "So you're getting more calls but not more gators?" Add drama queen to Ray Naquin's list of attributes.

"I'm getting more calls because folks are hearing rumors about gator attacks. I haven't seen more aggressive gators. Just more paranoid people."

"The last two attacks were down on lower Bayou Pointe-aux-Chenes," Mac said. "You had any calls out that way?"

Ray reached beside him and dragged a pile of papers onto his lap. "Damned paperwork." He rifled through the stack. "One of our hysterical dog owners lives east of Chauvin off Highway 665, not too far from where you found that Grummond guy. She's called several times claiming to see a gator nearby, but I been out there at least twice and I ain't seen nothing. Plus, it's just one of those places that gives you the creepin' willies, y'know?"

Actually, no. Mac had gotten a few willies with some up close and personal bear encounters in Maine, but it was hard to figure what would creep out a tough dude like Ray Naquin. After all, the guy caught angry gators for a living. "What's so creepy about the place?"

Ray tossed the papers aside. "It's just a dirt road behind a couple of old cane fields. There are a few shacks there, and one of 'em butts up to an inlet off Bayou Pointe-aux-Chenes. Nobody lives out there now but the poodle lady and some guy she says is a hermit." Ray tossed the papers aside. "And maybe a gator. Who the hell knows? Want me to let you know if she calls again?"

Mac nodded. Why not? Maybe they'd luck out and find the gator that ate poor Dave Grummond's arm, although that wasn't likely. The arm was probably digested by now. "You get to sell the gators you have to put down?"

The licensed nuisance hunters had a lot of leeway. If they deemed a gator dangerous to humans, they didn't need a state-issued tag in order to kill it like gator hunters did during the one-month season. All the nuisance-gator hunters had to do was file some paperwork and they got to keep the profits.

As long as people wanted to buy alligator boots and shoes and purses, gators would bring in big money.

Ray's boots—which appeared to be alligator themselves—came off the table and hit the floor with a thud. "If you're hintin' that I'm putting down gators just for the money, th—"

"No, no, no. Relax, man." Mac held up a hand in a gesture of peace. Jeez, but this guy was touchy. "I just wondered if you had a particular seller you took them to. A seller might know if there were any other gators being brought in from one of the neighboring parishes."

Ray relaxed. "Yeah, sorry. It's been a long day already and it ain't even lunchtime."

Mac thought that, long day or not, Ray had overreacted, another indication that he bore watching. Still, the guy seemed to have a good reputation and the LDWF nuisance-alligator program had a great track record.

He wasn't letting the question go, however. "So is there one particular seller you work with, or do you spread the business around?"

Ray's tense shoulders visibly relaxed. "I spread it around. Take some up to Thibodaux, some to a place over in Bourg, whoever's closest to where I catch the gator. This time of year, though, I usually take 'em to Gateau's. It's a bigger place, on the east side of Houma."

Mac made a note of the name. "Any particular reason you take them there? Isn't Patout's bigger and closer?"

"Yeah, I used to take them there." Ray picked up his beer and took another sip. "But Amelia Patout—she's run the place since her husband died—has the cancer, and one of her two boys has some kind of thing . . . I don't know what you call it. But he don't quite think right, y'know? So she's not there a lot and her oldest kid's trying to run the place. It's easier to drive a few extra miles to Gateau's."

Mac nodded and got to his feet. "Don Gateau's a good guy; I've met him a couple of times, so maybe I'll stop by and talk to him. Might stop by Patout's too, in case they've seen something from one of the other hunters."

"Yeah, maybe, but like I said, she ain't there most of the time anymore. But suit yourself."

Mac didn't think he was going to get any more out of Ray Naquin, at least not today, so he headed toward the door. "Thanks for your time. I'll definitely talk to Mr. Gateau."

"Hey," Ray called from behind him. "I heard Jena Sinclair was already back at work. How's that long, tall, sweet thang doin'?"

She was doing well enough to beat the shit out of him if she heard him call her a *long, tall, sweet thang.* Halfway down the front steps, Mac turned. "She's been back in the field a week or two. We're partners right now. You got a message for her?" *Since you disappeared after she got shot, asshole?*

"Sure, tell her Ray says he's still waitin' on that rain check for dinner one night soon." He followed Mac down the stairs and stood in front of the porch. "Heard she got that pretty face o' hers scarred up a little, though. And probably some other body parts."

A flush of anger spread over Mac's skin to the point where he slammed his truck door as soon as he'd climbed in and immediately turned on the air conditioner to cool himself off. Otherwise, he'd be tempted to turn around and punch Ray Naquin square in his stubble. Mac didn't know the extent of Jena's scars, so he sure as hell figured Ray Naquin didn't have a clue—the man was fishing for information that was none of his business.

Punching someone while in uniform—or even off duty—would not be considered appropriate for a wildlife enforcement agent, his first partner, Paul Billiot, would have told him without a hint of a smile. Not that Paul ever smiled.

So Mac had to settle for putting on his sunglasses and spearing Ray with his best inscrutable look.

"On second thought, guess you better deliver that message yourself," he said through the open window. "I'm sure Jena would be glad to hear from you." *And rip you a new one, asshole.* "Have a nice afternoon."

CHAPTER 5

Jena paced the tiled foyer of the house that Daddy bought, wishing she were at work, staking out a poacher, counting fish—anything except waiting for Gentry and a sheriff's deputy to ambush her little brother and take him in for questioning.

Jackson didn't know it was coming. Jena had thought about warning him; she'd spent her whole life serving as the mediator between Jacks and her parents. Taking the blame for his screwups. Standing up for him.

But he'd scared her last night with his erratic behavior before he'd stormed out, leaving Gentry and Mac to calm her down. She'd always been the tough one and he the mellow one, but last night, she'd felt threatened. Gentry had been through the whole guilt trip over shooting his brother in a drug-related incident several years ago, before he'd transferred to Terrebonne Parish. She'd seen enough of his guilt to know she didn't want to live through it herself.

Jacks had slammed into the house about 3:00 a.m. She'd been sleeping fitfully and instinctively had slid her hand beneath her pillow and wrapped her fingers around the familiar handle of her SIG Sauer.

Then, all had grown quiet. Her brother had slept until noon, and now the soft sounds of his favorite indie folk band wafted down the hall from behind his closed door. She'd heard the shower. She'd heard him humming.

She hadn't smelled pot, but if he felt like singing with Mumford and Sons, he must be past his Black Diamond rage. She didn't know how long it would take the drugs to leave his system, though, and didn't want to risk setting him off again by admitting she'd turned him in to the sheriff, or at least she'd ratted on him to Gentry, who called the sheriff.

No, she didn't want to face Jackson until she had backup.

Maybe it had been a one-time thing, an experiment. That's what she kept telling herself. Maybe some dealer had given Jacks the plastic bag of drugs, hoping to get him hooked and to get his claws into a new client.

Problem was, Black Diamond wasn't a hook-'em-slow kind of drug, or so said all the reports being issued through the different agencies on an almost-daily basis. Like flakka in South Florida, Black Diamond was cheap, extremely addictive, and lethal. It could be shot up or smoked or swallowed or snorted—an equal-opportunity drug.

Black Diamond had been streaming into Terrebonne Parish for the past two months, spreading west all the way to Houston and east to New Orleans and beyond. Officials weren't any closer to figuring how and where it was coming in, or who was behind it, than they had been two months ago.

A woman high on Black Diamond had run through oncoming traffic on I-10, stripping off every stitch of clothing as she ran from what she described as demons. A guy in Bourg had tied his toddler's tricycle to the back of his pickup before driving it down Highway 55 at eighty miles per hour. He finally ran into a ditch. Thank God, he'd forgotten to put the child on the trike, although it had taken several very tense hours to establish that and locate the toddler, safe with his mother.

Then there was the formerly mellow pothead computer genius doing naked cartwheels on top of a brick wall at his sister's home in Chauvin. Jena guessed she'd gotten off easy, but Jackson wasn't going to think so.

The sound of approaching vehicles propelled her to the front window of the ballroom-sized foyer, where she pulled aside the heavy white brocade curtains to see Gentry's black LDWF pickup followed by a squad car from the Terrebonne Parish Sheriff's Office. She was relieved to see Adam Meizel emerge from the TPSO vehicle; he and Gentry were buddies. Adam wouldn't get too rough with Jacks.

She opened the door before they could ring the bell. Gentry's dark-eyed gaze honed in on her face with a serious glint, but his voice was soft. He even gave her a glimpse of his dimples, and his curly dark hair, as usual, needed a trim. "How're you doing, Red? Any more problems? You look like shit, by the way."

Jena laughed for the first time in what seemed like forever. Mac had made her smile when he'd barfed on the boat, and now Gentry had made her laugh in the middle of a family crisis. A real laugh, not the fake one she put on to assure everyone she was okay. And he'd used his favorite nickname for her.

Only her partner—make that her former partner and forever friend—would tell her how awful she looked and know that's what she needed to hear.

She loved these guys, and it made that moment of darkness when she tried to kill herself feel selfish and shortsighted. How had she let the blackness swallow her?

Because it was so damned hard to climb toward the light when you sank low enough and felt there was no way out, that's how.

"It wasn't my most restful night; let's leave it at that. Hey, Meizel." She stepped aside to let the guys in. At almost six feet, Jena was a couple of inches shorter than Gentry and at least two inches taller than Adam. Despite having spent a couple of decades in the parish, the deputy still sounded more like the folks up around Shreveport than a local, which is to say his accent was more Southern than Cajun. At least he didn't say "eh."

He nodded at her. "Glad you're back on the job, Sinclair. Bein' on sick leave seems to have been"—he looked around the gaudy foyer, which was almost the size of Jena's old efficiency apartment in Houma—"prosperous."

Jena laughed again. She had missed this, the camaraderie, the incessant teasing, the *family* of law enforcement, and vowed to cut Mac Griffin some slack and stop being so judgmental. It wasn't his fault he was an insanely cute womanizer from Maine. Well, the womanizer part was his fault, but it had nothing to do with Jena.

The vibe between the three of them grew awkward. Jena couldn't avoid the issue of Jackson any longer. "Okay, confession time. I didn't have the guts to warn him you were coming, but I'll get him now." She glanced down the hallway, where her brother had shifted into a boisterous sing-along with an old Nickelback song they'd both loved back in the day, "If Everyone Cared."

She *did* care. The instinct to protect Jacks lay deep inside her, born in childhood when she felt the need to take the consequences and criticisms herself so he wouldn't grow up with her neuroses. She'd always sensed he was more fragile than she, that she was the one who understood their parents' own peculiar, detached form of love.

Maybe, in the long run, however, she'd done him no favors. What was about to happen would be best for everyone, even though she was sure Jacks wouldn't see it that way. He'd feel ambushed, and she couldn't blame him.

Jena headed down the hallway to the end room Jacks had claimed as soon as they'd arrived at the White Rhino. She knocked on the door and waited. The music cut off abruptly, and she sent a silent prayer heavenward that the brother who opened the door would be the one she'd loved and protected his whole life. Not the other one.

The door swung wide and, even then, she wasn't sure. Jacks's hair, dark and thick, had been pulled up into one of those man-bun things Jena hated. Somehow, though, it suited him. He wore his orange *Let Your Geek Flag Fly* T-shirt and a pair of dark-green cargo pants. Black Chuck Taylors.

In fact, he looked just like Jackson Sinclair usually looked, except for the sullen expression in his blue eyes and the cold tone of his voice. "You took my stash."

So this was how they'd play it then, the misunderstood brother and his straight-arrow sibling.

"I took your *drugs*, and we need to talk about it." Jena kept her tone level, using her enforcement-agent voice, not her sister voice. "In the living room. Now."

Her attitude seemed to take Jacks by surprise. He'd already turned back toward his bed of white tangled sheets and balled-up pillows, but stopped.

"Talk about what? Who's here? I heard cars earlier."

"A senior enforcement agent and a sheriff's deputy, and they're here to see you. They're both part of the Black Diamond Task Force."

"Of course they are." Jacks brushed his shoulder against hers on his way out the door, turned, and whispered, "Fuck you, *Agent Sinclair*."

She flinched inside but showed no emotion as she followed him down the hallway. "I'd suggest you drop the attitude."

He didn't respond.

Gentry and Adam had remained in the foyer-slash-ballroom, looking uncomfortable and out of place. "Gentry, I think you met my brother, Jackson, while I was in the hospital last fall." She turned to Jacks. "Gentry is a senior enforcement agent and my former partner, and this is Deputy Adam Meizel of the Terrebonne Parish Sheriff's Office."

Gentry nodded and remained silent; Adam shook Jackson's hand, and was also silent. The way things had been going, Jena was thankful Jacks hadn't refused the polite handshake.

"Why don't we go in the living room and talk?" Jena walked ahead of them, cringing at the bright, sterile white of the tile floors, walls, and furniture when she turned on the lights. Her mother's handiwork. The woman equated color with dirt.

Jackson walked in behind her and slouched in the overstuffed white leather armchair. "You wanted to talk. Okay, talk."

Gentry remained silent and looked at Adam to take the lead, which told Jena more than anything that this was a TPSO case. It wasn't a family matter. Gentry was there for her, not Jacks.

"Mr. Sinclair, we have in our possession a small quantity of a synthetic drug known as *Diamant Noir*, or Black Diamond," Adam said. "It's my understanding that your sister found this in your room and turned it over to Agent Broussard, who brought it to the sheriff's office."

Jacks turned cold eyes toward Jena, and she suppressed a shiver. How much of that shit had he done to have changed so much, and how had she been so self-absorbed for the last month that she hadn't noticed?

"That's bullshit," Jacks said. "If these drugs even exist, Jena found them when I wasn't at home. They're probably hers and she's trying to cover her ass. You might want to follow up on that. You might want to have a *talk*."

A long silence followed. This, Jena hadn't expected. "Seriously, Jackson?"

He wouldn't even look at her.

"Jena, tell me what happened." Meizel turned equally impassive eyes toward Jena, but in his, she read only professionalism, not hostility. Well, maybe a little anger, but she knew it was directed at Jacks, not her.

"Sure." She went through the exchange of the previous night, including the fact that her brother had been trying to do cartwheels on top of the brick privacy fence in back. "Naked," she added. "If you make him strip down, you can probably see the scratches from where he fell in the crape myrtles."

Only a slight twitch from one tight corner of Meizel's mouth gave away his urge to smile. Gentry stared at the carpet as if in deep contemplation. Jacks's face turned the color of a Creole tomato.

She wasn't finished with him, the little shit. "I wouldn't have found the drugs at all if my brother hadn't shoved me to the floor," she added, a ball of heat growing behind her eyes. He wasn't throwing this back on her. "It was tucked beneath the corner of his dresser. You can probably find some residue if you search his room."

"My word against hers, dudes," Jacks said, getting up and walking toward the foyer. "Unless you wanna press charges, I'd suggest you get your asses out of here. I've got things to do, places to go, people to see."

Gentry caught up with Jacks a foot from the front door and put a hand on his shoulder. "Jackson, we don't want to arrest you. All we want to do is find out where you got the stuff. Do you think it was easy for Jena to call us when what she wanted was to protect you?"

Jackson shrugged off Gentry's hand. "You want to worry about drugs in your parish, Agent Broussard, why don't you check my sister's bag? Or is it okay for your agents to be racing around with guns while they're buzzing on painkillers? Is it okay for her to work four months after she tried to slit her wrists with a fucking utility knife?"

A chill washed across Jena's shoulders. Who was this person? The brother she'd known her whole life would never try to throw her under the squad car.

"We aren't talking about your sister, who, by the way, is a skilled law enforcement agent who took two bullets in the line of duty a few months ago, son." Gentry's voice was low, but serious. "We're talking about you, an unemployed twenty-four-year-old who had almost an ounce of an illegal synthetic drug stashed in his bedroom, not to mention what's probably still in your system. All we'd need is one simple blood test."

Gentry paused. "We're talking about jail time, Jackson. Do you understand what kind of trouble you could be in?"

Time seemed to stretch into slow motion. Jackson turned like an enraged devil, tightened his fingers around Gentry's throat, and squeezed. He moved so fast that Gentry wasn't able to get his hands up to protect himself and was left trying to breathe and pry Jacks's hands off at the same time. Jackson wasn't nearly as strong as Gentry, so it had to be the drugs. Jena had heard stories of users having almost superhuman strength.

She ran toward them, but Adam got there first. He kicked Jacks's legs out from beneath him and, by the time her brother hit the floor, Meizel was kneeling on his back, one hand pressing his head against the tile. The handcuffs clicked shut with a loud scrape of metal, and Meizel jerked Jacks to his feet, with Gentry's help. It was over in a matter of seconds.

All four of them stood still for a moment. Until Jacks, his chin bleeding from hitting the floor, began spewing more accusations at Jena, laced with a liberal dose of f-bombs. Then life sped up again. Meizel held one of Jacks's arms while Gentry held the other. The deputy had started his Miranda warning by the time they'd gotten Jacks out the front door, shoving him toward the patrol car none too gently.

Jena followed them out, torn between being a sister and a cop. She settled somewhere in the middle, not interfering while Meizel shoved a cursing Jackson into the back of the patrol unit but blocking the doorway when the deputy tried to close it.

"Keep your mouth shut and don't pull any more crap," she warned Jackson, who gave her a sullen stare. "I'll call Dad."

"You bitch, don't pretend you care about—"

Jena slammed the door, leaving her brother alone in the patrol car to curse to his heart's content. She turned to Gentry, whose neck already sported the beginnings of finger-shaped bruises. "You okay?"

"Yeah, let's go inside a minute. We've gotta talk."

"Later, Gentry. I need to go to the jail and see about Jacks."

"No, you need to sit down and talk to me first. Let Meizel take care of Jackson." Gentry's voice softened. "Adam knows he's your kid brother, Jena. Nothing's gonna happen to him."

Jena drew in an unsteady lungful of air and nodded. Gentry was right and she needed to show him the respect he deserved. She had to tell him the truth that Jackson had begun with such a twisted version. Turning, she went back into the living room, unconsciously straightening a white vase standing atop a white marble stand.

"This place doesn't look like you," Gentry said, sitting in the chair where Jacks had been, his dark-green uniform stark against the white upholstery, the black SIG Sauer tucked into its holster. It reminded Jena of her own gun, which she'd slept with last night for the first time in her life. It reminded her that Gentry and Adam had both shown a lot of restraint by not being a lot rougher when Jacks went off on them.

Gentry leaned back in the chair but his posture remained tense. "Before we deal with Jackson, tell me how much truth he was talking back there."

Jena sighed and rubbed her throbbing temples with the tips of her fingers. "I had a prescription for painkillers, but I've already gotten rid of them as well as the antianxiety meds. I haven't taken any prescription painkillers since I went back on duty; you know I'd never do that. I've been getting by on ibuprofen. The muscles are still sore sometimes from the gunshot wounds."

"What about the rest?" Gentry hadn't taken his eyes off hers. He was testing her, and it was a test she needed to pass.

She looked down at her hands. "It was so awful there, back in my parents' house. I fell into a dark, dark place, Gentry. The damage from the gunshot wounds left me disfigured and . . . damaged." She just couldn't go into the details yet, not even with him. "I'm not proud of what I did, but I'll get over it and it will be okay. You don't know how good it's been to get out on patrol again this week. It's helped me see my way back into the light."

He moved next to her on the sofa, gently reached over, and took her left hand. He turned it palm side up and raised her sleeve to expose the vertical cuts on her wrists. "I fucking hate your parents, you know that?"

Jena gave a weak laugh. She wished she could truly hate them, but they *were* her parents. Like it or not, they were part of her life. "They love us in their own way. But they're control freaks, and it drives them crazy that they can't control Jackson or me." As a result, they behaved like entitled bullies. "How'd you know to look on my left wrist?"

"Because you're right-handed." Gentry leaned forward and propped his elbows on his knees. "Do you need to be back on duty? Do I need to be worrying about you? Honest answer."

She shook her head. "I've felt more alive and more like myself in the last few days than since I was shot. If I even suspect it's getting the better of me, I'll take myself off duty and get help. I promise."

Gentry looked at her with a long, probing question in his deep-brown eyes. Whatever he saw seemed to satisfy him. "Okay, that's all we'll say about it. Does Warren know?"

Jena nodded. "I didn't feel right even talking to him about coming back on duty if he didn't know." He was the only one besides her parents who knew everything. She smiled. "The lieutenant's keeping an eye on me."

Gentry gave her a hug. "So am I, Red. And if I see something I don't like, we're gonna revisit this conversation. Fair enough?"

"Fair enough."

"Okay then." Gentry's gaze flicked toward the front door and back to Jena. "Tell me how long Jackson's been acting this way. He doesn't even seem like the same guy I met after you got shot."

"He's not." Jena rubbed her eyes, which stung from too little sleep. "I don't recognize the person Adam just hauled out of here."

They both looked toward the front window. Meizel still stood outside his unit, arms crossed, face blank. Inside the patrol car, her brother's mouth moved in violent, dramatic motions. He was trying to give the deputy an earful of crap and the deputy wasn't listening, or at least he wasn't reacting.

"This drug is ugly. It's so damned addictive, and it works fast." Gentry turned back to Jena. "It doesn't work *that* fast, though. No way last night was his first encounter with Black Diamond."

Jena nodded. "As much as I want to think it was a one-time thing, I realized this morning that it couldn't be. We've hardly been here a month, though. Think he got started on it back in New Orleans?"

Gentry's gaze on her was serious and steady. "You're the one who knows him best. What's your take on it?"

Jena thought about her parents sending Jackson to stay with her at least until summer semester at UNO started in June, which had been weird. They'd let him skip a semester of college. As much as she might like to believe Jackson's presence was prompted by parental concern—so Jackson could take care of his stubborn older sister—she didn't think so. That dog didn't hunt.

"I think Jacks was in some kind of trouble in New Orleans, and that's why my parents sent him here to cool his heels for a few months." She thought it through as she talked. "I don't think it was Black Diamond, though. He's a pothead—has been since he hit fifteen. He's too smart for his own good. He's spoiled rotten and unmotivated and doesn't even know the meaning of ambition. But he's never been violent. I've never, ever seen that side of him."

Wouldn't have believed he was capable of it.

"So you think your parents sent him here with some ulterior motive, but that he didn't get into the Black Diamond until he hit a local source?"

Jena nodded. "When we first got here, he was his same old normal slob of a self. I wish I could say when he started changing, but"—and it sure hurt to admit this—"I was too preoccupied with my own crap."

Which meant she had to do something that, for her, was worse than spending time in ICU with bullet wounds or being chewed out by her lieutenant for not following protocol with Gentry and Ceelie's situation six months ago. Or just about anything.

She had to talk to her parents.

Maybe she'd better go ahead and do it now, while Gentry was here for moral support. Pulling out her cell phone, she paused, weighing the pros and cons between calling home for an unpleasant conversation with Mom or calling the firm for an unpleasant conversation with Dad.

In the end, it didn't really matter. She called the law office of Sinclair and Mattingly and recognized Dad's longtime secretary when she answered.

"Hey, hon, your dad's in a meeting with Mr. Mattingly. You want me to have him call you back?"

Oh hell, why not just piss him off even more? She rolled her eyes for Gentry's benefit and said, "It's important, Sandy. I need to talk to him now. Interrupt their meeting and tell Dad I said it was urgent."

Jackson Sr.'s polished uptown New Orleans voice came on the line in a surprisingly short time. "Jena. Sandy said you had a problem. Have you had a . . . relapse?"

Which was probably as close to an admission of fatherly concern as she'd get, but she would take it. "No, I'm fine. It's about Jackson. He's been arrested, or will be soon."

The pause hung heavy between them. "On what charges?"

"Don't know yet. Probably battery on an officer. Felony drug possession." Gentry wouldn't press charges, but that didn't matter. The fact that he had marks on his throat and Jacks's chin was bleeding meant her brother would be booked. What happened to the charges after that would be up to the sheriff and Jacks's attorney. Plus, there was the drug issue.

Dad's voice grew more irate. "Damn it, Jena. Couldn't you keep him in line for three months without letting him fuck things up?" The clear response was *Obviously not*, but Jena wasn't leaving it at that.

"It might have helped if you'd told me I needed to keep him in line. Why did you send him here in the first place?"

Another pause passed before her father spoke, back in his unflappable attorney mode. "Tell Jackson to keep his mouth shut, if you can manage that much. I'm on my way to make this cluster-fuck disappear. First Jackson knocks up a street punk with social aspirations and now this. Your mother will have a few words for you."

Jena disconnected the call without responding and glanced at Gentry's raised eyebrows.

She shrugged. "That went well."

And she was going to be an aunt.

CHAPTER 6

Cole sat at the eastern edge of his weathered wooden porch, the side nearest the branch of water that intersected with Bayou Pointe-aux-Chenes and the path to his workhouse. He sipped from a cold bottle of water, letting the sweat run down the sides of the plastic container and send cooling streams over his tired hands.

For the past three hours, he'd been in the workhouse, taking care of his newest culinary and financial acquisition. He'd trimmed the lean gator meat into chunks and strips, lined the pieces up on cheap tin cookie sheets, then set them in his freezer. Once they were frozen, he'd bag them up and take out only as much as he needed for a meal. One day next week, when he could catch the neighbors away from home and didn't have to worry about arousing their curiosity with the smell of smoked meat, he'd thaw the longer strips and smoke and cure them for jerky. Never knew when hard times or emergencies might hit, plus he could take them on his jaunts through the parish.

Splendid isolation, as the old Warren Zevon song said. That had been Cole's sole purpose in life the past five years. Learning the fine art of self-sufficiency. Learning to live with himself, to come to terms with who he'd become and the life he'd chosen. Learning to need no one and have no one need him.

He'd made peace with his choices.

This little corner of Terrebonne Parish, hidden between the abandoned sugarcane fields and the bayou, had afforded him those choices, along with the blood money that kept the lights on and the water running. The blood money that paid for his commercial freezer and truck and freaking Wi-Fi. The blood money that bought what he couldn't catch or build himself.

The gator hide, he'd slowly scraped free of meat and sinew. He'd found another bucket to toss the remains in and, after dark, he would take them down the inlet to Bayou Pointe-aux-Chenes and dispose of them, feeding whatever was around and hungry. It was far enough from his house that he didn't worry about creating nuisance animals.

The skull and feet, he stuck in the cooler to deal with later. For now, Cole spread a thick layer of salt over the inside of the leathery hide with reverence. He took no joy in the death of such an amazing animal, especially while such ugly human beasts walked the earth freely. He didn't hold the ingested arm against the gator; it had simply been following the instincts God had given it.

As for the guy who'd once called the arm his own, well, bad shit happened to people who didn't deserve it. Where God fit into *that* equation, Cole had no clue. Once, he'd believed everything happened for a reason. Until he came across a thing whose reason escaped him.

Finally, his work done, feeling hot and sweaty despite the pleasant high sixties of the late afternoon, he'd settled onto the porch with the water. Next to him, propped against the house, rested his shotgun. A man never knew when he might need a shotgun.

Down the inlet, where it joined Bayou Pointe-aux-Chenes, Cole spotted a small boat. It held only one person, as near as he could tell from almost a half mile away. All he could tell about the guy was that he had light hair, maybe a light hooded jacket, and appeared to be looking through binoculars—toward Sugarcane Lane.

A chill ran along Cole's shoulders—a sign of danger he'd learned not to discount. His first instinct was to grab his shotgun, but that could get him shot as well. Instead, he shifted the position of a big, ancient aluminum bucket he kept on the porch in which he grew tomatoes. He'd planted them early because he knew he could always drag them inside in the case of a rare freeze. The thick, fuzzy vines didn't have anything on them but leaves, but they made a decent camouflage.

Paranoid much, Ryan?

Well, yeah. He glanced through the heavy leaves of the tomato plant, held upright by a wooden stake to which he'd attached the vine with a strip of cloth, and decided his spy's attention was not directed at his house after all.

Instead, the binoculars seemed to be pointed toward the other side of Sugarcane Lane, so he relaxed, leaned against the side of the house, and closed his eyes. His tomato plant would keep him safely hidden.

All was quiet for a couple of minutes, until a cringing screech from down the dirt road interrupted his reverie on the meaning of life— mainly, that he was no longer convinced it had a meaning.

Damn it, the witch was home. That must be who the guy with the binoculars had been watching.

An empty shack sat to the left of Cole's house, the edge of the bayou branch sat at its right, and a small empty lot took up the space across the dirt road—he'd bought both pieces of property, along with the one he lived in, to make sure they stayed empty. But next to the vacant lot was a small wooden house on stilts high enough for the occupants to store their small boat and, next to the boat, a pickup almost as decrepit as his own.

He hated to tell them, but it wouldn't take a flood of biblical proportions to bring down their elevated palace. A good gust of wind would blow it to hell.

Hopefully, it would take the witch with it. Cole's neighbor—he had no idea of her real name, only that she referred to him as The Hermit—sported a straw-like mop of bleached hair, a sharp nose and chin, a perpetual cigarette hanging from her mouth at a forty-five-degree angle, and a voice that would make a joyful noise unto no one.

"Chewie, you get away from that goddamned gator right now. Chewbacca—here, now, you good-for-nothing mutt!"

Cole leaned forward for a better look. They'd had a brief, hard shower not long before and, sure enough, a gator sat in the middle of the mud pit that now made up Sugarcane Lane. The gator hissed and backed up a few inches as the witch waved a big stick of some kind in its direction. Chewbacca, a cross between a poodle and something reddish-brown and hairy, barked in a high-pitched yip.

If the damned gator had any sense, it would turn around and head back toward the water as quickly as possible. Cole might join it, just to dull the noise. He glanced around at the shotgun. He could probably shoot the ground near enough to scare the gator back toward the water, but with his luck, he'd hit the witch and get his ass arrested.

"Chewie, hush." The witch's voice rose another octave, making Cole glad he'd gotten the double-paned glass for his windows; otherwise, they might shatter from the pitch. "Ronnie, call them game wardens this time. That no-good Ray Naquin couldn't find a gator if it was sitting on top'a his ass."

A man's gruff voice rang out from the vicinity of the house. "Done called 'em—dey's on da way."

Great. Wildlife agents, after Cole had spent the afternoon butchering an out-of-season gator and the morning burying some guy's chewed-up arm. He sighed, looked down the bayou to make sure the guy with the binoculars was gone, and climbed to his feet, holding the water bottle in one hand and the shotgun in the other.

"Chewie, you . . ." The witch spotted Cole. "You there! Hermit! Bring that shotgun over here and kill this gator." She paused and assumed what she must have thought was a coy tone. "You can eat it after you kill it. Ain't nobody has to know."

"It's illegal, and hermits don't break the law," he called, against his better judgment. *Don't engage. Engagement leads to familiarity, and familiarity leads to obligation.*

And with that, he went inside his house and slammed the door behind him, ignoring the outraged outpourings of one angry witch.

A shower couldn't wash away everything, but it could scrub off the stench of gator and drown out a lot of noise.

CHAPTER 7

"Where the heck is this place?" Jena leaned forward, trying to spot a dirt road that cut through the cane fields. "I've never heard of Sugarcane Lane, and I swear I've driven every road in this parish."

Mac squinted through the mud-spattered windshield. "I'm not quite sure. Maybe we should've gone in by boat, eh? I think it's pretty close to that part of Bayou Pointe-aux-Chenes where we found the body."

Great. She felt as if she'd spent the past eight hours with a pack of hungry pit bulls, aka lawyers, as her father and two of his assistants had descended on the Terrebonne Parish Detention Center en masse. They had left, hours later, with an arrangement for an emergency hearing that would no doubt have Jackson on his way back to New Orleans in record time.

It had been Jena's first experience on the receiving end of an official interrogation by her father, and she hoped it would be the last. To Dad's credit, he didn't give any credence to Jackson's insistence that the drugs were hers. He'd simply buy his only son out of trouble again, probably thinking a pregnant girl with social ambitions paled beside drug possession and assault.

Now she could wrangle an aggressive alligator on a backwater dirt road to top her highlight reel for the week.

"Damn it. This is a mud hole and I just washed this truck." Mac took a slow turn onto a wide swath of brown that, before the midafternoon gulley washer a half hour ago, had probably been a road. He switched the truck into all-wheel drive and weaved around the worst of the puddles, trying to keep at least one wheel at a time on ground that looked vaguely solid.

Around them, crowded against the road on both sides, stretched sugarcane fields that in years past would already be lush and green, the stalks about shoulder high. Maybe a quarter of the cane still stood sentinel against automation, economics, and saltwater from too much oil drilling. The rest was a mass of black dirt and scraggly ground cover.

"You're from here," Mac said. "What kind of person would want to live sandwiched between these empty cane fields and the water? They'd have a hard time getting out of here after even a small rain."

Jena glanced over to see if he was joking, but he looked serious. "Mac, first of all, I'm from New Orleans, not Terrebonne Parish. Same state, different world. Not better or worse, just different. Why does anybody want to live in an isolated place?"

Mac was silent for a few moments, then seemed to realize it wasn't a hypothetical question. "Well, maybe it's convenient for the way they live—fishing from that inlet off the bayou, maybe, or working the cane fields."

Jena nodded. "Except most of the sugarcane harvest is done by machine now. What else?"

He shrugged. "Maybe they got something to hide. Or maybe they're crazy. You know, like some kind of anarchist. The Unabomber, only hiding in the swamps instead of the mountains."

Jena smiled. "Well, maybe. More likely your first guess."

He took his hand off the steering wheel long enough to snap his fingers. "I know. Maybe it's a guy who brings his girl out here when they want to be alone. You know, rollin' in the mud or having sugarcane sex. I bet that's it."

Jena clapped her hands over her ears. "Stop it. Oh my God. Sugarcane sex."

They reached the end of the cane fields, and Sugarcane Lane stretched to their left. More mud, marked by a handmade road sign. Mac slid his gaze her way and grinned. "At least I got a reaction out of you. You looked pretty down-and-out when we met for a late lunch in Chauvin."

"You talk to Gentry since last night?"

"No, but I knew he and someone from the sheriff's office were going to talk to your brother this morning."

Jena watched the mud splatter the truck as they made the slow turn onto the road. "Yeah, Jackson was so out of control that Adam Meizel arrested him and charged him with assaulting an officer." Jena shook her head. "It's my word against his about the drugs since he hasn't changed his story. He stopped talking altogether as soon as my dad arrived."

"Your dad's a big-shot attorney, right?"

"He's a big-shot something," Jena muttered. "He waved his magic legal wand and will probably have Jacks back in New Orleans by the end of the day. Anyway, I see where our complaint came from."

A few yards ahead of them, a woman stood in the mud, wielding a stick.

"What's she holding—is that a wooden ruler?" Mac squinted through the mucked-up windshield.

"No, I do believe that's a table leg." Jena looked in the small notebook she kept in her shirt pocket and flipped the pages. "And I assume the woman threatening the gator with the table leg would be Doris Benoit. Her husband, Ronald Benoit, called it in. Said the alligator was attacking his wife's dog, whose name is Chewbacca, and he didn't care if the gator 'ate the goddamned thing'—that's a direct quote."

She smiled at the sight of Mac chewing on his bottom lip, his attempt at remaining professional. Even so, he had to clear his throat a couple of times as he got out of the truck.

"State wildlife agents." He waved at the woman. "I see you've got an unwanted visitor." He walked to stand beside Doris just as she poked at the gator with the table leg and caused it to hiss and back up again. "Ma'am, would you please not poke the gator anymore? Hissing is his way of telling you he doesn't much like that."

The well-named Chewbacca—a gnarled mop of mud-brown fur on four legs—barked incessantly.

"Mrs. Benoit, could you take your dog inside while we handle this?" Jena already wore her LDWF baseball cap, but slid on her sunglasses when she thought Doris was looking at her face—at her scars—too closely. "Any reason you called us instead of the nuisance hunter?"

"Ronnie, come get Chewie and take him in the house!" Doris's voice could carry for miles out in this quiet, flat landscape, although the only other place that looked occupied was the spot where the road ended and a few yards of sparse grass tried to hold on to life before the water took over.

"As for the nuisance hunter"—Doris turned back to Jena—"that Ray Naquin's done been out here two or three times and he ain't done nothing. Same dang gator keeps on comin' back."

Jena looked around. "Who else lives around here? Think somebody's feeding it? Gators don't usually hang around humans unless there's a food source. It hasn't eaten any dogs or cats, has it?"

"No dogs live here but Chewie." Doris looked up and down the street. "There used to be some folks that lived down to the end of the lane in that blue house. Morales or somethin' like that, but they moved. It's just us and that crazy man at the end of the road, near the water. I wouldn't put it past him to feed a gator. Matter of fact, I'd lay down money on it. I asked him to shoot the dang thing and he slammed the door in my face."

Jena looked at the road's final house. It was a wooden structure on short brick piers, narrow but stretching far back on the deep lot. It reminded her of the shotgun houses in New Orleans's older neighborhoods, only no self-respecting New Orleanian would paint a shotgun house white, and this one was white. Well, technically, it was gray. No one had painted it recently. It wasn't in terrible shape, though. Definitely looked solid. If the guy was crazy, he at least took care of his house.

First problems first. Something was wrong with this gator. It was fairly young, judging by its size of five or six feet, and had enough fight in it to hiss at Doris. Although to be fair, Jena kind of wanted to hiss at Doris herself. The alligator didn't try to leave, which was odd, especially for a young gator. It should've hightailed it toward the water at the first sign of Doris and her table leg.

It also apparently hadn't tried to charge at Doris, and Jena had no doubt the gator could catch her if she ran. A motivated gator could run thirty miles an hour. Doris was pure dumb lucky.

Jena was glad Ray Naquin hadn't been called first. She didn't want to put this gator down and have it used for meat and hide. She wanted to have it examined and then autopsied, if necessary, to see what was wrong with it.

"Mac, would you get the duct tape out of the truck? And some rope?"

Mac had been overseeing the Chewbacca handoff to a sullen dark-haired man with a cigarette hanging out the opposite side of his mouth from the one in his wife's mouth. Smoking bookends.

"We're going to catch him instead of shoot him?" Mac had taken off his sunglasses and hung them from his pocket, so those chocolate-brown eyes gave away his excitement. Why did he make Jena feel so ancient?

She still wanted to prove herself worthy of wearing the enforcement badge again, but after falling in Jackson's room and dealing with her parents all morning—Dad had brought her critical, razor-tongued mother with him as well—she didn't have the energy. There was proving yourself fit for duty, and there was being stupid. Today, she'd settle for not being stupid.

"Yeah, if you don't mind. Just get a rope and tape—I think that's all you'll need. This guy's hissing but he's not moving very much."

While Mac jogged back to the truck, Jena kept an eye on the gator, which seemed content to take an occasional step to the side but didn't seem inclined to make a run for the water. Weird.

"So, what's the man's name?" She jerked her head toward the house at the water's edge. "Does he live there alone?"

"I dunno. I just call him The Hermit." Doris took a last puff of her cigarette, dropped the butt, and ground it with the toe of her already-mud-coated running shoe. "He's just a funny old hippie type. Lives over there by himself. Don't talk to nobody. Don't want nobody talking to him. Don't get no visitors. Even Chewbacca won't go over there. God only knows what he does all day. Maybe feeds gators."

Maybe. Or maybe Chewie and Doris were not his cup of tea.

"Here we go." Mac walked up with two rolls of silver duct tape, enough to secure the mouths of a dozen bull gators. "Okay if I go ahead and catch him?"

"Go for it. Just watch his tail—he can knock you flat before you see it coming. Been there, done that."

Mac was probably disappointed by his first alligator catch in the wild. Once Jena had finally shooed Doris out of the way, the gator closed his mouth and didn't even react when Mac looped a noose around its snout and pulled the line taut. When he sat on its back and wrapped the duct tape around its jaws, the alligator did little more than give its tail a couple of halfhearted swishes.

"You gonna take this to Ray or send it to the forensics lab?" Mac asked. "Something's wrong with this little guy."

"Definitely the lab." Jena looked at her watch. "Call and let them know we're bringing him in. Think you can get him in the back of the truck by yourself? I'm not supposed to do much lifting." She hated admitting that, but here she was, being responsible and not stupid.

"Yeah, he's not that big, and kind of scrawny." Mac slid his arms beneath the reptile's belly and lifted him, getting a good whack of the animal's tail across his back in the process. "Damn, that hurt."

"Told ya. Better secure his feet too and make sure nothing in the back will fall on him and hurt him."

Mac glared back at her. "Want me to give him a pillow and blanket as well?"

Jena ignored him, and had to admit to herself she kind of enjoyed being the team's most experienced agent. She only had a couple of months on Mac as far as Wildlife and Fisheries was concerned, but she'd spent several years before that as an officer with the New Orleans Police Department—the choice of career that had set off the worst of the conflicts with her parents. Well, until she joined LDWF, went through their tough paramilitary-style enforcement training, and moved to Terrebonne Parish.

Grace and Jackson Sinclair had been, and were still, horrified by her career choices. Jena's mother still clung to the futile hope that her daughter would come to her senses and move back to the city. She also had hoped that move would be the outcome of the shooting—that Jena would realize she needed a safer job.

The purchase of her monstrous house might have been their final acceptance.

"Come down to the house next to the water when you're finished, or wait by the truck and stay alert," she called to Mac over her shoulder. "I want to talk to the guy who lives there and make sure he's not feeding gators."

Jena left her partner wrestling to secure the gator's feet, the whole operation overseen by Doris, and walked to the edge of the water.

She couldn't resist the pleasure of watching the way the bright-orange beginnings of sunset behind her illuminated the water in front of her. Everything was so close to the earth out here. There was a purity to it, a serenity.

Maybe the guy who lived here wasn't a hermit or a crazy. Maybe he could look past the poverty and see the rich, savage beauty all around him.

She glanced over at the house and saw him. He stood in the open front door, leaning against the jamb, wearing a pair of jeans but no shirt. Watching her.

"Hey, I need to talk to you for a minute. State wildlife agent." She turned and walked toward him, barely registering long silver or blond hair and a tall, muscled body before he turned and went inside, slamming the door behind him.

Oh hell no. That wasn't happening.

Jena sped up.

CHAPTER 8

Cole stood inside the door, knowing she'd be there any second. She would knock, probably with a firm rap to remind him who had the authority here, and it wasn't him. She would expect to come inside, and while he could deny her entrance without a warrant, he wouldn't. It would raise too much suspicion.

His fists clenched and unclenched. Again. Again. The press and release of tension filtered out some of the stiffness from his arms and shoulders. The woman was striking, her wistful expression had resonated with him, and he had wanted to look at her. He'd looked long and hard enough that she'd caught him standing in the doorway like an idiot. Otherwise, he could've pretended to be gone and not answered his door. Now, hiding wasn't an option.

The last thing he needed in his life was a woman. Especially a woman with a badge and a gun.

Though expected, the sharp knock made his shoulders jerk upward, and his fingers clenched again into fists. Weapons his body provided to protect itself, to protect him, to keep everyone away.

"Sir, I know you're in there. I'm Agent Sinclair of Louisiana Wildlife and Fisheries." Her voice was clear and no-nonsense. He tried to place her accent—she wasn't from Terrebonne Parish but didn't have a typical Southern accent either. "I want to talk to you about the gator in front of your neighbor Doris's house. It'll only take a minute or two."

Damn. Now that he knew his neighbor's real name, the Wicked Witch was dead. Now she was Doris.

He took a deep breath, turned, and opened the door an inch. Maybe two inches.

A hazel eye, heavy on the green, and the bill of a dark-green baseball cap came into view, peering through the crack. A strand of hair that trailed over her forehead from beneath the cap shone like pure molten fire.

"You can open it all the way, you know. I don't bite. I'd like to come inside for a few minutes and talk, or you can come out on the porch. Having a conversation isn't optional, but where we have it is. For now."

Damn it. Cole had to admit he was stuck and it was his own damned fault for standing in the doorway and watching her for so long. He opened the door wide, dread giving way to curiosity when he finally saw her face up close. She was beautiful but lightly scarred, more on her cheeks than her forehead, so she'd probably been hit by flying glass rather than having her head go through a windshield. Fairly recent too. The spots were still pink, but they *were* scars and not wounds. Five or six months old, he'd say. Eventually, they'd fade and, with her fair skin, would easily cover with makeup. If she hadn't been so close—not to mention his fixation on her face—he wouldn't have noticed them even now.

"Are you going to let me come inside, or are you coming outside, or do I need to make it an official order?"

Stop being an idiot, Ryan.

Cole stepped aside and motioned her in, just a man with nothing to hide. She pulled a notebook from her uniform pocket and handed him a business card. When he reached out to take it, their fingers brushed, and Cole jerked back his hand as if shot. He hadn't been touched in a long time, even in the most innocent of ways. That brief brush of fingers awoke memories he'd spent five long years sweeping out of his head—or so he thought. Apparently, he'd merely been sweeping them into a corner.

He looked at the card, then back up at her. "What can I do for you, Enforcement Agent Jena Sinclair? Is it pronounced *Jenna* or *Gina*?"

She cocked her head, causing sunlight from the open doorway to reflect on hair almost as deep red as the sinking sun—at least what he could see of it beneath her baseball cap. "It's pronounced *Jenna*; my parents didn't want to waste consonants. But I'm at a disadvantage. Do you have a name?"

Panic filled Cole for a moment before common sense stepped in to take its place. He had no reason to hide his name. Not here. "Cole Ryan. Come on in so I can close the door before my neighbor gets too curious."

For the first time in five years, another person other than a contractor or electrician walked into his living room, into his house. The place seemed to shrink in half.

"So you and Doris don't get along?" Jena looked away from him for the first time and glanced around the room. It probably looked rustic to someone like her, because she sounded like an educated city girl. Maybe New Orleans—the accent sounded right. More Brooklyn than Southern. He'd made the furniture himself, except for cushions and a couple of lamps. Everything was oiled unfinished wood or pale-blue milk paint. He found the combination soothing.

Now she was looking into his eyes again. Staring at him because she'd asked a question and he'd never answered. *Idiot.*

"I have no problem with Doris. I didn't even know her name." He shrugged. "We don't really talk."

"You don't like to talk to people, do you? I mean, slamming the door in my face was a clue that was hard to miss. I'm perceptive like that."

That made him sound like a psycho in the making and, hell, maybe he was. Cole needed to get off Jena Sinclair's radar, not further on it.

"Yeah, sorry about that." He forced himself to try to recall the fine art of conversing. "I moved here about five years ago, just wanting to get away from everything. Doris struck me as somebody who'd always be . . . around." Needy, asking for something, forcing him to talk to her.

He tried a smile, but didn't think he quite remembered how. His face felt contorted. "I didn't think Doris and I would have much in common."

Jena looked at him more closely—all of him. When her gaze returned to his face, he expected disgust but if he had to put a name on her expression he'd say *intrigued*.

"So why were you trying to move into the middle of nowhere and get off the grid? Something bad happen? Running away from something or someone?"

They stared at each other a second beyond awkward. She probably thought he was on the run, would end up doing a background check on him, and learn the whole sorry story that made up the life of one Coleman Thomas Ryan, until five years ago a lifelong resident of Yazoo City, Mississippi. Then again, she was a wildlife agent, not a regular cop. Maybe they weren't so keen on background checks or even flipping Google searches.

As for him, he found her intriguing as well—something he didn't want. All he wanted from Jena Sinclair was a hasty departure.

"I thought you needed to talk about Doris's alligator. Not much I can tell you. I'd been working around the house"—most decidedly *not* dressing an illegally obtained alligator—"when I heard her yelling at that brown rag mop of a dog. I went to the porch and saw her in the street batting at that poor gator with a big stick of some kind." Cole shrugged. "That's all I know, except it was weird that the gator wasn't running from her. Hell, *I* would've run from her."

He'd intentionally left out the guy with the binoculars, probably a bird-watcher, but he hadn't meant to add that last part. It made Jena laugh, however, so he was glad he'd said it, then chastised himself. He had his life planned and there was no room in it for an intriguing red-haired wildlife agent who, judging by her scars, had a past of her own.

"It was a table leg, actually," Jena said. "And I thought the same thing about the gator. We're loading it up to send to the state lab for testing because its behavior is so odd. Have you noticed any other weird things about the alligators around here while you were, what did you say . . . working around the house?"

Smart cookie, Jena Sinclair. Yeah, there had been a dead bull gator lying just off the bank by his house this morning with a human arm in its belly. He didn't plan on volunteering that tidbit of information.

"Not really. That same gator's been showing up off and on for a couple of weeks. At least I assume it's the same one; at least it's the same size. I thought Doris might be feeding it."

"Hmm." Jena removed her baseball cap and ran a long, slim hand over her hair, smoothing a pinned-up, braided mass of deep red. Cole imagined it would be about shoulder length if she wore it down, and would feel like fine silk if he ran his fingers through it. He tracked her movement with what felt disturbingly like hunger. "She thought *you* were the one feeding the gator."

Cole grunted. "I know better. You leave a gator alone, and it'll do the same for you."

"Exactly." Jena turned toward the door. "Well, I'll let you get back to whatever you were doing. You have my card. Will you call me if you see anything unusual with another gator?"

"I don't have a phone." *And it would be better if we never spoke again.*

Except Cole couldn't help asking one question after noticing that her reach to open the front door seemed stiff, as if her back hurt or she was trying not to move her upper body with any abruptness.

"Mind if I ask what happened to you? The scars on your face look like you might've been hit with flying glass, and you're moving as if you're in pain."

She'd stepped onto the front porch but now turned to study him with a slight frown that drew fine dark-red eyebrows together with a little wrinkle in between. One look at the blush on her face told Cole he'd trampled all over a sore spot—literally.

"Just a minor injury on the job," she said. "Good day, Mr. Ryan."

Jena Sinclair turned and walked down the stairs and out of his life with a square-shouldered gait that told him she was making a concerted effort to hide whatever was wrong with her. She reached the black pickup, where the other agent waited with his gaze trained on Cole's house. She turned back to look at Cole, still standing in the doorway.

He had no idea how to read her expression, but he could take his own emotional temperature and he didn't like the results. Jena Sinclair had taught him a couple of things about himself in the past few minutes that he didn't want to know.

First, sometime in the past five years, a deep fatigue had wrapped itself around him—not the fatigue that could be slept off with a soft bed and a warm blanket, but the fatigue caused by a tightened harness that restricted. That promised no end to long days and longer nights. A harness of his own making.

Cole had realized another surprising thing too. Very surprising for the man who needed nothing and no one.

He was lonely.

CHAPTER 9

Mac was animated on the drive to drop off the gator at regional headquarters in Thibodaux, where it would be sent to the LDWF Wildlife Division lab in Baton Rouge for testing.

Using about 10 percent of her brain, Jena managed to make appropriate "hmmmmm" and "you think so?" responses when needed. The other 90 percent was busy thinking about Cole Ryan. So much about that man simply didn't add up.

When she'd seen him in the distance, standing in his doorway for the first time, she'd mistaken him for a different kind of man, the type she thought of as a Terrebonne Hard Case. Usually, Hard Cases were guys that were long on hair and short on teeth, and who lived as much off the land as possible. They ate what they caught and weren't that picky about what it was. They might boil a mess of crawfish in an iron pot one night, sharing the feast with the whole neighborhood. Two days later, dinner might be a lone bullfrog or a squirrel.

There were lots of Hard Cases in the parish, although not nearly as many as there used to be, Gentry had told her. Most of them were as warm and big hearted as any other people in Terrebonne—maybe even more so. Hard Cases just lived the way they lived, often the way their parents and grandparents had lived, eking out a living and relying on the bounty of the parish for each meal.

She'd been utterly and absolutely wrong in her assessment, though. Cole Ryan was no Hard Case. He looked to be in his early to mid thirties and was clean shaven but for thick blond hair that reached almost to his waist. Parts of it were pulled into braids, but those strands struck her as more practical than cosmetic, like he wanted to keep his hair off his face. What she'd mistaken for gray-streaked locks were sun streaks in thick amber-gold hair most women would kill to have. He spent a lot of time outside.

And the man had the clearest, bluest eyes Jena had ever seen outside the brilliance of the sky during a cloudless day in Louisiana winter.

She didn't want to think about the six-pack on display or the muscles that moved beneath the tanned skin of his biceps when he opened and closed the door—or crossed his arms over his chest. The man even had perfect teeth, what little she'd been able to see of them from his brief attempt at conversation, a skill in which he was clearly out of practice.

Cole Ryan, if that was his real name, did not have a South Louisiana accent either. He talked like a Southerner, but one who hailed from Shreveport or Jackson or Birmingham—certainly nowhere south of I-10. And he talked like an educated man, or at least one who knew how to think on his feet. He'd danced around that story about why he'd moved to Terrebonne more smoothly than an Olympic skater on ice. He'd also been observant about her injuries, and not just the ones visible on her face.

No, Cole Ryan was not the kind of man who lived like a hermit on the edge of the water behind an abandoned sugarcane field, not unless he was in trouble with the law or had mental health issues.

He was eccentric, for sure. *Everything* about him said: "Leave me alone."

"What's going on up here?"

Mac braked fast, startling Jena back into the real world, where it had grown dark. Ahead of them, blocking the highway, lay a sea of flashing red and blue lights from SO patrol cars, an ambulance, even a couple of Houma PD sedans. And a ladder truck from the Montegut firehouse.

"I don't know, but isn't that one of our trucks up there—with the boat hitched to it?" Jena craned her neck but the license plate was hidden by the boat; each of their trucks had the agent's unit number on the plates. "I can't tell who it is."

Mac pulled over. "I've been monitoring the radio but whatever's going on is being kept vague. Just telling people the drawbridge up there is open indefinitely and people should plan alternate routes. Let's check it out."

Jena shivered when she got out of the truck. First, because she'd been so preoccupied with Cole Ryan that she hadn't been paying attention. Second, because the last time she'd climbed out of the passenger side of a department pickup on the narrow shoulder of this same parish road, she'd been shot, waking up in the hospital in Houma with two bullet wounds, a lot of glass cuts, and a missing friend.

She spotted a pair of familiar figures—Gentry and the Terrebonne enforcement unit's other senior agent, Paul Billiot. She pointed them out to Mac, and she and Mac made their way through a tangle of officers, each on a radio or, more often, a phone. Everybody was crouched behind a car or blocked from view of the bridge by a truck or SUV.

Jena had spent her first year intimidated by the intense, dark-eyed Paul Billiot, an active member of one of the parish's indigenous Native American tribes. He had fought like hell to find Ceelie when she was kidnapped, though, and he'd even driven to New Orleans a couple of times with Gentry to see how Jena was recuperating. Now she didn't fear him, but she definitely respected him.

Mac, however, who'd spent his first year in Terrebonne as Paul's partner, hadn't moved past the intimidation stage. Paul had probably traumatized him on purpose; the man had a very deeply guarded, but wicked, sense of humor. When they reached the two senior agents, Mac stood off to the side and kept his mouth shut, not noticing Paul looking at him with what Jena would call the Billiot version of a smile. He knew the junior officer was afraid of him and enjoyed it.

She stood next to Gentry and nudged him with her elbow. "What's going on?"

He didn't look at her but jerked his chin toward the highway ahead. "I think Black Diamond is about to claim another victim."

Jena frowned, scanning what she could see of the roadway. An old VW Beetle sat on the narrow shoulder just before the drawbridge at Highway 55 and Exxon Company Road, and the bridge was raised. Patrol cars blocked the roadway on the south side, just ahead of them, and Jena could see glints of flashing lights lining the road on the bridge's other side.

No one appeared to be in the drawbridge operation tower.

Standing on the other side of her, Paul leaned over and said, "Top of the bridge. This side."

"Oh no." She drew in a ragged breath. The kid could've been anywhere between fifteen and twenty because he still had that skinny, gangly look teenage boys always got until they filled out, like puppies with oversized feet they hadn't yet grown into. He walked the ragged, toothy edge of the raised bridge as if it were a circus high wire, teetering between the grooves that locked into the opposite side when the bridge was lowered. He wore baggy jeans but no shirt. His lank dark hair flopped in his eyes, and he'd stretched out his arms on both sides for balance.

Finally, Jena saw why no one was trying to force him down. In one hand he held a gun, its outline unmistakable. The weapon was a semiautomatic, the spotlight from a couple of the cars bouncing splashes of light off its shiny barrel. Every once in a while he'd shoot in the general direction of the line of patrol cars, and the officer in charge would remind everyone to stay down and hold fire. He didn't seem to be shooting *at* anyone, but that didn't mean someone couldn't get shot.

"Let us get you down from there, son. All you need to do is drop the gun. You can climb down the ladder onto the fire engine."

The voice boomed from somewhere, and Jena again looked at the tower next to the drawbridge. "They got an officer in the tower?"

"Yeah, several," Gentry said. "The negotiator has been trying to talk him down for at least half an hour. Nobody's sure how he even got up there. He was singing and talking for a while, but for the last ten minutes or so he's been quiet. His movements have grown more erratic."

"How do you know it's Black Diamond?" The image of Jacks singing and trying to cartwheel across the brick wall behind Jena's house wouldn't leave her mind. What if he'd been on this bridge? What if he'd had a gun? What if she'd still had her gun on her when he knocked her down?

"We don't know for sure." Paul glanced over at Mac, who remained quiet. "Something wrong with you, Griffin?"

"No, sir, just observing."

"Good."

Jena shook her head at Paul, who gave her a raised eyebrow in return. She'd been around Mac enough to realize he was upset by this boy's situation and not just intimidated by his former partner.

"The kid claimed it was Black Diamond before he stopped talking," Gentry said. "All we can do is take his word for it. He's sure as hell acting BSC."

The boy yelled something Jena couldn't understand. His movements were clear, though. He'd stopped walking. He held the gun's barrel to his temple.

The officer with the bullhorn stood and held up his free hand in a placating gesture. "Son, don't do that. Please drop the gun, and it'll be okay. I promise, we want to help you. Nothing bad's gonna happen to you. We just want to make sure you're safe."

Jena was just thinking the sheriff's negotiator was offering the kid an awfully big target to shoot at when a sudden shot rang out. Blood and tissue from the boy's head sprayed in a red-black arc, backlit by the spotlights. They heard a splash seconds after the boy disappeared over the bayou side of the open drawbridge.

"Shit. Damn it!" Paul's fist cracked down hard on the hood of the truck, but Jena couldn't take her eyes off the bridge. The boy was gone. No way he'd survived that shot.

"We've got a boat and drag hook over here!" Gentry shouted, striding toward the bridge. "Clear a path for us to launch next to the tower."

Paul jumped into the truck, but stuck his head out the open window. "Sinclair, Griffin, call the lieutenant and make sure he knows what's going on. We'll call it in as soon as we find the kid."

"Got it." Jena hadn't realized she was crying until a tear dropped off her chin and tickled its way down her neck. "You need us to do anything here?"

He looked back at Mac's truck. "You got a boat hitched to that truck?"

Jena shook her head. "No, we've got a gator on his way to the lab in Baton Rouge."

"Go ahead and take it around the long way. We got plenty of deputies here. Don't forget to call the lieutenant."

Back in Mac's truck, heading south to cut around via a detour of at least forty miles, Jena filled in Lieutenant Doucet on the situation, then sat staring at her phone.

Mac glanced at her. "You okay?"

She should be the one asking him. Jena had never seen Mac look so shaken, even after finding the gator victim, but she probably didn't look much better. "I think I need to make another call." One she didn't want to make.

Finally, she dialed Jackson's cell number.

Her mother answered, however, instead of her brother. Great.

"Good evening, Jena."

Jena was too tired to play her mother's passive-aggressive steel magnolia games.

"Hi, Mom. How is Jackson? Why are you answering his phone?"

There was a pause during which Jena imagined Grace Sinclair, dressed in tasteful winter-white slacks and a matching angora sweater, relaxing by the fireplace with a glass of wine and pretending life hadn't gone on a house call to Satan, riding in a handbasket.

"Jackson, I'm afraid, is at Oschsner, although we're trying to keep it as quiet as possible."

Jackson had just been released from jail that morning. Why would he be in the hospital unless he'd gotten more drugs? Unless . . ." The answer came to her. "You had him committed, didn't you? I need to see him. Will they let me see him?"

"Of course not. You've done quite enough by turning him over to the authorities before we had a chance to handle it quietly. They're not letting anyone see him or talk to him for the next two weeks."

Jena couldn't ignore the implication that Jackson's predicament was her fault. "Mom, I couldn't handle him. I'd never seen him so aggressive or angry, and he needed help. No one at all can see him, or just me? Not even you or Dad?"

"No one." Grace Sinclair's voice dripped acid. "He's been threatening to kill himself—more specifically, to slit his wrists. I wonder where he got such an idea?"

Jena would have hung up on her mother, but her mother beat her to it. Grace Sinclair might love her kids in her own way, but sometimes it was hard to see it.

CHAPTER 10

Mac fidgeted in the back row of the big muster room at the Terrebonne Parish Sheriff's Office. He'd never seen such an assortment of law enforcement officers crammed into a single room—state police, Houma cops, wildlife enforcement agents, sheriffs' deputies. They weren't just from Terrebonne either, but also the neighboring coastal parishes of Lafourche and Saint Mary. Men and women wore an array of uniforms, plainclothes, suits and ties, shorts and tees.

Pacing back and forth across the front of the room, walking with clipped steps to match his clipped voice, was the lead DEA agent on the case, a guy named O'Malley.

Mac sat with Jena on one side. Between him and the aisle sat EZ Caine, short for Ezekiel Zebediah. "Dad was kind of religious," he'd explained when they met, proving he was a man with a gift for understatement.

EZ, who wore his head shaved, had the squarest jaw Mac had ever seen, and sported the biceps of somebody who worked with weights—a lot. He had come over from Golden Meadow in Lafourche Parish to fill in for Jena after the shooting. EZ had applied for a permanent transfer to Terrebonne, and probably was going to get it.

They needed more agents—Wildlife and Fisheries personnel were dealing with whacked-out alligators as well as helping with the influx of Black Diamond, which seemed to be growing and showing up in places drugs didn't usually go.

Like the kid who'd killed himself last night on the drawbridge. The seventeen-year- old was an honors student at a Catholic school in Houma, not unlike the school Mac had attended just south of Presque Isle. The kid also was only eight years younger than him—just a year or two younger than Mac's youngest brother.

A small plastic bag with an ounce of Black Diamond had been found in the kid's room under his mattress, but nobody had any idea where he got it—or at least nobody was saying. The tox results weren't back yet, but there wasn't much doubt that the black powder in the bag under his pillow had sent him on a quest to climb the drawbridge and shoot himself.

Gentry and Paul had pulled him out of the water within fifteen minutes, but the kid was way beyond saving.

Mac felt as if he'd aged ten years in the last ten hours, witnessing the boy's mother sobbing openly on the starched shirtfront of his pale father, who struggled with a shaky voice to make a statement to the media.

That wasn't all. The DEA task force leader said there had been three other shootings in the parish last night where Black Diamond had been a factor.

LDWF and the Coast Guard had been searching every boat they could find coming into the parish in the southern half of Terrebonne, but almost 50 percent of the 2,100-square-mile parish was water. The state police and sheriff's office were crawling over the more solid northern half of the parish like ants. So far, nothing.

For now, Mac and Jena were staying on routine patrols, but the lieutenant had asked him to reschedule his time off next week. He'd planned to rent a cabin down near Cocodrie and spend a few days with

Cassie, a hot attorney he'd met in a Houma nightclub a few weeks ago. Cassie had been disappointed, but there were always more Cassies in the world, and Mac hoped his postponed time off meant Warren was going to bring him in on the Black Diamond case.

The vibration from his cell phone brought him out of the semi-stupor he'd been sent into by Agent O'Malley's dry explanation of the chemical properties of Black Diamond, and why DEA officials felt sure it was imported from China rather than being cooked up inside the parish.

As he pulled his phone from his pocket, he saw Jena pulling out hers as well. They held the phones side by side; both screens displayed texts from the wildlife biology lab in Baton Rouge. Mac was closest to the aisle, so he squeezed in front of EZ and slipped into the hallway.

"You guys might want to get up here and get the report about your hard-partying gator; I can meet you in Thibodaux." Maxie Renaud, the biologist who'd taken possession of the animal last night, was one of the first women Mac had dated after moving to Louisiana. He liked her, but she was too brainy for him. It wasn't that he disliked smart women, even women smarter than him. He just didn't want it thrown in his face. Jena was brainy but didn't feel the need to prove anything.

"What'd you find?" Better be something good for him to drive up to Thibodaux and potentially ruin his shot at getting in on this drug case.

Maxie laughed. "Bring someone from the sheriff's office if you want to make a bust. I'm still running tests, but I think your gator was stoned. I'm surprised he didn't have the munchies; probably thought he was hallucinating the old lady and her dog."

Considering he'd been listening to the hallucinogenic properties of Black Diamond for the past hour and a half, Mac wasn't amused. "How do you know it was marijuana? Did you find a stash in its stomach? Could it be something else?"

The uncharacteristic sharpness of his tone stopped Maxie's jokes. "I'll bring the tox results to Thibodaux and you can take a look for yourself—it's an odd mix of stuff." She paused, her voice filled with uncertainty. "Anything in particular you want me to test for before I leave?"

Mac glanced up as Jena slipped out of the muster room and walked toward him, eyebrows raised in question. He had a bad feeling about this whole thing, not that he could possibly be paranoid after the past twelve hours.

"We're on our way. You got any way of checking our gator for Black Diamond?"

CHAPTER 11

Cole had postponed handling the head and feet of the gator until the guts, meat, and hide were taken care of, but this morning was the day to deal with the bony parts. He had done some research on gator taxidermy when he'd first moved to the parish, but decided it was better to sell the parts to people who knew what they were doing.

Some skills, he just didn't want to acquire.

The heads and feet had to be tanned, cured, oiled, and sanitized before they could be turned into wall mounts or back scratchers to be sold in the markets throughout the state. Tourists snapped them up. Cole guessed visitors from the Midwest or New England believed owning a shiny polished skull or tooth or claw made them real badasses.

He'd get more for the parts at the taxidermy place up in Theriot if he could scrape out the head pretty clean, which was smelly, tedious work. He'd started after an early-morning fishing trip, and didn't finish until midafternoon. He put the slivers of already-spoiling scrap meat in another plastic bin, then moved on to his next job: preparing the feet. This had been one huge gator, with feet larger than Cole's hands, and that didn't account for the inch-long claws at the end of each of its four toes on the back feet and five on the front.

He cleaned off the first three feet carefully, then set them to dry on a rack before he put them into bags and returned them to the cooler.

One more foot and he could rid himself of the bin's contents upstream, giving swamp denizens another meal. Tomorrow, he'd drive up to Theriot with everything in the portable cooler that fit in his truck bed. First, he'd sell the head and feet, then stop off at a buyer to sell the hide. He didn't really need the money, so he'd find someplace in the parish to donate it anonymously.

The midafternoon sun sent trails of light through the open door of the workhouse, and caused something to glitter on the bottom of the fourth gator foot—a right front clawed monstrosity that had probably snagged his poor human victim long enough for Mr. Gator to twist off the guy's arm.

A stone must have gotten stuck in the webbing between the toes, which would bring down the price if he couldn't pry it out without damaging the scaly digits. Cole turned the foot over and saw nothing, so he took it to the door of the workhouse. Stretching the toes apart in the sunlight, he got to the webbing between the first two toes and saw it again.

It wasn't a stone, but what the hell *was* it?

Even though the day was mild and pleasant, too much air and sun would ruin his gator haul, so he left the mystery foot on the worktable, and made sure everything else had been stashed in individual bags in the freezer. This one foot, he'd sacrifice in the name of curiosity.

He pulled out his knife set again, choosing a small blade along with a pair of tweezers the size of his pinkie. Taking them to the table where he'd left the foot, he pulled over the bright lamp he used to illuminate his work during the gloomy days of winter. Time for a more thorough examination.

There—the light had caught on something orange. A round piece of glass or a . . .

Cole clutched his knife more tightly and leaned in closer, trying to make sense of what he'd seen. The round orange bead—maybe an eighth of a dime in size—blinked at him like an inflamed eyeball. So it was something with a watertight battery. But what? Maybe a transmitter from a child's toy or a cell phone? Had the gator stepped on it on the bayou bottom?

Cole didn't think it had contributed to the animal's death; the treble hook had been enough to do that.

Changing to an even smaller blade, he bent over the foot and cut around the blinking light, trying not to damage the metal base that had been embedded in the webbing. He loosened it enough to remove with the tweezers and held it under the light.

The thing was some kind of electrical device, but it had been embedded too deeply to be anything the gator had stepped on. Flipping the foot over, he studied the webbing between the toes on the top side of the foot and found what could be an imprint or stamp—as if someone had used a stapler of sorts to insert the device.

Another mystery, but one that would have to wait. Tomorrow, he could ask the taxidermist if he'd seen anything like it. Mystery or no mystery, it was too late to make the drive tonight.

A shave and a shower left Cole feeling clean but not relaxed. The fact that every beat of the warm water on his skin had drummed up the image of Jena Sinclair's shiny dark-red hair spilling from beneath her baseball cap? That hadn't helped. Nor the scrape of the razor across his jaw that made him think of her long, elegant neck, the peaches-and-cream skin beneath those glass scars, the way she'd blushed when he'd blundered in like a bull gator himself and asked what had happened to her.

For the first time in five years, Cole felt the stirring of an erection, or at least one that biology didn't push on him upon waking each morning. No, this one was all about her. Of all the women to capture his interest, it would be a fucking law enforcement officer. Yeah, she was a wildlife agent, but Cole knew about the Louisiana Wildlife and Fisheries enforcement division. Those officers went through tough training; the harsh conditions they worked in demanded it.

So Jena Sinclair was smart and strong. She knew how to shoot. She knew how to survive. And damn it, she wore a badge.

She was also beautiful, and she was damaged inside as well as out. He recognized the signs. She was in pain, and it wasn't just physical.

He'd never been so happy with his decision to not get another phone. The one from his old life lay at the bottom of the Mississippi River at Vicksburg, or at least it had been headed that way the last time he'd seen it. He'd tossed it over the rail at the rest stop when he left his home state behind. People kept looking for him, wanting to talk to him, and he didn't want to be found. He sure as hell didn't want to talk.

Now, thanks to that impulsive iPhone toss, he couldn't do anything stupid and equally impulsive like call Jena Sinclair. Plus, what would he say to her? He could chat about the man's arm he'd found in the stomach of a dead gator, which he'd decided to bury. He could tell her about finding a flashing orange light in the dead gator's foot when he was getting it ready to sell.

No, Cole and Jena Sinclair had nothing to discuss.

He pulled on a clean pair of jeans and a black sweater that was snugger than it had been last March—he kept adding muscle from all the manual labor it took to run this place. Then he settled onto his rustic but oh-so-comfortable sofa to read the news.

The tablet computer was one of the few indulgences he'd allowed himself, purchased at a discount electronics store in Houma. He might have cut himself off from the world, but he still needed to know what was going on in it and whether any of those goings-on potentially involved him. Or at least that's what he told himself.

If he were to be honest, he'd have to admit it provided him with some link, however tenuous, to the human race. It also could have exacerbated that loneliness he hadn't acknowledged until today. Or maybe that was just his response to Agent Sinclair.

Cole opened the bookmarked *Houma Today* newspaper. Politicians were doing nothing on Capitol Hill—no surprise there. The feds were making overtures that could further damage the state's fishing industry. No surprise there either.

The third headline stopped him cold: *Black Diamond Epidemic Rises, Results in Teen Suicide*. A story about a synthetic drug that officials described as reaching epic proportions in the parish was accompanied by a photo of a pile of powder. It looked like black sand—or coarse black pepper.

It looked a lot like what had been in the stomach of his gator. The gator with a blinking device embedded in its foot.

Cole slammed the tablet case shut and padded into the kitchen, his brain on overdrive as he poured himself a glass of the wine he'd made from last season's haul of wild blackberries. Why hadn't he looked more closely at that powder? He'd been so intent on finding the treble hook to see if the meat was edible that he could have overlooked something much more lethal.

He sliced some chunks of dried gator sausage left from last season and set them on a plate with a hunk of crusty bread and a few cold new potatoes spicy with crab boil. He'd become a decent, if rustic, cook out of necessity. The black earth in the small garden out back wasn't conducive to the cultivation of anything that didn't enjoy growing in mud, which limited him to mostly what he could raise in pots or other containers. It fed critters that wandered in out of the water as much as it fed him.

He did well enough, though, and at least the food wasn't filled with chemicals and shit.

That thought brought him full circle, back to the bag of black powder and the orange blinking light. Chewing mindlessly, he reached for the salt and the movement caused a white card to flutter to the table—something he'd stashed between his hand-carved salt and pepper shakers.

Jena Sinclair's business card.

CHAPTER 12

Jena had changed her ringtone to a wolf howl when she'd gotten to New Orleans after the shooting. It had a dual purpose: to annoy her parents and remind them—and herself—that she was a wildlife agent. Even a couple of bullets wouldn't turn her into an uptown socialite in the making. She hadn't changed the ringtone back to something more professional, so when the howls erupted from her uniform pants pocket halfway to Thibodaux, Jena just gave Mac a deadpan look and said, "Not. One. Word."

She pulled out the phone and frowned at the screen. "Ray Naquin. Wonder what he wants."

"He wants to get in your pants, that's what. The guy's a lounge lizard. Stay away from him."

Right. This coming from the lips of the LDWF's own unofficial lounge lizard himself.

She touched the red "Answer" button. "Sinclair."

She'd forgotten how to answer a telephone with anything other than her last name—another reason she was unfit for a different occupation. Assuming the call concerned a gator, she put the phone on speaker.

"What's up, Ray? You got a gator we need to know about?"

"I'm truly hurt. I'm calling about that dinner date your partner promised me. Well, he at least said you'd be glad to hear from me if I called."

Jena shot a beady glare in Mac's direction. He shrugged and gave her innocence-filled brown eyes. "Oh he did, did he?"

"He did. How about tonight? I know it's short notice, but we can go up to A-Bear's in Houma, have a nice meal, and see what happens after that."

A choking sound reached her from Mac's direction, followed by a cough wrapped around two words that she'd never been able to resist: "Dare you."

Damn it. How many times had she gotten in trouble because she couldn't resist a dare? This wasn't going to be one of them.

"Afraid I can't tonight. I already have plans." Thank God she'd called Ceelie Savoie last night and invited her to dinner tonight. A-Bear's sounded like a good idea, though. "Maybe another time."

"You bet, sweetheart." Ray didn't sound too disappointed.

Sweetheart, her ass. Jena would rather have her teeth pulled than go out with Ray Naquin, even if she were ready to date again, which she wasn't. Thanks to her scars, she might never be ready. She'd always ignored Ray's flirtations, figuring he was all talk. He was handsome in a rugged, he-bear kind of way, but his shtick sounded more like a used-car salesman than a rugged gator hunter.

"You really got plans tonight, or is our gator guy not your type?" Mac grinned.

"Both. I'm meeting Ceelie Savoie for dinner, but this"—she pulled off her baseball cap and whapped Mac on the shoulder—"is for telling him to call me."

"Hey, I thought you might need to get out." Mac laughed. "Besides, I was hoping he'd call you a 'long, tall, sweet thang' to your face, which is how he referred to you in our conversation."

God help her. "Well, in the future, leave me out of your conversations, eh?"

The *eh* got a chuckle out of him, and they continued toward Thibodaux in silence.

She was looking forward to meeting Ceelie for dinner instead of eating frozen pad thai at the White Rhino and feeling sorry for herself, plus she had no doubt Ceelie would go for A-Bear's. The place had great food.

She and Ceelie had agreed to meet at a restaurant at eight since Jena was on shift until six and Gentry went on duty at the same time. She'd call and suggest A-Bear's.

Enough about dinner and dates. "We still need to talk to Don Gateau and maybe Amelia Patout—even if Ray's taking his gators to Gateau's, other nuisance hunters might still be going to Patout's. Want to do that tomorrow?" Jena didn't want another day on the water if she could avoid it, or at least her sore body didn't. Cole Ryan had been right; she was achy and then some. Not that bouncing around in a pickup on these roads was a big improvement over bouncing around in a patrol boat. At least it jostled different muscles.

What would it be like to have dinner with Cole Ryan? He was the anti–Ray Naquin, closed off and taciturn, but fascinating. Handsome. Really handsome. She'd gone to sleep thinking about him last night, trying to solve the puzzle he presented. He was too tightly wound to be a back-to-the-earth hippie type, too sharp and observant to be a Hard Case. And, yeah, sexy.

Ray Naquin oozed oil; Cole Ryan oozed testosterone.

Back off, Sinclair. The man's eccentric and he's hiding something, and so are you. She wasn't saying she'd never again get naked with a man, but facts were facts, and she was disfigured. Even oily Ray wouldn't want any part of those puckered scars. At least she had makeup that would camouflage most of the damage on her face.

Eventually, if she could dig up the cash, she'd have plastic surgery, even if it was pure vanity. Her parents would pay for it in a second if she asked; her mom had already offered. Jena didn't want to encourage them to show love through money, though. For now, she'd have a nice, quiet dinner with a good friend. It would mark another tentative step back into the world of the living.

Mac had been singing over the sound of the LDWF and sheriff's office radios—some indie/folk/coffeehouse stuff she thought all sounded alike. She'd grown up in the city of Dr. John and the Neville Brothers, of Wynton Marsalis and Louis Armstrong and Nathan and the Zydeco Cha-Chas. She didn't do New England coffeehouse. Finally, he stopped singing and looked at her. "You got the printout?"

She dug in her bag and pulled out a list reflecting the makeup of Black Diamond. Different suppliers might tweak the recipe, but the active ingredients remained the same. Agent O'Malley had promised to have her badge if she didn't call him the second they got the toxicology report, and he'd have her badge again if the tox lab didn't get the final written report to him in seventy-two hours, like she had any control over what happened in Baton Rouge.

Warren had been standing next to her when those ultimatums were issued, and the lieutenant had clearly not liked one of his agents being threatened on his own turf by the same DEA guy who'd treated every one of them like half-witted yahoos, including Warren himself and the sheriff.

But Warren had kept his mouth shut, so Jena followed suit.

"I heard Paul Billiot say it acts like heroin in some folks, crystal meth in others, and a few hit the jackpot and go on a hallucinogenic trip swinging from superhigh to suicidal." Mac was talking and looking straight ahead, so he missed the tears that sprang into Jena's eyes. She kept her gaze on the passing scenery and blinked them away, swallowing down the image of Jackson locked up in a psychiatric wing. Trying not to think that he might have considered suicide because of what she'd done to herself.

Jackson had shown a devious side, though, so chances also were good he was just using the threat to push their parents' buttons, and he'd gotten locked up for it. The only bright light in the whole mess was that he might have a real shot at moving past his Black Diamond adventure if the doctors managed to keep Grace and Jackson Sinclair Sr. away from their son long enough.

Mac pulled into the parking lot of the LDWF regional office in Thibodaux, just down the street from the Mudbug Brewery, which they'd all visited more than a few times when they were up this way on the weekends. King Cake Ale with cinnamon sugar on the rim was Jena's favorite of the local brews, and everyone made fun of her for it.

Maxie Renaud met them in the lobby of the building. There had been no need for them to meet in person, so Jena suspected the woman wanted to reconnect with Mac. The forensic biologist was petite and blond—which seemed just her partner's type—so Jena saw why he'd hit on her. And after hearing her sum up the preliminary findings about the odd contents of the blood in *Alligator mississippiensis* 232D, as their gator had been named, she also understood why they'd flamed out so quickly as a couple. Dr. Renaud was smarter than Mac and probably not afraid to show it. He'd be just the guy to find that annoying, if not intimidating.

Or maybe she was selling Mac short. He'd surprised her this week with a perceptiveness and sensitivity she hadn't expected.

"Anyway, our gator was only about five or six years old," Maxie said, leading them back to the biology wing and into an office just off the double doors. She pulled a couple of sheets of paper off the printer. "You got that list of Black Diamond's chemical structure and components?"

Jena pulled out the DEA printout and handed it to the toxicologist. Maxie scanned it and whistled. "Your gator was definitely flying on Black Diamond. No wonder this stuff is so nasty. The difference between a pleasant high and full-out crazy would be minuscule."

"It's one of the bath salt drugs," Mac said. "I've been reading about them. They're synthetic versions of this amphetamine-like plant product sold legally in Asia and parts of Africa. They ship 'em over here and head shops sell them disguised as bath salts or plant food—at least until they kill or injure enough people for the politicians to get involved."

Maxie nodded. "They're also mixed with stuff like formaldehyde and—bingo—trouble, especially if the user's also been drinking. It's a lot cheaper than heroin or cocaine, doesn't show up on standard drug tests, and creates instant addicts. It's the perfect drug. We found something more weird than just the drug, though. It's why I wanted to talk to you in person."

They settled into chairs in the office, and Maxie perched on the edge of the desk. "Okay, first of all, we found this in the gator's belly." She handed over a clear plastic bag that looked to be about a foot square in size. Inside it, in a standard sandwich bag, was a large amount of black powder. Jena held it up: maybe as much as ten or twelve ounces of the stuff.

"This isn't a recreational amount." She handed the bag to Mac. "It's a shipment."

"Exactly. How the alligator got it is beyond me." Maxie took the bag from Mac and pointed to a bottom corner, where a few grains of black powder had escaped. "The gator's stomach acid could have started eating into the plastic or, more likely, it snagged on something in its belly. The poor guy was carrying a couple of small hooks where someone had tried to catch him." She held the bag up to the light. "The hooks weren't big enough to have killed the animal, but any one of them would have been big enough to tear a hole in that bag."

"Let me look at it again." Jena took the plastic bag and studied the small hole in the corner. "Any way to tell how much escaped into the gator's system through this hole?"

Maxie shook her head, retrieved her evidence bags and the DEA report, and locked them in a case on wheels. "I'll take this back to Baton Rouge and see what else I can find. We won't be able to pinpoint a precise amount, but now that I have the exact makeup of Black Diamond, or at least this iteration of the drug, I can give you a better idea of how much was in the gator's system."

Jena's biggest question was how the gator got the drugs in the first place. "Any way to tell how long the bag had been in his system? Wouldn't his stomach acids have started breaking it down pretty soon after swallowing?"

Maxie shook her head again. "Hard to say, but my guess is no. Human stomach acids won't eat through plastic; chances are, neither would an alligator's or, if they did, it would take so long he'd poop it out beforehand."

"Even what little he ingested was enough to make him sluggish and not too worried about a crazy woman, a barking dog, and being poked with a table leg," Mac said. There wasn't an ounce of flirtation in his voice—or his face. Jena finally saw the agent beneath the flirtatious exterior. "What was the other thing you found so interesting?"

Maxie reached behind her on the desk and handed them another evidence bag, this one with a small metallic rectangle in it. A light in the middle of the device blinked orange in a slow, steady rhythm.

Jena examined it and handed it to Mac. "So this was in the gator's belly too?"

"No, embedded in its right front foot, between two toes. That one's out of my field of expertise to examine, so I thought you could take it back to the Terrebonne Sheriff's Office since the gator was in your parish."

Mac leaned toward the window to get more light on the device. "It looks like it could be a receiver or transmitter of some kind. Any way the gator could have stepped on it accidentally?"

Maxie thought for a moment, blew out a frustrated breath, and shrugged. "Anything's possible, but I don't think so. It was embedded too far between his toes, for one thing, plus your ordinary transmitter probably wouldn't work underwater and, as you can see, that one's still blinking."

She stood up and grabbed the handle of her rolling case containing the Black Diamond. "Anyway, that's what I have for you. I want to get this printout back to Baton Rouge and officially get your gator on record as a Black Diamond user."

They walked back to the lobby with her, Mac distracted and still looking at the tiny metal box with its blinking light. He glanced up at Jena. "I got a buddy down around Bourg who knows a lot about electronics—he's into all these remote-control toys and stuff. Mind if we make a detour on the way home?"

"Fine with me." Jena had plenty of time before picking up Ceelie for dinner. Plus, the whole idea of a shipment-sized bag of Black Diamond inside a gator bothered her. Either they had a really careless drug supplier who'd lost a big chunk of his shipment somewhere in the water, or it was intentional.

Could an alligator be used as a drug mule?

CHAPTER 13

Mac had met Jerry Pourfon the first night after completing his six months of training in the LDWF Academy. He'd been sore, exhausted, and ready to chill out in some way that didn't involve trekking through mud weighed down in heavy boots and a ton of gear, or driving dirt roads in the middle of the night with his lights off, looking for illegal hunters or poachers.

He'd stopped in the Bayou Honey, an absolute dive in the worst sense of the word, somewhere between Houma and Thibodaux. The only other customer that Tuesday night had been a commercial fisherman home off a long run and trying to shake off his own exhaustion.

Except where Mac was thinking beer and the company of a woman, Jerry had been thinking bourbon and the slow, meticulous dismantling of the remote control for an Air Hogs toy helicopter.

Since the bar had no women in it other than a middle-aged brunette with silver roots and dark circles of exhaustion under her eyes, Mac asked the bourbon drinker if he could join him. They'd both slowly gotten drunk—well, it hadn't taken Mac very long—and talked about remote controls.

As a means of celebrating his graduation from his grueling enforcement training, the night sucked. As the beginning of a friendship, it was stellar. Mac could indulge his secret passion for dismantling things and reassembling them around Jerry as often as he wanted, comforted by the knowledge that he'd never reach his friend's level of geekitude.

"Who is this guy, anyway?" Jena stood by the truck with her arms crossed, studying the assortment of rusting robots, tin men, flamingos, and yard art that littered the front of Jerry's double-wide.

"Don't judge." Mac grinned and stepped around a metal squirrel the size of a kid's tricycle, orange with rust and wearing a hollow-eyed expression worthy of a Stephen King novel. "You'll love Jerry."

Actually, she'd probably leave Jerry's with an urgent desire to take a shower, but the place wasn't dirty—not like Ray Naquin's house had been. Jerry brought hoarding to a whole new level. His house might look like chaos on the inside, with stacks of parts and tools and unidentified-but-possibly-useful-someday objects, but he could lay his hands on a particular item in seconds. He was infallible in a filing system only he could understand.

Mac deliberately avoided looking at Jena when Jerry opened the door and welcomed them in. If she'd had any reaction, she'd gone back to a pleasantly bland expression by the time introductions had been done.

"What's up, dude? You get dat Swiss Army knife taken apart and put back together yet?" Jerry's shoulder-length gray hair, with only a few strands of black to hint at its original color, had been pulled back into a ponytail, and his solid-gray beard, which hung halfway down his chest, was braided and tied at the bottom with a blue ribbon.

"You take knives apart and reassemble them?" Jena wrenched her gaze away from Jerry's surroundings, which she probably equated with a warehouse for scrap metal, and raised her eyebrows at Mac.

"Just a hobby." Mac had always been secretive about his fascination with moving parts and how they fit together. Everybody needed a hobby. "Jerry, I have something that Jena and I wanted you to take a look at."

Jena reached inside her pocket and pulled out the plastic bag containing their mystery metal. She held it out to him. "Can you tell us anything about this?"

Jerry took the bag and held it up to the light, frowning. "Okay if I be takin' it out and lookin' at it?"

"No!" Jena and Mac reacted at the same time, which raised Jerry's antennae.

"Okay den, no problem." He held up the bag. "How 'bout you at least tell me what it is dat I'm supposed to be looking for?"

Mac looked at Jena and nodded. He trusted Jerry, but not enough to interfere with what she thought qualified as shareable.

"It's evidence in a case we're working, and that's about all I can tell you," she said. "Sorry. Mac thought you might know what it was."

Jerry's dark-brown eyes crinkled. "I done got an idea, me. Let's see if I'm right."

They followed him into what was probably supposed to be a dining room, but it held a broad, rustic worktable littered with all kinds of gadgets. Mac picked up a tiny spring. "Hey, this looks like what I need to finish rehabbing my knife. You using it for anything?"

Jerry had knelt to pull a box from beneath a table and glanced over his shoulder. "Nah, help yourself. Found another old knife on da table next to it if you want it."

Mac peered into a cardboard cigar box, its original bright cover faded and scratched. "This looks like an old Robeson. I'd love to have it. Sure you don't want it?"

"Nah. I like electronics more'n mechanics, me." A stack of books and papers toppled to the floor when Jerry pulled out the box. No, Mac decided, what Jerry pulled out was not a box, but an amplifier.

From a top shelf, Jerry retrieved a wire basket holding an assortment of microphones. He picked through them and finally selected a large handheld model, its black cord trailing like a snake as he pulled it free from the basket. "Yep, I think dis should work."

"What are you doing?" Jena's brow wrinkled in concern. "It's not going to mess up our evidence, is it?"

"No, ma'am." Jerry grinned at her. Mac watched to see if she reacted to his friend's front teeth, one of which had been broken halfway off when he got hit by a runaway winch on the shrimp boat a few weeks ago. Mac had been on the lookout for a dentist who offered a pro bono day since Jerry didn't have insurance. Mac made a decent salary with the state, but not enough to pick up a big dental bill.

Jena had no reaction to the tooth-impaired grin. She was too busy frowning at the sight of Jerry as he plugged the portable amplifier into the wall, then plugged the speaker into the amp.

"Okay, let's have a listen." Jerry sat at the table and motioned the others to join him. Mac pulled out a chair and settled in. Jena hesitated but eventually climbed on a nearby stool.

Jerry held the mic close to the bag. "It's gonna be muted, so I'll make some adjustments, me." Reaching behind him, he turned a couple of knobs on the amp until an unsettling electronic hum—almost white-noise static but not quite—filled the room. Mac shivered at the sensation, which felt like nails running across the tops of the nerves that ran down his arms.

Finally, Jerry held the mic against the bagged object again. A *ping* sounded with each blink of the orange light. "It done be a transmitter of some kind," Jerry pronounced, turning off the amp and leaving the room blissfully quiet. "My guess is dat somebody has a tracking device what's done set for whatever frequency dis transmitter is set to—it's low, so maybe it's meant to be used in da water. I don't have anything to measure underwater signals, but it could be somethin' like dat."

"Like for a kid's remote-controlled boat or something?" Although Mac didn't figure a child's toy would require anything so elaborate.

"No, more like if you wanted to fill a bottle with water and set it loose in da Gulf with one of dem little transmitters inside," Jerry said, handing the bag to Jena. "Den you could sit on your boat and tell exactly where it was. Maybe one'a them scientists is tracking da tides or something."

Or tracking an alligator being used to transport drugs? Even as he entertained the idea, Mac thought it sounded nuts. Why not just bring in the drugs and leave the gators out of it?

Which is exactly what he shared with Jena once they were back in the truck and headed for Chauvin, where he planned to drop her off at that white travesty she called home.

"Well, except our units and the sheriff and the Coast Guard are all over every vessel coming up the main bayous right now. *Everything's* being searched, even people we know." She spoke slowly, reasoning it out as she talked. "Then again, so what if you get caught illegally setting bait for or catching a gator? You get a fine. Only reason we knew about this gator was because his haul sprang a leak and he got stoned in sight of Doris Benoit."

Seemed to Mac that it was still pretty far-fetched. "Maybe whoever was running the drugs into the parish accidentally lost a bag and Doris's gator found and ate it." He thought that more likely. Much more likely. "Gators aren't picky eaters, after all." They even ate each other, which made them the badasses of the swamp.

"Yeah, you're probably right. Setting up that kind of trafficking system would take a lot of coordination and a lot of money—and would need to make sense, which it doesn't." Jena's brows were knit into a frown when she turned away from Mac to stare out the window at another picture-perfect orange sunset gathering in the west. "But that doesn't explain the transmitter."

CHAPTER 14

Cole had driven into Houma for the afternoon. He'd stopped by a generic megastore on the edge of town and bought food to supplement what he could produce. Mostly milk and eggs, which he packed in the ice-filled cooler in the back of his truck.

He'd passed a farm with a CHICKENS FOR SALE sign stuck next to a dirt driveway, and stopped to explore the idea of buying his own chickens. As much as he liked the notion of fresh eggs and the challenge of building a coop that would allow the birds to range when they wanted, after talking to the farmer and watching the birds in their habitat, he decided a backyard full of squawks and chicken shit held little appeal.

He'd picked up a few tools at a hardware store outside town, even though he didn't need them. One could never have too many wrenches, right?

He'd gone by the parish library, using their free Internet access to do faster research on Black Diamond and the whole class of drugs called "bath salts" than he could do with his own slow mobile-service Wi-Fi and outdated tablet. Those drugs hadn't even been on the scene when he'd decided to leave society to its own devices.

He had stopped at a mini-mart and pumped the old red-and-rust Ford truck full of gas. He'd gone inside and bought one of those snack cakes he used to love, but had to spit it out after one bite. Years of living on real food had made it taste to him like chemicals and sugar. Had they always been that sweet? He used to put away two or three of the things at a time.

What he had *not* done was sell the hide, the head, or the feet of Big Bull, as he'd named his alligator find. Yeah, he liked things to have names, maybe because he knew so few people's names now. Big Bull had earned his moniker because of his size, that blinking light in his front foot, and the bag of powder Cole had found in his stomach, along with the human arm. A gator that size would've been king of the swamp—until he swallowed the wrong thing.

He'd thought a lot about Big Bull as he'd tossed and turned all night, wondering what really killed the big gator. Was it the treble hook or had some of that powder leaked out of the bag and been enough to kill him?

He'd wondered if the powder he'd found was Black Diamond, as he feared, or was something as innocuous as he'd originally thought.

He wondered if there was any relation between Big Bull and that crazy little gator that had wandered into the neighborhood and had the misfortune of running into Doris Day, as he'd renamed his neighbor. That had been a Doris kind of day when the gator had been caught, after all, and he still didn't know her real last name.

He wondered what the state wildlife biologists had discovered about Doris's gator and whether they might have found something similar from Big Bull if Cole had turned him in instead of trying to turn him into a profit.

He wondered why he couldn't just let the whole thing pass. Why he couldn't throw away or bury the rest of Big Bull and be done with it. It was none of his business, and he wouldn't dare eat the gator meat now that there was a possibility that drugs had been the cause of death.

He knew the answer to the last two questions, and those answers had prompted his rare trip into Houma. It was time to pull his head out of the South Louisiana mud and deal with hard truths, however inconvenient.

He couldn't let it go because of that boy, Morgan Tyler. The kid had been only seventeen years old and had blown off the top of his head because of whatever that black powder had done to his brain. From all Cole had read since—which had been a lot, thanks to his tablet and the library visit—this drug was very, very bad news. It was the kind of drug that turned kids into killers.

Maybe they killed themselves, like Morgan Tyler had.

Or maybe they went into a theater and started firing on a bunch of strangers.

Or maybe they went into a department store looking for someone with whom they had an ongoing feud, maybe an ex-girlfriend or a class bully, and began a deadly rampage of death and blood.

Cole had seen it happen, and he couldn't just sit back when there was any chance of it happening again, not here in this place that, somehow, he'd come to love even if it was rife with poverty and the people talked funny and the land was slowly sinking into the Gulf of Mexico. If he didn't tell someone in authority about Big Bull and the wrong person got hold of that drug, he'd feel responsible for the consequences. It was as simple as that.

Profiting from an illegally obtained gator was one thing. Keeping quiet about a potentially deadly drug was on another moral plane. It was as simple as that.

As simple as telling the truth.

As simple as holding on to whatever humanity, and sanity, he had left.

Still, after spending years extricating himself from society, he was reluctant to do something like pick up the receiver of a pay phone, assuming he could find one, plug in some change, and dial a number. He'd been working his way up to it.

Thus, the shopping.

And now the pay phone.

He'd been sitting outside the mini-mart on Highway 55 south of Montegut since his failed snack cake adventure had ended fifteen minutes earlier. In front of his truck sat what might be one of the only pay phones left in Terrebonne Parish. In his right hand he clenched a fistful of quarters. In his left hand he clenched Jena Sinclair's business card. Jena Sinclair, who for the last few days had taken up residence in whatever part of his brain and body wasn't otherwise occupied.

He could do this. It was just a phone call.

Cole opened the truck door and approached the old-fashioned pay phone as if it might itself be lethal. Maybe it wouldn't work. He'd take that as a sign.

He grasped the receiver, pulled it free of the tangle of its heavy metal cord, and plugged his coins into the slot. Damn it. A warbly dial tone filled the ear he'd pressed so hard against the receiver it would probably leave an indentation.

He punched in Jena's number, listened to several rings, and then let out a shaky breath at the message: *You have reached Wildlife and Fisheries Agent Jena Sinclair. Please leave a detailed message and I'll get back to you as soon as possible. If this is an emergency, please call . . .*

No, he didn't think he'd be doing that. Maybe he'd read her demeanor and body language wrong—God knew he was out of practice—but he thought Jena Sinclair would believe him when he said he'd found the gator and the drugs. She wouldn't take one look at him, toss him in jail, and do the fact-checking later. Not that local law enforcement wouldn't do its job, and not that he wasn't innocent. But people were freaked out and the paper made it sound as if the task force was desperate for an arrest.

For some reason that had nothing to do with *reason*, he trusted Jena to stand behind him.

He could come back tomorrow and try her again, but would he? Or would his deep-seated paranoia and distrust of life in general win out if he gave it another day?

No, he needed to see her tonight, or at least make the initial contact. Leaving a message on the phone didn't feel right, though. If he couldn't talk to her directly, he needed to see her.

He plugged in the change again and this time called a number dredged from deep inside his memory. Pressing those buttons still felt natural; he'd done it so many times his fingers moved from muscle memory. When Mike Leonard answered, the voice of his best friend took Cole back to a time that robbed him of breath for a few moments. Long enough for Mike to call him a perv and hang up.

Damn it, you don't need chickens to get chicken shit, Ryan. You are chickenshit.

He went into the store and got more quarters, then slipped them into the pay phone slot before he could think about it too hard.

This time, Mike sounded pissed. "Look, buddy, whoever you are, you—"

"Mike, it's Cole." And just in case his old friend had forgotten: "Cole Ryan."

The pause seemed to stretch forever, but he finally heard a heavy exhale of breath. "Cole? Oh, thank God. Man, is that really you? Where the *hell* have you been? Where the hell *are* you?"

If he was going to ask a favor, at least he could be honest. "I've been living in South Louisiana since . . . since I left Mississippi. I'm sorry to call after all this time. I know I don't have any right—"

Mike's voice grew softer. "Cole Ryan, you don't owe anybody an explanation, especially me. I was there, remember?"

Like he could forget anything that happened on March fifteenth, five years ago this month.

"Cole, are you ready to come home?" Mike's voice sounded tentative. "Because if you're not, that's okay, man. I'm just glad to know you're alive and somewhere, even if it is in Louisiana. What's going on with you?"

Cole's throat muscles had grown so tight he sounded like a frog. "I'm okay. It's just . . . been hard."

"Do you need anything? You only have to say the word."

He knew Mike meant it.

"Can you find me an address for somebody?"

Fifteen minutes and a pile of quarters later, Cole had what he needed: the address of one Jena G. Sinclair of Chauvin, Louisiana. She'd only been at the address a month.

He hung up the phone, walked back to his truck, and sat behind the wheel, staring out the front windshield into another life. God, that had hurt, but in some ways he felt better. He'd never told Mike where he was, but the man was no idiot; he'd probably already known and was testing to see if Cole was ready to be found.

He trusted Mike to let what little family he had left know he was alive and relatively intact without revealing where he was. He couldn't see any of them yet, even Mike. Until today, he'd thought he never would. Now, maybe. Maybe he could at least think about coming back from the unthinkable.

One step at a time, however. He flipped over Jena's business card, where he'd written down the address. He probably wouldn't have the guts to stop, but he'd at least see where it was.

The house took him by surprise. Jena hadn't struck him as the show-pony type, but the house was a monstrosity. Painted a stark white, it had a fountain in the center of its circular front drive and a double stairway leading in a curve around either side of a first-floor entry. The glorious excess culminated in a grand second-level front door with an elaborate arrangement of windows and columns surrounding it. Door and windows? Also white.

Maybe he'd misjudged her. Badly.

There was no sign of a vehicle, which gave Cole a few minutes to size up the place. A high brick privacy fence, also painted white, circled the massive backyard.

He was here, though, and he'd do this before he backed out.

Digging in his glove compartment, he found an old envelope and pulled out a Sharpie he'd bought at the convenience store.

Have info that might help drug case. Will drop by again tomorrow abt 5. Will only talk to you. No other officers. Please.— Coleman Ryan

No woman with a lick of common sense—or man, for that matter—would respond to that kind of note, but Cole didn't have anything else to write on. He could wait for her, but . . . no, not a good idea. Waiting would put him in stalker territory.

He added: *P.S. I know this sounds nuts, but I am not dangerous.*

Yeah, like that would help.

He climbed the curved stairs and left the envelope on the mat in front of the entrance. Someone had slipped up and introduced color into the place; the mat was dark green. He anchored it down with one of his new tools from the hardware store.

Then he got into his truck and drove back to the house on Sugarcane Lane as fast as he dared. He needed a drink.

CHAPTER 15

After returning from the trip to Thibodaux and the bizarre visit to Mac's buddy in Bourg, Jena stood in front of her full-length mirror, sizing up the fourth outfit she had tried on: simple jeans and a lightweight sage-green sweater.

Tonight would be the first time since she'd been shot—well, longer, if she were to be honest—that she'd tried to make herself look attractive. Working in often-uncomfortable conditions, whether by herself or with her primarily male colleagues, she found playing up her looks both counterproductive and ill-advised. Except for a good SPF, makeup and swamps didn't mix, and she had no desire to impress her colleagues in any but a professional way.

She'd grown up trying to be girly because her mother was all over the makeup-and-heels thing, and whatever Grace Sinclair wanted, Jena tried her hardest to give her. It was never enough.

The inner Jena, at thirty, was no kinder than her mother: *You're six feet tall, and the biggest curve on you is the puckered scar where a bullet got dug out of your breast.*

She'd carefully covered the facial scars with makeup. She couldn't completely smooth her skin out without spreading foundation on like pancake batter, but she could manage a consistent color.

The things she'd always had going for her were her legs and her hair, so she'd learned early how to play up her assets. Her legs were a mile long and had a nice shape, so if she'd been meeting a man for dinner—and damn her as an idiot that Cole Ryan's face popped into her mind—she'd go girly with a dress. Nothing too short but enough to show off her long legs.

She pulled her hair back in a ponytail, wishing she could put on her baseball cap. Ceelie wouldn't care, but somehow tonight felt important to Jena, this first foray back into polite society. To mark the occasion, she even put on honest-to-god earrings, and . . . Jena looked around her room, realizing she might not own a purse.

What kind of woman didn't own a purse? Certainly no daughter of Grace Sinclair's.

Digging through the half-unpacked boxes, she came across two backpacks, a rolling suitcase, and a black camera case that might have been a possibility except that *Nikon* had been emblazoned across the front in bright yellow. No way to pass that off as a purse.

Finally, she shrugged and placed her wallet and her SIG Sauer in a plastic evidence bag, keeping out one credit card. She slipped the card into one of the jeans' slit pockets and, when she got to her truck, tossed the plastic bag through the open door onto the passenger seat. She'd stash it in the glove compartment when she got in. Ceelie was engaged to an LDWF enforcement officer, after all. She was used to riding in trucks filled with guns and electronics.

A few minutes later, she pulled her truck into the drive of Gentry's raised house on Bayou Terrebone in Montegut, parking alongside the beat-up two-toned pickup Ceelie had inherited from her great-aunt. Ceelie sat on the porch and waved when Jena pulled to a stop. "I'll be ready in just a minute. His Highness is searching for his spot du jour."

Since Gentry's truck wasn't in the drive, *His Highness* had to refer to Hoss, Gentry's bat-eared little French bulldog. Sure enough, Jena spotted him deep in the shadows under the house, snuffling around for the best spot to pee. It was a ritual Gentry claimed to find amusing. After the first few times waiting for Hoss to do his business, however, Jena was convinced that she was, indeed, a cat person at heart. What Boudreaux lacked in obedience (he was a cat, after all), he made up for in affectionate indifference and a low-maintenance lifestyle.

"How about A-Bear's?" Jena asked when Ceelie joined her in the truck. "It's all-you-can-eat catfish night."

"God, I haven't been there in ages, and Gentry won't be home until sunrise. Let's do it."

They made small talk along the way into Houma. Ceelie was as petite as Jena was tall. With her blue eyes and dark skin that revealed her Native American, Cajun, and Creole gumbo of ancestry, she was gorgeous.

"You're letting your hair grow out. Are you going to grow it long again?" Jena had been in the hospital when Ceelie had been kidnapped last fall. Ceelie had walked away with no lasting injuries, but the monster had tormented her by using a knife to saw off the beautiful black braid that had hung to her waist. Now, her hair hung in curls to her shoulders.

"Probably not much longer than this. It's easier to take care of than the braid. Had to let it grow out a little, though." Ceelie slid her gaze toward Jena with a smile. "Y'know, so Gentry has something to hold on to when we—"

"Ack! TMI!" Jena held out a hand in the universal sign for *Shut up.* "No intimate details about my former partner, please."

Ceelie laughed. "You'll be partners again once this drug case is over. I'm pretty sure Paul wants Mac under his thumb again."

"Poor Mac. You know, he's really a good agent."

"I know—Gentry says so too. But Paul knows he's afraid of him and just enjoys it too much to give up the power."

Jena shook her head. "Paul needs a life."

"Paul needs a woman," Ceelie said.

"Poor thing."

They drove the rest of the way in silence. She and Ceelie had speculated on numerous occasions about what kind of woman it would take to loosen up the parish's most senior enforcement agent. Jena wasn't sure such a woman existed.

"Here we are." Jena pulled the truck into the A-Bear's parking lot, a gravel area the size of a postage stamp beside an old blue-painted wooden cottage. The porch pillars were made of unfinished wood, and beside the door sat a rustic rocking chair.

The sound of a Cajun fiddle reached them from inside. "I think there's music tonight, so let's see if we can get in a quieter area," Jena said.

The waitress managed to squeeze them into a table tucked as far from the Cajun band as possible, and by the time they'd ordered and gotten their iced tea, the band was taking a break.

"Good, we can talk. There's something I need to ask you," Ceelie said. They waited while the first wave of catfish arrived, then dug in.

"If it's about last fall, Ceelie—" Jena took a deep breath and set aside her forkful of catfish fillet. She knew Ceelie didn't blame her for the kidnapping, and neither did Gentry. Jena blamed herself, though, and she valued Ceelie's friendship. If there were any ill feelings, she wanted to know. "Just know that I couldn't be sorrier about—"

"Hush." Ceelie put her fork down as well. "That wasn't your fault. None of it. You were indulging me because I insisted on getting out and running around instead of staying safe. That's all we're going to say about it. I have something much more important to ask."

Jena blinked back tears. Even knowing Ceelie didn't blame her, she had needed to hear those words again. The world around her felt lighter. "What did you want to ask?"

"Well, okay, I know it sounds silly because I'm not the white-dress-and-fancy-reception type, but would you be my maid of honor when Gentry and I get married in May?"

Jena had taken her fork, speared a quarter of a fillet, and had it halfway to her mouth, but set it down again at Ceelie's words. Damn if she wasn't going to cry. Again. "Of course I will. I'd be honored to do it. But, uh, do I have to wear a pink dress?" Visions of the deep-rose chiffon monstrosity floated across her mental vision.

Ceelie laughed. "God, no. I might wear a dress, but I'm not even promising that. We have a couple of months to decide; you can help me plan it. Gentry's threatening to wear his LDWF dress uniform, but your only rule is *not* to show up in forest green."

"Well, our dress uniforms do have white gloves," Jena said.

"Yeah, and black ties. That would be a no."

"Well, well. Look who I found." A deep drawl reached them from above Jena's head. Jena almost swallowed her tongue when she looked up to see none other than Ray Naquin pulling a chair up to their table. "You told me you had dinner plans but didn't say we could make it a threesome."

"You know this . . . gentleman?" Ceelie asked, keeping her narrowed gaze on Ray and slipping into a heavier Cajun accent. "If not, I have a few spells I could be throwin' his way."

Jena stifled a grin at Ray's frown. "Celestine Savoie, Raymond Naquin. Ray's one of the parish nuisance hunters. Ceelie is Gentry Broussard's fiancée, and I'd recommend you not mention threesomes lest the news get back to him."

"Aw, I was just jokin'." Ray signaled for the waitress and ordered a tea. Jena and Ceelie exchanged exasperated looks. The guy had big balls, she'd give him that much, and he cleaned up well.

But he was no Cole Ryan.

Good thing Jena and Ceelie had gotten their most important talking out of the way, because clueless Ray was perfectly happy to carry the load by talking about his favorite subject, which was Ray.

They heard about the worst gator catch ever, the pug he'd managed to extract from a gator's jaws and rushed to the veterinarian in time to save the dog and the day, his growing notoriety for being able to catch venomous snakes while having been bitten only once (he displayed a twisted, scarred left index finger to accompany that story), and how Wildlife and Fisheries could help him do his job better by calling him whenever a gator was involved instead of handling things themselves.

"See, you shoulda called me when that old lady off Bayou Pointe-aux-Chenes reported that gator behind the cane fields." Ray punctuated his words with a fork, at the end of which dangled a French fry he'd taken from Jena's abandoned plate. "What buyer'd you take it to? What happens to the money if a gator's brought in by a game warden?"

Jena almost choked on an oversized bite of the peanut butter pie the waitress had just brought. "We didn't sell it," she said after her coughing fit subsided. "It was acting so weird, I sent it to Baton Rouge to be examined and autopsied. If we had sold it, all the meat would've gone to a local shelter and proceeds into a special aid fund."

Ray frowned and set down his fork. "It was acting weird how?"

"The gator just sat in a mud puddle in the middle of the road, if you can really call it a road. The woman—Doris Benoit—said she'd called you before."

"Yeah, but I never saw no gators out there. Just her ugly mutt."

Yeah, well, even ugly mutts could be lovable, although Chewbacca was a pretty good Ugliest Dog candidate. "It was there this time, just hissing every once in a while. Doris was yelling, jumping around, even poking it with a table leg." That got a raised eyebrow from Ray and the beginnings of a smile from Ceelie. "Gator just sat there. Didn't try to fight. Didn't try to run back to the water even though it had a clear path."

"You make the call to send it to Baton Rouge or did your high school partner?"

Snarky much? "Mac's a good agent, and he's not as young as he looks." He was only a year older than Jacks, Jena realized, and next to Jackson, Mac Griffin was the soul of maturity.

"Seems like a good enough guy. Hey, you ladies want to go have a drink somewhere? I'd like to hear how the Black Diamond investigation is going."

"Not me. I gotta get home." Ceelie gave Jena a questioning look while Ray gave her a semi-leer beneath raised eyebrows. He gave used-car salesmen a bad name.

"How 'bout you, Jena?" He leaned closer, speaking in an exaggerated whisper. "We could go somewhere private. I know you probably got some scars from being shot, but you can't see a scar in the dark, right?"

The dickwad was offering her a pity fuck in a darkened room?

She smiled. "You'll never know, will you?" Then she gave him the easy out he didn't deserve. "Sorry, but my younger brother has just moved in with me, and I told him I'd be back before eleven to help him get settled. Besides, I'm not involved in the drug task force." Like she'd tell him anything.

"How little is this little brother? Too little to unpack by himself?"

"He's twenty-four, but not feeling well." She gave a conspicuous sniffle. "Hope it isn't contagious. Ceelie, you ready to go?"

They managed to escape the restaurant without further contact, and only after Jena burned rubber pulling her truck out of the parking lot did she let loose a stream of expletives that had Ceelie on the floor laughing.

"Let me guess. You don't like this guy, right?"

"Of all the condescending, sexist things I've heard in my life—and remember I worked patrol for NOPD—this was the worst."

"You want I should throw da bones for you, sha?" Ceelie slid easily into the swamp patois, and she'd learned a few voodoo spells from her great-aunt Eva. "Put a little curse on dat coonass, him? Take away his ability to get dat thing up?"

Jena laughed. "That man is not worth wasting your mojo on, and I don't care what he can or can't get up. But I'll let you know if I need some mystical intervention."

Jena kept the tone light until she dropped Ceelie off, but the closer she got to Chauvin, the madder she got. By the time she parked in front of the architectural monstrosity she called home and climbed the front steps, she was ready to punch someone.

Until she saw what looked like an envelope from Terrebonne Parish Waterworks on her doormat, which was the only thing she'd bought for the house so far. The envelope had been weighted down with what looked like a socket wrench, still new and in its packaging with the Ace Hardware price tag. Did it have any significance or was it the note writer's version of a paperweight?

She read the note, did a slow one eighty to look around the property, unlocked the door, and went inside. After making sure the deadbolt had been thrown and the house was in order, she poured herself a glass of sparkling water with fresh lime juice and settled on her sofa. She read the note another ten or twenty times. What did Cole Ryan know about the drug case? Why would he only talk to her—she wasn't even involved in the case except for the unexpected connection of the gator.

The gator found near Cole's house.

She hadn't felt threatened by Cole Ryan earlier, but Mac had been right outside, along with Doris Benoit and her odd little family.

Another item on the creepy list: somehow, Coleman Ryan had found out where she lived. It wasn't as if she was in any directories; she hadn't been here long enough. No one from LDWF would give out her private info. Not directory assistance, even though Dad had installed a landline. The number was unlisted and she hadn't given it to anyone.

She couldn't call Cole, but he could've called her without showing up at her house.

Maybe he had tried; she hadn't been able to hear a lot inside the restaurant. She had carried her mobile phone with her, but it had sat on the table next to her plate the whole time. She could've been in a stupor from the stories of Ray's heroics and missed a call.

Which is exactly what had happened. When Jena tugged her phone from her pocket, there was a call from an unknown number with a south-central Louisiana area code, made around eight thirty. Would it have killed the guy to leave a message, if that was even him? Talk about doing things the hard way.

She dialed the number and eventually a young boy answered with a tentative "Hello?"

"Hi, I got a call from this number earlier tonight. Can you tell me where this phone is located?"

The boy's voice grew muffled as he talked to someone who turned out to be his mother and took the phone. "Ma'am, this is a pay phone outside the Kwik Mart on 55. You must have the wrong number."

The woman hung up, not realizing she'd told Jena all she needed to know. Cole Ryan had tried to call her; she'd bet on it. Why he'd creep her out by leaving a message at her house instead of on her phone, she had no idea. Not to mention how he'd found out where she lived.

Then again, she knew nothing about this man, did she? Her instincts told her she could trust him, but her instincts were not very trustworthy themselves these days.

She'd be here at five tomorrow to talk to him, but she wasn't sure she should be alone.

CHAPTER 16

When Mac picked Jena up at 6:00 a.m., she'd been preoccupied and quiet. They'd planned to spend part of the day hiding out in their patrol boat on Bayou Pointe-aux-Chenes, seeing what kind of activity the place was attracting. Then they'd drive up to Houma so they could talk to Don Gateau and Amelia Patout.

"I need to get home by four thirty," she'd announced when Mac asked if she wanted to hang out with EZ and him after their shift since their stint as full-time partners was ending soon. He admitted he'd miss her. Lieutenant Doucet had finally cleared her for solo patrol next week, so Mac would be back on his own part of the time, with Jena part of the time, and—God help him—would spend a couple of night shifts each week under the silent glare of Paul Billiot. That, he wasn't looking forward to.

In the meantime, they had their alligator case to figure out. One Jena feared might just intersect the DEA case. She had laid out her theory on the way back from Thibodaux yesterday, but they agreed to keep it quiet unless more evidence piled up. Making the leap from one gator with Black Diamond in its belly to an elaborate system using ill-tempered reptiles as drug mules? That leap was the size of the Grand

Canyon. They'd both be laughed out of the division if they came in with that crazy idea and no proof.

They drove to the boat launch in silence and set out with a trolling motor, which was slower than the outboard but also quieter. As they proceeded south down the main bayou, growing closer to the branch that cut off toward Sugarcane Lane, Mac scanned the banks for gator lines.

His heart rate spiked when he finally spotted one in a bank overhung with branches—heavy-duty fishing line attached to a limb, a baseball-sized lump of what looked like rotten chicken hanging from the bottom.

"Look over there." Mac slowed the boat and pointed at the baited line.

"Damn." Jena picked up a pair of binoculars and studied the area. "Let's settle in and watch for a while. Might be a poacher, or might be worse."

"Sounds good." Mac maneuvered the nimble mud boat against the opposite bank, hidden from view in either direction. He turned off the motor, used a pole to push the boat as far against the bank as he could, and tied off.

Now they waited.

"If nobody shows up, we should take a closer look at the bait." Jena kept her voice low. "If the drug traffickers are using gators as a mobile delivery system, it makes sense that their bags of drugs would have to go inside something a gator would want to eat."

Mac shook his head. "It's a wild-sounding idea, using gators to deliver drugs. Why wouldn't the supplier just bring the drugs in by boat and turn them over to the local distributor? You know, like in the real world."

"Because between us and the Sheriff's Office and the DEA and the Coast Guard and the State Police, we have every major waterway covered. The only way to get drugs in by water is to come in a minor route."

There were thousands, literally, of small inlets and waterways coming in from the Gulf and snaking around southern Terrebonne.

"What if the supplier caught the gator somewhere else, fed him the drugs, stuck on a tracking device, and then released him up here?"

Jena nodded. "Exactly. The risk to the supplier is minimal since all he has to do is meet one of the locals somewhere in an isolated spot offshore, hand over the goods, and leave. The local idiot catching the gator-mules only has to use his tracking device and nab the gator, so his risk of getting caught is minimal because even if we caught him, we'd assume he was a poacher."

"Except that a couple of bags of drugs got caught on treble hooks and the stoned gators' weird behavior tipped us off."

Jena raised her binoculars and looked at the bait again. "Which means our rotten chicken over there could be bait for a poacher, or it could be bait for someone looking to trap a gator full of drugs." She gave Mac a rare smile—at least it was rare these days. "I think it's a plausible theory. Everybody on the task force is focusing on boats coming in through the major waterways along the coast, not a guy in small bayous trapping gators out of season. But who's the supplier? Who's catching the gators? And who's taking the drugs out of those gators and distributing it?"

Mac shrugged. "That, I don't know." But he was going to keep thinking about it.

They sat quietly for a while, watching and waiting—something Wildlife and Fisheries agents did a lot. Waiting for a poacher or illegal hunter to show up. Patrolling, looking for trouble. Mac figured that was true of a lot of law enforcement agencies. It sounded exciting, and it was—about 5 percent of the time.

"So, how'd things go on your dinner with Ceelie last night?" Mac asked.

"It was great until Ray Naquin showed up." Jena's expression was that of someone who'd just smelled a bucket of fish guts. "He might be a fine nuisance-gator trapper—just ask him, and he'll confirm it. But what an absolute sleaze bucket. I should slap you for daring me to go out with him."

Mac returned the grin. "You didn't take the dare, so I'm blameless. What'd he do? And how'd you pay him back?"

Jena's smile faded. "He suggested it would be okay to go someplace private and dark after dinner—you know, because you can't see scars in the dark."

Mac clenched his jaw and looked away from the pain that showed on her face. "I might have to beat the crap out of that asshole. Bet Gentry would help me."

Jena's voice turned fierce. "I told you that as my friend and my partner. You don't go blabbing it around, hear me? Or I swear to God I'll never tell you anything again."

Mac glanced back at her with surprise. "You consider me a friend? I thought you hated me, like the rest of them."

"Mac Griffin, stop right there and take that hurt look off your face. You're gonna make *me* beat your ass, and don't think I can't do it." Jena's voice grew stern. "Nobody hates you. People only tease the agents they like; you should know that. Even Paul doesn't hate you; he knows you're intimidated by him and he thinks it's funny. So he pushes your buttons on purpose."

Mac let that sink in a moment. "No, you're lying. Paul doesn't think anything is funny."

Jena smiled. "Yeah, he does. He's a nice guy under all that serious silence. And as improbable as it seems, yes, I consider you a friend. You're a good agent."

Mac gave a short nod, but inside he was doing a Snoopy dance. He'd come so close to quitting and crawling back to Maine, but damn it, he liked it down here where nothing came easy and people fought and clawed for whatever they had. Maybe there was a chance for him to succeed here after all. He just wanted to fit in.

"Hey, I hear something—not a motor, but water moving." Jena moved to get a better view from the prow while Mac grabbed his own binoculars. "I think it's from the south."

Actually, it turned out to be more from the west, from the bayou outlet that dead-ended at Sugarcane Lane. And Jena was right; this was no motorized boat but a simple pirogue, being propelled by pole by a tall man with long blond hair tied in the back with braids.

"Is that the guy who lives down by our last gator call? Ryan something or other?" Mac had never gotten a visual on the guy, just a description from Jena.

She gave him a squinty-eyed look. "Yes it is." She dropped her voice to a whisper. "Stay down and be quiet. I want to see what he does without him knowing we're here."

The Ryan guy poled his pirogue around the bend, then took out an oar to propel himself in their direction along the bigger bayou. He had a couple of fishing poles on board, and Mac spotted a life jacket. He didn't see any alcohol. Those were his automatic responses to seeing a boat, and Ryan had passed those basic tests.

As he got closer, Mac got a better look at the hermit of Sugarcane Lane. The guy was younger than he'd looked from a distance, maybe early thirties, his hair blond, not silver. Great physique if you were interested in male physiques. Mac could be jealous of a six-pack as much as the next guy.

Ryan paddled his boat along slowly, but stopped short at the baited gator line. He sat still in the water, his boat bobbing slowly southward with the light current. He stood up in his pirogue, staying in the center and balancing his weight in the light boat as if he'd done this a lot. And he had his own set of binoculars.

The guy studied the baited line, then sat down and slowly swiveled, using his binoculars to examine the areas all around him. He stopped for a few seconds when his line of sight reached their hiding spot, and

Mac held his breath. He shifted his gaze toward Jena without moving and she subtly shook her head: *Stay hidden.*

After what was probably five seconds but seemed an eternity, the Ryan guy turned his pirogue and rowed back toward the south. He didn't turn into the inlet toward his house, but kept going.

"You going to tell me why we didn't stop and ask him about that bait line? At the very least he could be a poacher. Or maybe he's seen something." Mac turned toward Jena, who still had her binoculars trained on Ryan's progress down the bayou.

"I have a meeting with him later today, and I didn't want to scare him off," she said. "Let's wait here for a couple more hours, then we'll talk to the gator buyers in Houma. If nobody shows up before we leave, we'll examine the bait and cut the line. Either way, it'll put somebody out of business today—poacher or drug trafficker."

The next two hours were boring as hell, and Mac fought to stay awake, much less alert. A few boats with outboards sped past but had either not seen the baited line or not felt the need to stop since the gator hadn't fed on it yet.

Finally, they emerged from cover and crossed the bayou, confirming that the bait was not only plain-old rotten chicken, but someone had added an extra dose of rotted something-or-other juice to enhance its stench. It contained no Black Diamond. Just enough nastiness to make Mac glad he hadn't eaten in a few hours. If he barfed in their fish cooler again, Jena would never let him hear the end of it, friends or not.

He waited until they were back in the truck and on their way to Gateau's in Houma to ask her the obvious. "Why are you meeting with that Ryan guy today, and who's your backup?"

"He left a note for me last night while I was at dinner. It was lying on the mat outside my front door." Jena watched the passing scenery and didn't look at Mac, which told him she was measuring her words and didn't want her face to give anything away. "He says he has information on the Black Diamond case but he won't talk to anyone but me. He wants to talk to me alone."

Mac let that process for a minute. Maybe half a minute. Maybe ten seconds. "He left a note at your freaking *house*? How would he know where you live, Sinclair? That's just one of a dozen reasons not to meet with him, much less alone."

Jena gave him a brief glance. "Yeah, it bothers me too. I have an unlisted landline number. He called my cell from a pay phone, but didn't leave a message. Instead, he drove to my house and left a note."

"So I repeat, who's your backup?"

"Mac, if he sees another officer there, he won't talk. I can guarantee you that from my one conversation with him."

He took a deep breath. She was his senior officer, but this had to be said. "Jena, there's an easy solution to this. We call the sheriff's office and tell them this Ryan guy could be a person of interest. Then you're out of it. He'd never even have to know you had anything to do with it."

She twisted in her seat to look at him, her hazel eyes serious. "No. I mean it, Mac. No. There's something about this guy that's on the level; I can just feel it. He's . . . I don't know . . . *fragile.*"

"Fragile? Fragile? He's built like a solid fucking tank, pardon my *Français*. He's as fragile as a bull gator in a small bayou."

"I don't mean physically fragile. Obviously." She smiled. "I mean emotionally fragile. We connected in some way the day I talked to him, and I don't want to scare him off."

"You are not talking to this guy alone, even if I have to park a half mile away and hide in the bushes."

At that, she grinned. "Only if I get photos."

He pointed at the laptop computer lying atop a pile of paperwork on the center armrest of the truck. "In the meantime, have you run a search on him? Even a simple Internet search? See if he shows up?"

"No, things have been too crazy with Jackson and . . ."

Jena pulled the computer into her lap and began to type and scroll. "Oh my God." Her eyes widened with each click of the keypad.

Mac almost lost control of the truck trying to crane his neck to see the screen. "Did you find him?"

She closed down the page she'd been reading and twisted the laptop back to its usual resting place. "Oh yeah, I found him, all right."

CHAPTER 17

When Jena and Mac had been trying to figure out what kind of person would live in a middle-of-nowhere outpost like Sugarcane Lane, one of their options had been a guy who was on the run.

She'd been thinking *criminal*, as most law enforcement officers would. But there were other types of people on the run. She'd bet her next year's salary that Cole Ryan was running from a past he hadn't been able to face, something that had shaken his faith in humanity.

Jena was aware that Mac was waiting for an explanation, but she wasn't sure what to tell him, not until she talked to Cole. It felt too personal.

"For now, will you just accept that I feel even more sure he's not a drug trafficker, nor is he the least bit dangerous?" Jena finally asked. Trauma could turn victims violent, but she got no violent vibe from him at all. Just the opposite. He wanted to stay as far away from people as possible, which made his willingness to seek her out even more intriguing. "Will you let it go at that for now?"

Not that Mac wouldn't look Cole up himself the first chance he got.

Mac didn't like it, she could tell. His brown eyes darkened; there was no light of animation in them. "No matter what you found out about

Cole Ryan's past, people can change. Take *my* word for it. Something snaps and they can change on a dime. I will be at your house by five, like it or not."

Damn it. She was trying to navigate a delicate balance. She wanted Mac nearby, but not in the room with them. She'd like him in close range but out of earshot and out of sight, especially since she knew who Cole was now. At the same time, Mac was following protocol. No, he was giving her leeway. Protocol would be to call the lieutenant.

Mac had also injected a lot of fire into his words. Jena knew virtually nothing about his background, but someone, somewhere, had turned on him. Someone had snapped. But Mac Griffin's past was a topic for another day.

"Okay, fine. But you have to stay out of sight unless something goes wrong. I want him to talk to me on his own. This is not an interrogation."

That might come later, but not yet. Now that she'd learned who he was, she felt protective. The fact that he'd reached out to her had been a huge step for him. She understood being pulled underwater and deciding how and whether to survive. When she'd hit her own lowest of lows, she'd seen no way out and had tried to end her life. Cole Ryan had ended his life just as drastically, only without the blood or the blade.

Mac didn't have time to argue more because they had reached Gateau's, which Jena could immediately tell was a dead end. The parking lot was empty, and there was a handwritten sign on the door. Mac pulled his truck alongside it:

CLOSED UNTIL GATOR SEASON. REOPENING AUGUST 30.
IN AN EMERGENCY, E-MAIL DON@DONGATEAU.NET

"I'll e-mail him." Jena wrote his address in her notebook. "In the meantime, we might as well try Patout's."

Located on the far west side of Houma, Patout's Seafood was a cinder-block building the size of a football field with a small brown-painted public store across part of the front. WE BUY, PROCESS, AND SELL YEAR-ROUND! read a handmade sign taped to the glass front entrance.

A big, closed bay door stood next to it; during gator season, Jena had seen lines of pickups and boats full of gators, ready to back up to that bay door, one by one, where they'd unload and weigh their daily hauls. Being near the Lafourche Parish line, Gateau's catered more to that parish's hunters, while most Terrebonne hunters working gator season sold their catch to Patout's.

Mac's conversation with Ray Naquin had been the first time Jena had heard about Amelia Patout's cancer, but she knew Amelia's husband had been murdered about two years ago. As far as she knew, the case had never been solved.

A tinkling bell rang overhead when they opened the glass door to the store. There were no other vehicles in the front lot, but Jena had spotted a van and a pickup in the back, the latter with maybe a fourteen-foot white fishing boat hitched to it.

"Be right with you!" yelled a male voice from somewhere in the back. Not Amelia Patout, obviously. While they waited, Jena scanned the contents of the refrigerated display cases that spanned a room about the size of her bedroom—maybe twelve by fifteen feet. Behind the counter stretched a wide blackboard with various notes scribbled on it: *Last day for oysters: April 30. Redfish in season through March 31. Alligators bought only from licensed nuisance hunters through August 29. Hunting season for wild alligators starts August 30 and ends September 30.*

Good. They were adhering to the state hunting and fishing laws, or at least their signs said so. It was a pretty big operation to run year-round; Jena had done her homework and hadn't found any negatives about the owners or their business.

A teenage boy emerged from a door behind the counter. He had close-cropped light-brown hair, wide sky-blue eyes with a telltale slant, and a smile that was filled with sweetness. He wore hearing aids in both ears. "Help you?"

Jena pasted on her professional smile. "Hi, we're agents Sinclair and Griffin from Wildlife and Fisheries. How're you doing today?"

The boy smiled wider. "I'm real, real good. My name is Slade. Does that mean you're game wardens?"

Jena's homework had told her Amelia's youngest son was named Slade, but not that he had Down syndrome. "Hi, Slade. Yep, we're game wardens. We wanted to talk to your mother. Is she here?"

"She is not here, but she will be back." Slade looked down at the display cases. "I can sell you fish. We have oysters this week."

"I'll buy a pound of oysters," Mac said, taking Jena by surprise. He seemed to do that to her a lot. "How old are you, Slade?"

"I am fifteen," he said, carefully opening the case and weighing out an exact pound of oysters on his first try. He seemed comfortable behind the counter, as if he worked it a lot. Probably a big help to his mother if she was battling cancer.

"I have a brother about your age," Mac said. "His name is Lee."

Slade placed the oysters in a plastic bag and then wrapped the whole thing in white paper.

"Does Lee live in Houma?"

"No, he lives way up north, in Maine."

"You folks getting what you need?" While Mac paid for his oysters, an older boy came out of the back. Jena judged him to be maybe eighteen or nineteen, with hair so blond it was almost white, cut short and spiky. He'd started his question in a friendly tone, but got less so when he noted their uniforms. "Game wardens. You here on business or just buying?"

The older son, as Jena recalled, was named Martin, and she'd bet this was him. "Are you Martin Patout?"

"Maybe." Nothing sweet about this teenager, who had five or six tattoos that weren't covered by his LSU sweatshirt and blue jeans. "What you guys need?"

Jena handed him a business card. "We actually wanted to talk to your mom, but Slade says she isn't here."

"No, she had a doctor's appointment," the boy said, looking at her card. "Is it hard to become a wildlife enforcement agent? What's the difference between that and a regular game warden?"

A lot of hard training that only about 10 percent managed to get through before dropping out, even fewer women, but Jena didn't feel the need to share that. "They're the same thing, basically. It's a great job. If you think you might be interested, I can drop some information by for you one day."

Finally, he stuck out his hand. "I'm Marty Patout. Slade's my little brother."

"I ain't little."

"Yeah, you are." Marty grinned at his brother, and Jena liked the easiness between them.

"Anyway, Mom should be back in a few minutes. Until then, I'm in charge."

Jena thought his tone held both resentment and pride. "You having to do that a lot these days? I heard your mom had been sick."

Fighting cancer was hard enough without worrying about a son who might not be able to live independently. Slade Patout was clearly comfortable in these surroundings, but outside his familiar zones? Who knew? She didn't envy anything about Amelia Patout's life right now. Maybe Marty was working harder than he thought he should have to these days. She didn't blame him. He was carrying a heavy load for someone so young.

Again, she couldn't help a fleeting thought about her own little brother, so lost and void of ambition. *What will become of Jackson?*

Mac handed Marty a card. "Mac Griffin. Think we could ask you a few questions about gators since your mom's not here?"

Marty took the card and stuck it in his pocket along with Jena's. "Suppose so. They ain't in season right now, but I guess you know that."

Jena walked around to look in the cases while Mac asked the questions, but she listened closely. Sometimes one could hear a nuance in a voice better if one wasn't looking at the speaker. Sometimes it worked the other way around.

Business might be a little above normal with nuisance gators but not a lot, and Marty didn't recall anything odd about them. "You might wanna talk to Eddie Knight from over 'round Dulac—he's a new nuisance trapper and brings us some business," Marty said, shooing Slade into the back to pack some newly arrived finfish on ice. "And a lot of folks go to Gateau's, but he's closed until gator season starts back up."

Jena looked over her shoulder. "You know why Don Gateau closed? I thought he was one of the ones who stayed open year-round."

Marty shrugged. "I dunno. Seems like I heard he was about to retire or something."

He probably made most of his annual income during gator season anyway, but if Gateau's was closed, why would Ray Naquin say he took his gators there to sell? Unless Don Gateau made some kind of special deal with him.

And Jena knew Eddie Knight. The man was one of the best-known commercial fishermen in the area; he was licensed as a nuisance hunter, but he was a last resort. He did it because he wanted to, not because he needed the money.

Last Jena had heard, Eddie had landed a lucrative contract with a seafood shipper in Lake Charles. She couldn't imagine him mixed up in drug running. He had too much to lose.

"What about Raymond Naquin?" she asked. "He said he brings you quite a bit of business because of your mom being sick." So, maybe she was lying. To his credit, Mac didn't change expressions.

"Did he?" Marty shrugged, his expression a blank. "Maybe he brings 'em in when I ain't here."

"Who would that be?" A woman emerged from the back. She looked about forty going on seventy, pale and thin, with a scarf tied around her hair and dark circles under her eyes.

"They was askin' questions about Mr. Naquin," Marty said.

"You go on back and help your brother while I talk to the agents."

As soon as Marty disappeared, the woman turned to Mac and Jena. "I'm Amelia Patout. Why are you folks asking about Ray Naquin?"

"We've had another gator attack in the parish, and I wanted to see if he'd come across any aggressive gators," Mac said. "He mentioned that he sold some of his nuisance gators to you—the ones that couldn't be relocated."

"I don't think so." Amelia pulled a laptop from beneath the counter and almost dropped it before Mac reached across and helped steady her.

"Would you like to do this another time?" Jena asked her. "Ray told us you had been sick."

Amelia laughed, and Jena caught a glimpse of who she might have been even a month ago—an attractive, lively woman with olive skin and smile lines around her mouth. Even the illness hadn't dulled the spark of intelligence she emitted.

"Honey, might as well call it what it is. Lung cancer." The smile faded. "Nothing's working so far. I wouldn't worry except for the boys, with my husband gone . . ."

She trailed off, then shook her head. "Sorry, you were asking about Ray. Let's see." She opened the laptop and began tapping the keyboard. "Moved the whole business onto a spreadsheet last year. My late husband, Martin Sr., he didn't like computers. Wanted everything written down in those heavy ledgers. I got a room full of those damned things."

Jena didn't remember much about Martin Patout's murder; it had happened about the same time she graduated from the academy and moved to the parish. He'd been the biggest seafood buyer and processor in Terrebonne at that time, so Amelia had to be sharp to pick up the business without missing a step. Or at least it seemed that way, judging by the size of the place and the amount of inventory in their display cases. Jena would have to do some research if she could squeeze it in between clandestine meetings with sexy hermits and fending off sleazy gator hunters.

And helping to plan a wedding. Couldn't forget that one.

"No, last time I bought a gator from Ray Naquin was in January, one he caught up around Theriot. Guess he's doing business with somebody else. He and my husband were good friends, but he ain't come around as much since Marty Sr. died—he'll usually bring in four or five gators a year. Why you wantin' to know? Ray done something wrong?"

Jena sidled a look toward Mac and gave him a slight nod. She was far from objective where Ray Naquin was concerned, and Mac was the one who'd gotten the paranoid vibe from him.

"He just had had a few inconsistencies in his account of where he was selling his gators," Mac said, giving Amelia the full benefit of his baby-faced smile. Who could suspect that face of being anything but transparent? "We thought maybe you could help us clear it up."

Amelia shrugged. Had Jena seen a flash of anger cross her face, or was she too being paranoid? "I wouldn't know. Anything else you folks need?"

Which was their cue to leave.

They weren't going to get any more out of Amelia Patout today, and Jena wanted to e-mail Don Gateau. If his biggest buyer had shut down, why wouldn't Ray know that?

Besides, Jena wanted to make sure Mac was good and hidden when she talked to Cole Ryan. Not only good and hidden, but out of earshot. The last would be harder to achieve, but she was a firm believer in that whole bit about the key to a man's heart being through his stomach. Working with Gentry Broussard had taught her it worked just as well with partners.

"Hey, Mac," she said, climbing back into the truck's passenger seat. "Let me buy you an early dinner before you stake out my house."

He handed her his packet of oysters. "Yeah, okay, but first let's find a Dumpster and get rid of these oysters. I wanted to see what kind of plastic bags Patout's uses."

Mac just kept surprising her.

CHAPTER 18

Cole sat on his porch facing the water, swinging his legs off the end and pondering the baited gator line he'd seen up on Bayou Pointe-aux-Chenes this morning. If the game wardens hadn't been hiding across the bayou, he'd have stopped to take a closer look at it. He only knew they were there because the sunlight had glinted off something metallic—a belt buckle or binoculars or a gun, maybe—and drawn his attention.

With the line under surveillance, he'd simply turned around and done his morning fishing farther down the bayou. Afterward, he'd cleaned his fish, fried up a few for a late lunch, and frozen the rest. Now it was time to think. He had some decisions to make.

In retrospect, the note he'd left for Jena Sinclair embarrassed him. As foreign as it felt and for reasons he couldn't identify—or didn't want to—he cared what she thought of him. He didn't want her to think he was a psycho, which is exactly how he'd sounded in that note. Downright certifiable. Why hadn't he left a message on her damned phone like a normal person?

Because he'd stepped away from normal five years ago, that's why. Since meeting Jena, he had promised to always be honest with himself, so he had to admit that stepping back into normal—hell, just taking a teetering stumble in the general direction of normal—was proving hard for him. Probably because he'd thought his withdrawal from the mainstream would be permanent. He'd intended it to be permanent, this solitary life as the self-reliant man.

One swing of silky red hair and a wistful look at the sunset from a woman with her own damaged heart had apparently killed those intentions. He didn't know what, or who, had hurt her, but he recognized a kindred spirit in pain. Only hers was fresher and—he had to be honest again—his had begun to fade. It would never disappear. Never.

But it had healed enough for him to voluntarily put himself back among the living, at least on a small scale.

The drugs had made him turn to her. Those goddamned drugs that he couldn't ignore. He'd never been a cop, but law enforcement had to feel as if they were fighting a losing battle against these synthetic drugs. As soon as they got a handle on one, some asshole cooked up another form.

Add the alligators into the mix and it made no sense. Big Bull could've gotten the stuff by accident, but Cole's gut said there was nothing accidental about it. It would be easy enough to bypass the boat searches the newspaper had talked about. Southern Terrebonne was full of places to hide or do secretive things. Cole knew, because he'd visited a lot of them.

Once a month or so, if the weather promised to be cooperative, Cole would load up a heavy pack of survival rations and set out in the pirogue with no plan beyond whether he'd turn north or south when his outlet reached Bayou Pointe-aux-Chenes. For a week or two, he'd practice runs in the bays and bayous, streams and swamps and wetlands. He'd repeat each route until it felt comfortable, make a note of which ones drew fishermen and which ones seemed pristine or deserted. Then he'd return home, give the route a name, and mark it on his big wall map of the parish.

A man needed a hobby, and navigating the swamps was his. That, and survival training. He wasn't one of those loony tunes doomsday preppers. He just figured that eventually, living in isolation as he did, a hurricane would catch up with him and he'd be on his own for a while, without even the meager comforts he'd devised for himself.

Chances were good that her partner would be there with handcuffs. Or the sheriff, more likely. Even the DEA, who'd set up a big presence in the parish.

Chances were good that Cole would be walking into a trap, and that his trust in Jena Sinclair would prove unfounded. Everyone would know his story, assume he'd come unhinged, and he'd be arrested. If he had any sense of self-preservation, he'd pack up his stuff and move on. Except, damn it, he didn't want to leave.

He didn't think he had it in him to start over again.

A heavy vehicle sounded from behind him, so he swung his legs back around to the porch and watched as Doris and her husband trekked in and out of their shack on stilts, carrying boxes and furnishings. It looked like the only other remaining residents of Sugarcane Lane were moving out.

He considered offering to help them on their way, not because he was antisocial and wanted them gone, but, well, actually, it *was* because he was antisocial and wanted them gone.

Instead, Cole watched a while longer and, about three thirty, went inside for a shower. He wandered around in a towel for a while because, really, what did one wear that conveyed sanity and also—being honest again here—might make him attractive to Jena Sinclair?

There. He'd finally let himself think it. He never believed he'd want another woman after Rachel, but he wanted Jena, and not just physically, although he thought she was beautiful. He thought about her at night. He thought about being with her, kissing her, touching her until he erased the sadness that seemed to settle around her, even in their brief conversation.

Yes, he wanted her. Which was simply pathetic, considering he'd given her every reason to think of him as a psychopath and she might very well have him in jail on suspicion of drug trafficking before nightfall.

He deserved whatever he got.

Still, he dug in the back of his bedroom closet for a box that hadn't been opened in five years. The sight of the few clothes he'd kept from his old life sent a shiver across his scalp, and he thought how stupid they'd look with his Swamp Man hair. He wasn't that guy anymore and didn't want to be.

Be who you are now, jackass. Who you were then is just a bunch of words on a page or a photo in a newspaper. Who are you now?

He had no answers.

Cole shoved the box back into the closet and instead chose a clean pair of jeans and a long-sleeved blue Henley. He laced up his boots. Considered whether to wear his hair down or tied into a long ponytail with the braids, and finally settled on the tail.

He was an idiot, treating this like a date when it was going to end up being an inquisition.

At four thirty, after pacing and fidgeting until he couldn't stand it any longer, Cole got in his truck and drove to Chauvin. The sight of two black LDWF pickups in front of Jena's house, perched there like two big predators, confirmed his worst fear: she'd brought in other agents. No, not his absolute worst fear. So far there wasn't a squad car from the Terrebonne Parish Sheriff's Office in sight.

Still, he kept driving a mile or two past her house.

Finally, he pulled into the lot of an abandoned gas station, the rust marks that ran halfway up its pumps telling him the place had flooded at some point. But what part of Terrebonne couldn't say the same? It was one thing that kept him here, on this land sliding slowly into the Gulf of Mexico but hanging on to everything it had with a fierceness that defied logic.

He wanted to hang on to it with the rest of the people who loved this land. And unless he planned to pack up and keep running, the time to claim his place had finally come.

He had to face his past in order to help the future of a land that had become important to him, despite his efforts to avoid it. And he had to do it with the only person who'd managed, somehow, to get through the thick wall he'd built up around himself.

He had to talk to Jena Sinclair, no matter who had arrived in that other black truck.

CHAPTER 19

Jena had asked Mac to move his truck behind her house so it wouldn't look like they were throwing their lack of trust right in Cole's face. When Mac refused, she ordered him to move it. The problem was, she had no real authority to order him to do anything and they both knew it.

They had argued all the way from the drive into the foyer. "You want to fill Lieutenant Doucet in on this whole thing?" Mac got in her face. "You want to let him know you're planning to have a chat with some off-the-grid hermit about the Black Diamond case without letting anybody know about it? I don't care what the guy's been through. People change."

She gave it right back to him. "Are we talking about Cole Ryan here, or someone from your past? Who changed, Mac?"

Jena would never have believed she'd see true anger on Mac Griffin's face, but he was angry, and she'd been right—he flinched when she asked the question. "This is not about me," Mac said, his voice low and furious. "So you want me to tell the lieutenant that if your partner insists on backing you up in a potentially dangerous situation, you want him to park out of sight and hide in the bushes? Well, then, put it on speaker because I want to hear Warren's reaction."

Then he'd sat his happy ass down on one of her white chairs, crossed his arms across his chest, and waited. He'd even refused to untuck his uniform shirt or hide the SIG Sauer. Mac Griffin was on duty and he intended for Cole Ryan to know it.

Damn it. If only he weren't right. Warren would jerk her back to desk duty before she could say "big white rhino."

This week, after talking to Ceelie and thinking about what had happened last fall, she'd finally let herself off the hook. She had reacted the way she'd been trained, whether she worked for NOPD or Wildlife and Fisheries. She had come to accept that sometimes, even when you did everything right, situations still went straight to hell.

So she had confidence in her gut instinct to trust Cole Ryan. At the same time, her training told her to not let her gut get in the way of common sense, even if it meant giving in to Mac Griffin, sitting there surrounded by his aura of smugness.

Her law enforcement training would not condone her talking to Cole alone, no matter who he was or what her gut told her.

"I take it all back—every word." She sat on the twin chair facing Mac's. "I am not your friend. I am the woman who's going to make your life a living hell by telling the rest of the guys that you have the hots for Paul Billiot. And you don't know this yet, but he's going to be your partner again as soon as the DEA case is wrapped up. Ceelie told me."

A fleeting look of alarm crossed Mac's face, replaced by the mulish expression she'd seen most of the afternoon. She hated that expression.

"Go for it." He gave her a Cheshire cat smirk because they both knew she would do no such thing, and so what if he did? Paul was handsome in a stern, silent kind of way.

"Fine." She rubbed her temples, the result of stress and too much time with Mac Griffin. "Will you at least go out and sit by the pool while I talk to him?"

"Maybe."

Who *was* this annoying man? He was the department playboy, the joker, the baby-faced smart-mouth who'd driven the lieutenant so crazy his first month that he ended up spending his off day washing all of their trucks. He'd turned into a . . .

Jena sighed. He'd turned into what he was supposed to be—an enforcement agent.

She walked to the front window, gazing down the long drive at the traffic zipping up and down the highway, then checked her watch. Cole was five minutes late. Had he seen the second LDWF truck and kept going?

Less than a minute passed before Jena had her answer. Her heart surged at the sight of the old faded-red Ford pickup she'd seen sitting behind his house when she met him. It turned into the drive and came to a stop alongside the two black trucks. She said a prayer for herself, for patience; for Mac, that he'd give them space; and for Cole, that he'd still trust her.

She opened the door as Cole exited his truck. He stopped when he saw her, and his eyes captivated her, as they had the first time, by their clear, rich blue—maybe even more so because of his blue shirt. His hair glinted golden arcs of light from the late-afternoon sun, and he wore it pulled back instead of down, tied back with his braids. She'd thought him striking before but she'd been wrong. He was beautiful.

Beautiful and so, so broken. Her emotions must have shown on her face, which meant she was letting this get way too personal.

"You know who I am." His voice wasn't accusatory, just resigned.

She nodded. "I felt I had to look you up, and when I did . . ."

When she'd done a simple Google search, she'd seen that photo before anything else. The image had run everywhere, from the local Houma newspaper to *NBC Nightly News*. Looking at it, even five years later, felt invasive. For several weeks, until a bigger story took its place, it had become the iconic photo of gun violence in America.

A young uniformed paramedic had been photographed at the scene of a deadly mass shooting at a mall in Mississippi, where more than a dozen people shopping in a department store had been shot and three dozen injured before law enforcement caught the shooter and arrested him.

"Massacre at the Mall," the news reports had called it.

In that iconic photo, the paramedic cradled a tiny, blood-covered girl against his chest, a cascade of blond curls trailing off his arm, a pink-and-white outfit and white sandals soaked crimson. Naked grief mingled with the tears and blood on his face as paramedic Coleman Ryan carried the body of his four-year-old daughter, Alexandra, whose life he'd been unable to save. His wife and mother also had died—all at the hands of a young man strung out on meth, trying to gun down his ex-girlfriend. Ironically, the ex hadn't even been injured.

An older version of that same face looked back at her now, only, instead of sorrow, his expression held defiance. Jaws clenched. Eyes unflinching. Waiting for meaningless words like *I'm sorry* or *How are you doing?* or *Why did you run away?*

Jena swallowed those words down. "I tried to get my partner to leave but he refused," she finally said. "I'm sorry about that. You never frightened me." Not quite true, but close.

He gave her a small smile, and she knew she'd been right to change the subject. It wasn't the murder of his family that had brought him here to talk. He'd probably talked it to death. Talked about it until the only way he could cope was to leave and reinvent himself. Leave everything and everybody behind.

If you didn't get attached to anyone, it didn't hurt to lose them, right?

"I understand about the partner thing." He glanced at the two mud-spattered black pickups. "I drove on past when I saw the second truck here. But I couldn't let . . . I have to tell you what I know and hope you'll believe me."

"Come on in." Jena moved aside, letting Cole pass close enough that she became even more aware of him physically. Of his height, maybe a few inches above hers, of the heat emanating from his muscled body, of some kind of electricity between them. She'd felt it when he was simply The Hermit of Sugarcane Lane, and it was as inappropriate to think about now as then. Inappropriate on so many levels.

Mac stood in the wide doorway between the entry hall and the living room. His uniform looked forbidding in the stark-white surroundings, and there was no missing the SIG Sauer in his hip holster.

Cole walked straight toward him without pausing and held out his hand. "I'm Coleman Ryan. I'm sorry to have asked Agent Sinclair to not . . . to break procedure and talk to me alone. It's okay . . . You did the right thing by staying."

The words didn't come out smoothly, but they sounded sincere. Apparently, Mac thought so as well, as he shook Cole's hand and introduced himself. Even handed him a business card.

They all walked into the living room together, Cole observing his surroundings in all their blandness. "This is . . . not what I expected, although I don't guess I know you well enough to have expected anything." Cole's mouth twitched as if caught between a laugh and a frown. "The inside looks like the outside."

"Plain as a pikestaff," Mac said. "Jena's mother decorated while my partner was on leave. The woman doesn't believe in color."

"And I haven't had time to do anything with it since I got back a month ago." Jena had to do something about this awful place; she'd trade it for Cole's comfortable little house in a second, which would serve her parents right even though they'd probably meant well. And what the hell was a pikestaff? "You want something to drink?"

Cole looked at her, and another spark arced between them. This was getting ridiculous. Then he doused it with just a few words.

"No, I reckon we better talk first."

Yeah, she reckoned he was right.

Mac seemed to have had a change of heart. "While you two talk, I'm going to sit out by the empty pool and enjoy the big white brick wall. Let me know if you need anything."

She gave him a small smile. "Thanks, Mac."

Pointing Cole toward one of the armchairs, she took a seat on the end of the sofa nearest him. "I just want you to know that, before I hear you out, I'm not going to take notes and I'm not taping anything. I want to hear what you have to tell me first. Then I will probably need to hear it again, and I will probably take notes, and I might tape it."

Cole fidgeted in the chair, crossed and uncrossed his legs, seemed unsure where to rest his hands. Jena figured this was probably going to be the longest conversation he'd had in five years if he'd been as isolated as she suspected.

He let out a deep breath and kept his eyes on the white carpet. "I go fishing in the morning most days." He glanced up at her. "I have a license."

Jena smiled and shrugged. "Not worried about it, at least not right now."

"The day you and your partner came out about my neighbor's gator, something had happened earlier in the day that . . ." He stalled out and Jena waited. He needed to tell the story in his own way and in his own time.

"I was going out early that morning because I'd wanted to do some work on my back porch that afternoon, reinforcing some flooring."

"Sounds like you're quite a handyman."

He shrugged. "You know my story. When I decided to . . . change my life, I wanted to be as self-reliant as possible. That meant what I didn't know how to do, I had to learn."

"So what happened when you went out early to go fishing?"

He took another deep breath, and Jena found herself watching his hands clench and unclench and clench again. "I found a dead alligator."

CHAPTER 20

Once he got started, Cole found the concept of stringing one sentence after another came easier than he would've expected. Jena's prompting helped.

"You found a dead alligator where?" she'd asked, and that had gotten him started. "I should have called you guys, but at the time, I didn't think there was any harm in keeping it—using the meat for food and selling the parts and the hide."

Jena's hazel eyes, with more than a touch of green, never left his face. Cole would bet she was good at her job; he could feel her gaze like a weight on him even while looking back down at the floor, at his hands, anywhere except at her.

"Cole, I don't imagine you set up this meeting to confess to a little unauthorized gator usage, especially if it's one you found already dead."

Cole shook his head. "No. I was really careful dressing it, because I wanted to make sure I understood what killed it before I risked eating it." He looked up at her again, struck by the irony of the whole mess. "Guess it sounds silly, but even though I went off the grid, I never had a death wish."

Some expression crossed her face he couldn't interpret. Pain, maybe. Regret. For the first time he was aware of, she looked away from him. What was that about?

"So you found something unusual?"

Here's where it got tricky. He scrubbed his hands across his cheeks and huffed out a deep breath. "I found something, all right. Too much. First thing was an arm."

Jena jerked her attention back to his face. "A human arm?"

He nodded. "I later found out there'd been a fisherman go missing a few days earlier and his body had been found. I figured it was his, but it was too late to do him any good. I buried it with the organs and the contents of the stomach."

Jena might have stared a hole through him if she didn't at least blink. She seemed to have no words in response to what he was saying. So he kept talking.

"There was something else in the stomach I didn't think much about at the time. Just figured it was something the gator found and swallowed whole—you know they'll eat just about anything. Figured it probably had fallen off a boat or had been thrown out by a litterbug."

Jena still didn't respond, so he plowed on. "It was one of those plastic sandwich bags—you know, the kind with a zipper."

"What was in it?" Jena's expression had gone blank and, if possible, her voice became more formal.

"A black powder. I thought it was black pepper or something like that." Cole closed his eyes. "Then I saw a picture in the newspaper of that Black Diamond drug. It looked just like it."

"Where is it now?"

"Still buried."

Jena got up and paced the room. Cole looked back at the floor to avoid watching her slim, angular figure stride back and forth with her hands crossed over her chest. She was sexy as hell, even with her hair tied back and probable plans to have him arrested. "Anything else?"

Yeah, the thing Cole had found weirdest of all. "I found something else strange when I was dressing the hide—well, the feet, actually. You know—suppliers buy them to make stuff for tourists. I'd been thinking I needed to call you anyway about the gator, but this on top of the drugs convinced me something weird was going on. Something bad."

Jena's eyes narrowed. "What else did you find?"

"I don't know for sure, but it looked like some kind of signal or transmitter. A little orange light, stuck in the webbing between its toes. I didn't know what to make of it."

"Where is it now?"

"I dug it out of the foot thinking it was a rock. When I realized it wasn't—and it was still blinking—I put it and the foot in a bag and stuck them in the refrigerator I keep in my workhouse."

"Good. I'm glad you kept them."

He'd been watching Jena closely as he talked, looking for any change of expression. She didn't look confused or surprised, which could be her training—or it could mean she wasn't confused or surprised. "Judging by your expression, I'm guessing my gator wasn't the first one to show up with that thing in its foot."

She didn't answer but sat on the chair facing him instead of on the sofa. She was widening the distance between them already, whether or not she was conscious of it. Which made him sad.

"Why'd you call now, all of a sudden? Finding the item in the alligator's foot?"

"Like I said, I was already thinking about it, and then, that night, I was reading about that boy who blew his brains out on the drawbridge and saw a photo of Black Diamond and . . ."

He closed his eyes, and the tumble of words halted as his mind withdrew beneath an onslaught of bloody images. Blood on mannequins, blood pooled in the aisles between racks of formal wear and into the children's department. The cries of the injured as soon as police had taken in the shooter and let EMS in to search the store for survivors, stalking those aisles of blood with handfuls of triage tags.

He pulled himself back to the present before the images went to the last one he remembered. The last image before some part of him had shut down.

He got up and began pacing himself. "Once I read that story and saw the photo of Black Diamond, I knew what it was that I'd buried back there. I knew I had to tell somebody." He turned to look at her. "I trusted you because I . . . I trusted you."

What could he say: Because you made me feel alive again? Because, somehow, you slipped beneath my defenses without even knowing it?

Jena smiled. "I get it. We connected that first day on some level. But after overlooking everything else, I still don't understand why the drugs and the boy's death made a difference. You could've just kept quiet and never have gotten involved."

This time, he moved closer to her. "I don't know how much you remember about it. About what happened in Yazoo City."

Her voice was soft. "Tell me."

"I was the first paramedic on the scene, first in the store. I didn't know they were there—my wife, my mother, my daught . . ." He swallowed hard. "My four-year-old daughter. I was zeroed in on triage. Moving from one person to the next, not looking at their faces, just at whatever the injury was, tagging them by color as to who could be helped and how serious it was."

"Black tags for those already dead?" she asked.

"Yeah. Black for the dead." His mom had been in another section of the store; he didn't find out until later that she'd died as well. By that time, he was too numb to process it. No, not numb—empty. Numb was what he felt when he bypassed a dark-haired woman in a red blouse and jeans, a woman who was clearly dead, to check on the child beside her.

His child. The one who everyone said was the "spittin' image" of her daddy, with blond curls and big, long-lashed eyes so blue they could melt your heart. Moments had passed—he didn't know how many—before he'd realized that her small, bloody hand was clutched in that of the woman beside her. Only then had he recognized Rachel. Between that time and when he drove his "new" used pickup out of town, everything was a blur. He didn't even remember picking Alex up and taking her to the ambulance, not until he saw that photo everywhere he looked.

Cole skimmed over most of that for Jena, though, and focused instead on his anger. "I was furious with the scumbag who walked into that store with a gun until I saw him. Jena, he was just a sixteen-year-old kid strung out of his mind on meth. He didn't have a clue what he was doing. He was being stupid and hotheaded, wanting to have it out with his girlfriend and lashing out in a way the drugs told him was okay. When he came down from his high and realized what he'd done, he killed himself."

"Kind of like the kid on the bridge?"

Cole nodded. "It was all such a fucking waste."

Until a teardrop hit his arm, he hadn't realized he was crying for the first time in five years.

CHAPTER 21

To hell with professionalism. Jena moved to sit next to Cole on the sofa and wrapped her arms around his shoulders. He leaned on her for the briefest of moments before she could feel him wrapping himself inside his familiar shell. He stiffened his shoulders first, then pulled away from her and took a deep breath. Then another. A third. "Sorry. I don't know where that came from after all this time."

"I do." Jena pulled her arms away from him but rested her left hand on the knot of his fingers twisted together in his lap. "People stuff hurt and pain away the best way they know how. You did it by trying to make yourself untouchable. Strong. Self-reliant. Invulnerable. But all it did was cover up the hurt—it was still there, hiding and waiting to find a way out. That's how you dealt with the unthinkable."

Cole leaned back and looked at her. His eyes were too perceptive, too probing. "And how did you deal with it, Jena?"

She moved her hand away from his. "I don't know what you mean."

"I just spilled my guts and you're gonna lie to me?"

But she was a law enforcement officer, and they had to deal with the information he'd shared. Mac would need to hear the facts, but Cole wouldn't show his raw self to Mac. That had been for her, because he recognized another wounded spirit.

"Okay." Jena's voice was little more than a whisper. Steeling herself for whatever reaction she thought he might have, Jena unbuttoned her left uniform sleeve, pushed it up, and turned her arm wrist side up. "My coworkers don't know." Except Gentry and Warren, and they would hold her trust as sacred.

Cole took her wrist in his hands and traced a finger over the neat row of scars with gentle strokes. "These aren't that old. Three months, maybe. You said you were injured at work; you did it because of that?"

She nodded. "Partly, at least. I was shot twice last fall."

"Ah." He stroked her wrist. "You were the agent with the woman who was kidnapped. I heard about that."

Jena gave him a weak smile. "You're awfully well informed for a recluse."

"A recluse with Wi-Fi and a tablet."

"And no cell phone." Jena shook her head, and moved to stand up. She needed to get Mac in here so they could decide how to handle this. Cole still held on to her wrist, however, and she either had to sit back down or stand halfway and look like a dork.

"So why this, Jena?"

Right, as if she would share the real reason. "It left me scarred, disfigured." She paused. "Not just my face. I was feeling sorry for myself."

Cole reached out and tugged her chin so she couldn't avoid looking at him. "I'm calling foul on that one. I don't know you that well, but I do know this: you're not the type to wallow in self-pity, and surgery can cover most scars these days." He released her chin and her hand. "You don't have to tell me. I can tell it's still raw. If or when you want to, though, I'll listen."

Jena almost blurted out the truth, of the real reason her world had gone black, but she couldn't.

Cole sensed it. Somehow, he *did* know her.

He let her off the hook. "You want to call your partner in and figure out whether or not you're gonna arrest me?"

Right. Black Diamond. Alligators. That little business of the law.

She wiped away tears on her way to the back door, and wasn't surprised to find Mac sitting not in a deck chair beside the covered pool but on the step nearest the door. He turned when she cleared her throat and asked, "How much did you hear?"

"Nothing," he said, clearly not happy about it. "Not a damned thing. The White Rhino has very thick walls. But if you had screamed I would've heard you." Mac stopped next to her and gave her a last hard look for good measure. "Except he made you cry."

"I have allergies."

"Liar."

For the next hour, Cole repeated his story while both Mac and Jena took notes, and she taped his statement.

"I need to call our lieutenant." Jena got up to use the landline in the kitchen so her side of the conversation wouldn't be overheard. After a terse chat with a pissed-off Warren Doucet, she returned to the living room.

"Am I under arrest?" Cole stood up, followed by Mac.

"No, but our lieutenant is not a happy man," she said. Never mind that Warren hadn't been a bundle of joy since DEA agent O'Malley came to town and, by all accounts, neither had Terrebonne Parish Sheriff Roscoe Brown. Jena figured one parish, even one as large as Terrebonne, could only stand so much legal testosterone within its borders at one time, especially with the outsider holding the trump card.

"How'd you swing that?" Mac asked. "I expected Warren to tell us to bring him in."

Jena grimaced. "I haven't swung anything yet. The sheriff's department will have someone meet us at Cole's house. Now. They'll probably get there before we do. They'll dig up the gator entrails and drugs, examine what you still have in your possession, and make a judgment call. It helped that you volunteered the information."

"Woulda probably helped more if you'd volunteered it when you found the gator." Mac gathered his keys and opened the front door. Cole followed, and they both turned to watch Jena transform back into official mode. She'd had her personal pistol in the drawer of the table next to her chair, within easy reach, but before Cole arrived, she'd removed her duty belt and her SIG Sauer. She'd been afraid too much official gear would scare him off.

"I guess we'll take all three vehicles out." She set the alarm and locked the door of the White Rhino. "It'll probably be the most traffic Sugarcane Lane has seen in a while." Like ever, or at least since the cane fields ceased production.

"There's plenty of parking," Cole said. "Doris and her husband moved today, so it's just me back there now. I was looking for an isolated spot when I moved down here from Mississippi. Guess I have it."

"If you don't mind my asking, how do you make a living, Mr. Ryan?" Mac was going to keep this formal and professional, probably because Jena had gone out of her way to make it personal.

Cole stopped beside the open door to his pickup and gave Mac a steady look. "My mother, wife, and daughter all had life insurance policies and I was the only surviving beneficiary," he said, his tone abrupt. "I guess you could call it blood money."

CHAPTER 22

If one of those nosy reporters had been around now, holding out their microphones and asking, "How do you feel, Mr. Ryan?" Cole wouldn't have a clue how to answer. Five years ago, "No comment" had been an easy out.

Now, he'd have to say, "Confused." The idea of people—law enforcement officers at that—combing through his home and his workhouse left him petrified. Other than Jena, no one else had set foot in the place for five years. He felt protective of it, maybe in return for the protection it had offered him, the solace and solitude it had given him when he most needed it.

At the same time, he felt more alive than he had since Rachel and Alex and his mom had been killed. It was like his brain had been an extinguished candle that someone had finally spotted and lit. The wick had sputtered but caught. His mind felt sharp, and he wanted to talk.

Maybe once this was over, if he didn't get made into an easy scapegoat, he'd call Mike again and really come clean this time. He wasn't ready to revisit Yazoo City yet. He might never be. But he'd like to see his old friend and former partner on Ambulance 23.

Mac Griffin's truck took the lead in their convoy, Cole settled into the middle because he thought it would make Mac feel better, and Jena was a couple of cars behind him as they left Chauvin, cut over to Montegut, and then headed down the narrow Highway 665.

Cole could tell Mac didn't like him, but his admittedly rusty instincts told him it was more personal than professional. If he'd truly been concerned for Jena's safety, he wouldn't have left them alone to talk and, had that been the case, Cole wouldn't have tried to interfere. They had a job to do, no matter what vibe was going on between Jena and him. Even she'd acknowledged the connection.

He didn't think it was jealousy either. Before his self-imposed exile from humanity, he'd been a pretty good judge of human behavior. You had to be, to be a good paramedic. People did something stupid or embarrassing, it backfired on them in some way that required a paramedic or EMT to get involved, and their first instinct was to lie, to avoid admitting they'd done something dumb. Every single time. The best paramedics could look past the words and quickly analyze the actions and emotions to get at the truth of a situation.

He'd been considered an excellent paramedic, at least until the day he found himself unable to save a single member of his own family. He knew now that no one could have saved them other than God, and He had chosen not to. Cole had lost more than his family that day. He had lost his faith.

No, Cole thought Jena's partner was being plain-old protective. She'd just come back from a serious injury and was fragile. If she'd been telling the truth about her suicide attempt, she might be more fragile than her partner suspected. Mac didn't like Cole because Jena did and he wanted to protect her. Cole could respect that.

They passed the Island Road cutoff that went to Isle de Jean Charles and finally reached the last road that crossed Bayou Pointe-aux-Chenes. The turnoff to Sugarcane Lane came up quickly after that, and from what Cole could see around Mac's truck, there was already a swarm of uniformed people around his house. Even though he had nothing left to hide, it made him nervous.

He pulled his truck in behind Mac's and killed the engine. He'd take his cues from the wildlife agents. Besides, if he'd gone barreling into his driveway, he'd look guilty of . . . something. There were so many options, from alligator poaching to drug trafficking.

Jena parked across the dirt road, and the three of them walked in silence toward the house with Cole in the middle.

"How should I play this?" Suddenly aware of his clenched fists, Cole forced his hands to relax and tried to release the tension from his shoulders.

"Just tell the truth and . . . oh shit." Jena looked around Cole and directed Mac's gaze to the end of the lane. "I think the sheriff himself is here."

"And Warren too." Mac pointed at the LDWF truck in front of Doris's former home. "The big dogs have come out."

"Hold up!" They turned and saw two other wildlife agents jogging to catch up with them. Good grief, how many people were going to be here? Cole stifled the urge to run like hell.

Jena introduced the newcomers as senior agents Gentry Broussard and Paul Billiot. Great. The more the merrier.

Both agents greeted Cole respectfully—more so than he deserved, given the circumstances. So he knew there was a pity factor at work. Jena had probably gone to the kitchen to call her lieutenant so she could explain who he was. He was being given professional courtesy that might not be extended to any other long-haired guy living so far off the grid.

He didn't know whether to be grateful for that or annoyed. Maybe a little of both. For now, he'd keep his mouth shut unless spoken to.

His greeting by the sheriff and the Wildlife and Fisheries lieutenant wasn't quite as warm. Both had the look of career, no-nonsense law enforcement officers, even if the lieutenant wore a dark-green uniform and was probably outranked by the sheriff, an imposing man, tall and broad and serious as a myocardial infarction.

Cole unlocked the doors to both his house and his workhouse, giving permission for the deputies and forensics teams to go wherever they wanted.

It wasn't quite dark, but it would be soon, so he suggested they first make a trip to exhume the nastiest part of the job. "There are lights in the workhouse so you'll be able to see everything in there, but we'll lose daylight fast."

A sheriff's patrol boat sat at the end of the outlet, and Cole agreed to ride with the officers to show them where he'd buried the gator's contents. He'd almost barfed the day he buried them, so he didn't want to imagine the odors that would be coming from that plastic bin when they opened it.

He borrowed a heavy-duty flashlight from one of the officers—the guy named Billiot, he thought—and found his burial spot with sure-footed ease. The marine patrol deputy handed him a shovel, and Cole and Agent Billiot did the work of digging up what he'd done way too good a job at burying. They were both sweaty by the time they pulled the plastic bin out of the muddy soil with a wet, sucking sound.

A brief lift of one edge of the bin resulted in a lot of coughing and cursing, and Cole was glad his stomach was empty. It at least spared him the humiliation of treating everyone to one more gross indignity.

After clapping the lid back on the bin and securing it with a cord from the boat, the sheriff's forensics team decided the whole bin and its contents should go back to their lab intact, where Cole suspected they'd foist its unpacking on some junior colleagues.

An hour later they arrived back at the workhouse, where Cole was surprised to find the sheriff and Jena's lieutenant waiting inside. Nothing appeared to have been touched.

Ah, right. They wanted the forensics team here. Cole opened the big commercial fridge and freezer in back and showed them the bags containing the hide, skull, and feet of the gator on one shelf and, on another, the meat.

"How were you so damned sure that meat wouldn't kill you?" the sheriff asked.

Cole shrugged. "I found a treble hook in the gator's stomach, so I figured that's what killed him and I had found him not long after he died. I didn't think anything about that plastic bag in his stomach until I saw a picture in the paper the day after that kid shot himself. As soon as I realized what it might be, I called J—Agent Sinclair."

Sheriff Brown crossed his arms. "You realize we're cutting you some slack out of respect for your past history."

If Cole hadn't been sure before, he was now. "Yes, sir, I do."

"But you're still gonna take a ride with one of my deputies. We're taking you to Houma, and we're gonna ask you questions. Then we're gonna ask you more questions. If you're smart and you've got nothing to hide, you'll go willingly. Up to this point you are not under arrest and you are not being charged with anything. Yet. You got that?"

Roscoe Brown got close enough in Cole's personal space that he had to bite his tongue to keep from stepping backward. He wouldn't be bullied. His time for running was done.

"Yes, sir."

"You are not off the hook even if we do believe your story about finding that gator. At the very least you can be charged with hindering an investigation. You cost us days that might have helped us figure out these crazy gators and our traffickers might be somehow connected. Do you understand? Days! You got that too?"

Cole didn't drop his gaze from that of the big man in front of him. "I understand."

"Get out of here, then. Meizel!"

"Yes, sir?" A dark-haired deputy stepped in from the back, where he'd been overseeing the unloading of Cole's cooler.

"Take our hippie friend to the justice center for questioning."

Cole realized he'd be dead meat if he smiled, but being called a hippie was pretty funny. He'd never given much thought to how his appearance would strike someone like the sheriff—in other words, someone who looked and dressed a lot like Cole had looked himself once upon a time, only older and way more tightly wound.

Sheriff Brown's voice had grown a few decibels louder with every word, so he and the deputy were back in the yard before Cole realized the man didn't seem to think he *was* one of the traffickers. He gave a silent sigh of relief. So far, they believed him.

"Meizel, what's going on?" Jena stood on the back stoop of the house, looking pale and beautiful but for the dark circles under her eyes. "Is Mr. Ryan under arrest?"

"Evening, Agent Sinclair." Meizel smiled at her, and Cole got the impression they were, if not friends, at least not enemies. "We're just taking Mr. Ryan in for questioning. If he isn't charged he'll be released later tonight or early tomorrow. Depends on how long it takes the sheriff to cool off."

"I see." Jena looked past them toward the workhouse. What was she up to? "I need to talk to the sheriff and my lieutenant about something, but will drive up to Houma afterward. For whatever it's worth, Mr. Ryan is my friend and I believe him."

"Duly noted." Meizel had been holding on to Cole's arm just above the elbow, but his grip loosened, or at least Cole thought so. The deputy still pulled him toward one of the jumble of squad cars. "C'mon, Ryan. Let's spend some quality time at the Terrebonne Parish Detention Center."

CHAPTER 23

Jena steeled her nerves and walked into the workhouse, interrupting a chaotic scene of movement and multiple voices. "Excuse me?"

Everything stopped, and Sheriff Brown turned a beady glare in her direction. Now *there* was a guy who intimidated her. "Agent Sinclair. Why is it that when something untoward happens involving both of our agencies, you seem to be involved?"

Lieutenant Doucet saved her from having to come up with an answer. "Don't forget, Roscoe. If not for Agents Sinclair and Griffin being smart enough to take that gator in for testing instead of having it put down, we wouldn't know a damned thing about a possible link between the gators and the drugs. What is it, Sinclair?"

"My partner, Mac Griffin, and I got a couple of pieces of new information today and put together a theory," she said, hoping her voice didn't sound as shaky from the outside as it did from the inside. She was glad the DEA agent hadn't been brought in or hadn't thought it was worth his time. "Admittedly, it's pretty far-fetched, but not when you consider we're talking about the possibility of using alligators as drug runners."

The sheriff crossed his arms and tried to stare a hole through her. She thought it was working since the simple act of breathing had become difficult.

"Let's hear it," Warren said. "Griffin's off duty, so you get to do all the talking."

Awesome. "Well, this morning we got the final results of the tests on that gator we took to Baton Rouge, the one that was caught here the same day Mr. Ryan found his gator," she said. "It had a partially opened bag of Black Diamond in its stomach—a big bag with a pound of the stuff, minus a very small amount that had leaked from the bag into its system. Its front right foot had been marked in the same place with a tracking transmitter like the one Mr. Ryan found."

Warren frowned at her. "One could be an accident; two, not so much. Still doesn't make sense."

"You heard of anything else odd around here? Anybody besides Mr. Ryan who doesn't belong?" The sheriff had stopped glaring and started to look interested.

Jena leaned against one of the worktables, her arms crossed. "When Agent Griffin and I took Mr. Ryan's statement, which we recorded"— she handed the sheriff a flash drive—"he said the same afternoon Doris Benoit called that alligator in, he saw a guy in a boat out toward the juncture of that same inlet off Bayou Pointe-aux-Chenes."

The sheriff handed the flash drive off to a deputy, who put it in an evidence bag and left the workhouse. "What did Mr. Ryan remember about this guy in a boat?"

"Just that he was standing up and looking toward their houses with binoculars. Mr. Ryan thought he was probably a bird-watcher. He was medium height, wore a jacket with a hood—a light color. White or tan. The boat was a white skiff of some kind, a small one that has the captain's seat in the middle. Maybe twelve or fourteen feet."

"Well, that narrows it down to about a million men and boats in the parish," the sheriff said. "Did he notice any kind of markings on the boat?"

Jena shook her head. She wished, for Cole's sake, he'd seen something that could lead to an arrest of someone else. Then again, being too observant might make him look guilty. "He said when his neighbor began chasing that gator with a table leg, he started watching her instead. Next time he looked toward the bayou, the guy was gone."

Warren leaned on the edge of the worktable next to Jena. "Anything else?"

"We also found a baited line up on the main bayou just north of the juncture with this inlet yesterday. Agent Griffin and I staked it out for a while, but when no one came we cut the line. We came up with a way that maybe the gators were being used to transport the drugs."

"Explain." The sheriff's brown eyes had gone from hard marbles to sharp and interested.

Here was the kicker, and she watched Warren. Jena knew him better and could better read if he thought their theory had any validity. "What if a trafficker catches multiple gators in one of those hundreds of inlets nearer the Gulf, feeds them the drugs and puts the transmitters on them, then releases them someplace like Pointe-aux-Chenes, which is easier and faster to reach? There's little risk because law enforcement is focusing on the bigger waterways."

Warren and the sheriff were both frowning, but she thought it was more out of interest than doubt. She plowed on. "Then a second person—maybe somebody who normally fishes the area anyway—finds the gators through their transmitters, hauls them in, and extracts the drugs for local suppliers."

Sheriff Brown scratched his head. "That's the craziest theory I've ever heard, Agent Sinclair. You've got two traffickers, some drugged-up gators, a buyer, and a distributor all involved. Not to mention whoever's supplying the goddamned drugs in the first place. That's too many people."

Jena had been thinking about that very thing. "Maybe not, if the buyer and supplier were the same person. A gator processor, maybe.

Like Don Gateau, who might be retiring because he had another source of income, or Amelia Patout, who had cancer and was worried about how to provide for her kids if she didn't make it. Or one of the nuisance hunters, who'd be able to catch gators out of season without anybody questioning him."

Jena didn't like pointing fingers at people without evidence, but she wanted Warren and the sheriff to understand this theory—crazy as it sounded—might have legs.

Jena was pleased to see Warren's eyes spark with real life as he propped his elbows on Cole's worktable. "You talk to Raymond Naquin or any of the other nuisance hunters? You talk to any of the buyers?"

Jena nodded. "Mac and I were following up on the aggressive gator attacks and talked to Ray first, then Amelia Patout. Don Gateau's closed till gator season, but I've reached out to him. Waiting to hear back."

"And?" Brown crossed his arms over his chest. "We can't go accusing some of the parish's important businesspeople without something more substantial than a theory and a couple of interviews that weren't even related to drugs."

Jena blushed. "Parts of Ray's and Amelia's stories didn't add up, so we intend to talk to them again."

"Not about drugs, you won't." Brown practically bristled. "My detectives will talk to them. Your business is alligators. Anything else you stumble across about the drug case goes to your lieutenant or me and nobody else. You got that, Sinclair?"

Feeling properly put in her place, Jena mumbled, "I got it. Thanks for listening," and edged past the sheriff and into the cool night air. It soothed the heat burning her cheeks to ash.

"Hey, Sinclair."

She turned to see Warren exiting the workhouse. "It's an interesting theory, and if he didn't agree, the sheriff wouldn't have claimed it as his investigation. Good work. Now, go home and get some rest."

Jena nodded, but went into Cole's house first to make sure everything was okay. She was pleased to see that the deputies searching the place were putting things pretty much back where they'd found them.

She ended up walking back to her truck with Gentry, EZ, and Paul. Gentry hung back when the others reached their vehicles and joined the procession leaving Sugarcane Lane.

Gentry leaned against Jena's truck, and even though his face was illuminated only by the moonlight and the faint glow from Cole's windows, Jena knew those dark-brown eyes were filled with concern. Gentry was her best friend, even more so than Ceelie; all the stuff that had happened last fall had forged a bond between them that went way beyond partners or fellow agents. "You doing okay?"

"I'm hanging in there." She wasn't sure if he wanted to gauge the status of her emotional state or was trying to confirm anything he might have heard from Mac about her relationship with Cole Ryan. Not that she knew what kind of relationship they had, exactly.

Gentry looked back at the house. "You might not be able to save him, Jena. Ryan has been isolated from people so long it's hard for him to even carry on a conversation."

"Not with me." Those words told Gentry more than Jena had intended, but they were true. With her, Cole lost a lot of his awkwardness.

Gentry's posture tensed and he leaned forward. "What are you telling me? That you and Ryan are involved?"

"No. Maybe. I don't know." Jena scratched through the dirt with the toe of her shoe. "There's some kind of connection between us—has been from the first time we met, even before I knew who he was."

Her voice softened. "Cole is a good guy, Gentry."

He stared at her a few moments and she held his gaze. Finally, he shrugged. "Hell, I'm the last one to talk about keeping a professional distance, as you well know. Just be careful. Grief and loss can change people. So far, he mostly seems socially awkward, but he's been out here alone a long time. The guy's probably got pain he hasn't even begun to deal with, much less put behind him."

Yeah, well, they all had pain they'd never dealt with, didn't they? Cole had come clean with her, or at least she thought so. His tears had been real, and his raw emotion transparent. Which is more than she could say for herself.

She needed to fix that.

"Hey, don't worry," she said. "Go home and tell Ceelie I said no pink bridesmaids' dresses."

Gentry grinned, but then it faded. "You aren't going home, are you?"

"No, I'm going to the justice center and check on Cole." He knew her too well.

Gentry sighed. "Do what you have to do, Jena. Just don't hand over your heart too easily. You've been through some shit of your own, remember?"

Like she could forget. "I want to make sure Cole's being treated fairly, that's all. I don't plan to bring the man home and ravish him. At least I don't think so." In another place and time, before scars and hurts and wounds, that might have been a good idea.

Gentry laughed. "Unless you run into trouble and need my help? That's way more than I wanted to know, Sinclair."

CHAPTER 24

Cole had never been run over multiple times by a tractor-trailer rig but imagined it must feel something like this. Too many emotions had been dragged all over the map since this morning, and his head pounded from the incessant questions. His tongue stuck to the roof of his mouth from having to answer those questions.

He'd cried in front of Jena, sharing things he never expected to put into words, even with himself.

He'd voluntarily opened up his home to not only strangers, but strangers who could destroy everything he'd built here, strangers he hadn't learned to trust because he was so out of practice.

Now he'd spent hours running the gauntlet of questions posed by different people and worded in different ways, but they all led to the same place: to see if Cole would trip up in telling his story from different starting points and in a different order. He hadn't. Truth was truth, and it was all he had.

Finally, they'd released him with a warning not to leave the parish while the case was still open. He was tired and had no idea how he'd get home, much less flee the hounds of justice, truth, and the American way.

Until he walked into the lobby and saw Jena sitting on one of the chairs lined up along the wall. She looked as exhausted as he felt, but it didn't make her one bit less beautiful. He felt a foreign warmth fill his chest but tamped it down before it could reach his tear ducts. He'd be damned if he was going to cry in front of her again—at least not today.

Yet some part deep inside him, a part he'd been afraid to acknowledge until now, had hoped she would be here, waiting for him. "You came."

She stood up and walked toward him, pausing for a brief, awkward moment before wrapping her arms around his neck. He circled her waist and held on tight, pulling a new sense of energy from their closeness. He felt as if they'd known each other forever. Or at least as if their souls had.

"I thought you might need a ride home," she said, stepping away too soon. His arms, which had been empty too long, wanted her back. But however fragile he felt, she was more fragile. He sensed it, and would never push her.

"Yeah, I was just thinking I might have to sleep in an alley before I tried that long walk in the dark without my gear. Or I might grow old waiting for a deputy to have time to take me home. So thank you . . . I had really hoped you'd be here."

Pathetic, but it had made her smile.

They walked into the parking lot, got in her truck, and were mostly quiet on the ride down the deserted eastern parish highway. She filled him in on her theory and the fact that the big dogs—the sheriff and her own lieutenant—seemed to think it was at least plausible. She didn't mention any names, and they wouldn't have meant anything to Cole anyway. He was just glad she felt comfortable using him as a sounding board for her theory.

They finally reached the cutoff and headed through the old cane fields toward the dirt road leading to Cole's house. Even he had trouble finding the road at night after five years, yet she slowed and turned with one smooth motion. "You navigate really well in the dark. That turnoff is hard to find."

She laughed. "Enforcement agents spend a lot of time driving in dark places with our lights out. It's the best way to catch poachers and illegal hunters. Your eyes adapt to it eventually, or else you find another job."

"Poachers and illegal hunters . . . and drug traffickers?" He looked out the window. As hard as the interrogation had been, at least his questioners had never made him think they considered him a trafficker. Like the sheriff, they were mostly pissed off that he hadn't come forward earlier. Maybe they realized, on learning his background, drug trafficking would be the last crime he'd commit.

"Was it bad?" Jena's voice sounded small amid all the gear filling most of the closed truck cab. It was a chaotic jumble of radios and wires, weapons, and equipment.

"Not in the long run." He smiled a little at the approaching lights of his house. His *home*. "At least I've gotten off their radar as a suspect, or I think I have."

"Yeah, definitely. I think the only reason you got held that long is because the sheriff wanted to make a point—to all of us."

She stopped the truck in front of the house. Midnight had come and gone, and Cole froze in place, trying to figure out the halting words to invite her inside while at the same time letting her know it was okay if she said no. Had interacting with people—with women—always been this hard? Or maybe it was just her; he was desperate to not screw things up with Jena Sinclair, a feeling he couldn't imagine having even a couple of weeks before.

Before he could pull his words together, she killed the engine. "Cole, is it okay if we go inside and talk?"

He smiled. She had a knack for it—making him smile. He could have sworn he'd forgotten how, unless it was the kind of smile one pulled out in appreciation for a beautiful sunrise or a pure, cloudless autumn afternoon.

With her, he could not only smile; he could tease.

"Sure, c'mon in . . . or is your partner standing guard?" He looked up and down the lane as they approached the front porch. "Your coworkers are really protective of you, in case you haven't noticed. Especially that guy Broussard. He kept sizing me up tonight. Never said a word. Just stood there and watched me like I was an ugly bug under a microscope and he might have to stomp me flat if I made a wrong move."

Jena laughed. "Mac and I have only been partners for a week or two, but Gentry's been my partner since I joined the division. We've been through some stuff together, and he . . . yeah, he's overprotective. They all are since I just came back on active duty, which is nice on the one hand and, on the other, makes me want to throttle them."

She waited until he unlocked his door and stood aside so she could go in first. "You should see Gentry with his fiancée. She keeps threatening to tie him to a chair just to get some alone time. Whenever she wants to go anywhere, he thinks he needs to go with her."

Cole found himself smiling again, pleased to know Broussard had a fiancée and not a thing for Jena.

He must be overly tired, or losing his mind altogether. He'd gone from *no contact* to *wants full contact* in a matter of days. "You want something to drink? I've got some blackberry wine I made that's pretty good. Tea. Water. Afraid I don't have Cokes or hard stuff."

"I'm medication free as of today," she said. "Not even ibuprofen. So yeah. I've never tried blackberry wine, but it sounds good. Did you grow the berries?"

"No, I made it from wild ones I found on one of my rambles through the parish. Hang on." He disappeared into the kitchen and returned with two mismatched tumblers half filled with dark-purple liquid. "When I came here, I brought one box with a few clothes and a toothbrush," he said, handing her a glass. "Nothing else. So most of my glasses and stuff—whatever I haven't been able to make—have been thrift-store treasures."

"Except for the tablet." Jena had spotted the computer on his rough-hewn coffee table.

"Yeah, I guess the fact that I had to hold on to one lifeline should've told me I wasn't completely ready to cut myself off. Anyway, I like to wander around the parish by boat a lot, and in spring I'll stay gone a few weeks at a time. I found tons of wild blackberries last year and brought them back for wine and jam."

Jena tasted the wine, then took a longer sip. "This is amazing. Rich, with an aftertaste of honey. Kind of like port, but not as heavy."

"Yeah, and to think I couldn't boil water before becoming a swamp dweller."

Jena took a seat on the sofa, and Cole found himself with another dilemma. Should he sit next to her or take the other chair? Such a decision shouldn't feel momentous, but it did. It felt as momentous as a choice between the past and the future.

It felt like a choice between friendship and maybe more than friendship.

He sat next to her on the sofa.

∗∗∗∗

Jena had come here to finish the story she'd begun this afternoon and now here she was, almost close enough to touch Cole, definitely close enough to feel the chemistry that seemed to spring up between them whenever they got near each other. It was as if he had some kind of heat field around him that she could absorb through her skin.

She sipped a little more wine and took a deep breath. The wine relaxed her, and she needed relaxing for this conversation. "I came back tonight because I realized I had been unfair this afternoon."

"Seriously? Your support was the only thing that kept me from getting arrested, which I thought was extremely fair—although the sheriff hung back and gave me another lecture that included not leaving the parish and pretty much not breathing without his permission until this was all cleared up."

"Sheriff Brown is a tough character, but I guess it's in his job description." Jena ran a finger around the rim of her glass. "No, you were really honest and open with me today about what happened to you, and I wasn't as honest with you. About why I tried to kill myself. About why I gave up. You said one time that you'd cut yourself off from everyone but never had a death wish. I can't say the same."

Cole set his glass on the end table and moved closer. Close enough that his energy field engulfed her and shared that inner strength she was pretty sure he didn't realize he had. "Jena, I meant it when I said only when and if you're ready. You don't have to tell me anything."

"Yeah, I do." She reached out to take his hand, wondering even as she did it whether he would flinch or pull away. Instead, after a momentary stillness, he twined his fingers with hers and held on. "We had some kind of connection from the beginning, and it meant a lot that you were able to open up and talk to me about what happened to you. I know it didn't come naturally and it wasn't easy. I considered it an honor that I was the one you could talk to."

Her gaze probed his face. "I hope the drug case wasn't the only reason you told me."

He reached out with his other hand and tugged on the band holding her ponytail, letting her hair fall to her shoulders. His gaze seemed to heat her skin as he leaned closer. "You know damned well it wasn't the case. I felt something pulling me toward you the first time you came here that afternoon. I sense some sadness inside you, and I wanted to fix it. Something about you resonated with me."

He looked at their hands, comfortably together. "No, it was even before that, when I saw you standing out there and looking over the water. Before you caught me looking at you. The expression on your face was one I understood."

Jena nodded. "Me too. Something inside me recognized you." She took another sip of wine. "After I was shot, I had to go back to New Orleans and stay at my parents' house while I recuperated. I knew it would be awful. My parents and I have never gotten along well. They love me, but they don't know how to show it in a way that makes me feel it. My dad throws money at everything and keeps his distance, and my mom hovers too close and tries to micromanage. As the bullet wounds healed and I realized how disfigured I'd be, my mom assured me someone might still want me if I found a good plastic surgeon."

Jena was aware of Cole shifting on the sofa, pulling her closer, but she kept her eyes on the far side of the room, on a knot in one of the pine panels that covered the walls. If she looked at him, she'd never get it out. "Then, during one of my last assessments with the doctors, they told me . . ." She'd never said the words aloud, but gathered them in her mind. "One of the bullets had damaged . . . They told me I'd never be able to bear a child."

Cole drew her close, wrapped his long arms around her, and folded her in his warmth. "And a baby is something you've always wanted?"

Jena relaxed in his arms; his warmth and the hand that rubbed her back simply wouldn't allow the tension to linger. "I honestly hadn't given it that much thought before, which is the stupid part." She pulled away so she could look at him, to try explaining something that sounded crazy, even to her.

"I want kids, or I always assumed I would have kids if I found the right person to have them with. I realized that not carrying a child wasn't the end of the story. I can always adopt a child or find a surrogate. But I didn't feel like a woman anymore. I had fallen so deeply into a dark hole that I couldn't think clearly enough to be logical."

His voice was soft. "I know that hole pretty well myself."

"All I could think was how I'd always failed my parents, and this was one more failure. I wasn't the beauty they wanted. I was a tomboy and refused to be a part of the debutante scene; believe me, in New Orleans, that's a huge deal. When I chose an academic field, it wasn't to pursue a respectable white-collar occupation like a doctor or lawyer or business tycoon. I wanted to be a cop. Even worse, after a few years with NOPD, I decided to train for wildlife enforcement."

Jena could feel him watching her, but she still couldn't look at him without crying, and she didn't want to cry. She might not be able to stop.

"What happened to push you over the edge?" Cole asked.

"I overheard my mom talking to one of her friends." Jena did her best Mom impression, assuming an uptown New Orleans accent. "'Well, thanks to her poor choices and obvious inability to do her job, Jena Grace will not even be able to present us with a grandchild. Honestly, I sometimes think she was a punishment from God for some wrong I did in the past.'

"That's what did it: my own mother seeing me as her punishment from God, as if I only mattered because of how I reflected on her. And I bought into it. Stupid thing is that now, I don't think she even realizes she said it. If she did, I don't think she'd understand why it would hurt me."

Cole pulled her back into an embrace. "We're programmed to believe our parents, but parents are just people who've had kids. There's nothing magical about them. They don't automatically become warm, nurturing people upon giving birth." Rachel had been a hard woman. Cole hoped she would've never said anything like that to Alex, but he'd never know. "Think of it this way. You were strong enough to escape and do the thing you loved, then you got sent back at a time when you were hurt and vulnerable. Whether she meant it or not, she pushed you into that hole and started shoveling in the dirt."

Jena's tears came anyway. "I guess."

Susannah Sandlin

"When I first met you, I saw sadness." Cole's voice was slow and calm. "But since then, here's what I've come to know about you. You're strong. You're a survivor. You're smart. You're beautiful." He paused. "Of course, you have to take into account that I haven't met anybody else in five years."

She shoved him away, and when she met his gaze, they both laughed. It had been the perfect response to stop the tears and let her know it was okay.

Until his smile faded and there seemed to be some kind of war going on behind his eyes.

"What's wrong?"

He didn't answer at first, but finally said, "I really want to kiss you."

Her first instinct was a flippant *Then why don't you, already?* Because she wanted him to. But she'd bet her last paycheck that the last woman he'd kissed was his wife. He'd probably climbed out of their bed that morning, given her a quick kiss, and headed to work. Never imagining it would be the last time.

The statement that he wanted to kiss her wasn't an idle flirtation, not coming from him, and she couldn't treat it that way.

"I want you to kiss me." She wasn't sure she was ready to be with a man, not with her scars, but her need to taste him overrode her fear of rejection.

He leaned forward, tentative, and pressed his lips to hers. Pulled away. Kissed her again, this time with more force. Jena opened her mouth to his, and he took the invitation. Even after such a long day, he smelled like fresh air and sunshine and tasted as sweet as the wine he'd made from the blackberries he'd found in the wild.

He scattered kisses along her jawline and down her neck, sending heat way farther south. God, could she do this? Could she stop?

A buzz from her pocket startled them both, and they jumped apart as if they'd been about to fall into some abyss, saved only by Jena's mobile phone.

176

Damned phone.

"Sorry." She pulled it out and read the text from Warren: *The sheriff wants you to present your theory to the full task force, noon tomorrow @ TPSO. Bring your A game.*

Cole brushed his fingers through her hair. "Don't tell me. You have to go?"

She couldn't tell if he was relieved or disappointed. She wasn't even sure about her own feelings. Maybe a little of both. If she stayed, they would make love, and she wasn't sure either of them was ready for that step. They'd taken an awful lot of steps today already.

"Yeah, a command performance before the sheriff at noon, and I have to meet Mac in a few hours to talk to a nuisance-gator guy." They were going to confront Ray Naquin about his claim of selling gators to a business that was not even open but, as ordered, never mention drugs.

Now *that*, she regretted.

CHAPTER 25

Ray Naquin's silver pickup was parked in his drive, with a shiny white fiberglass bass boat hitched to the back. Mac wished the guy would make it easy for them and have the back of it filled with Black Diamond, but no such luck.

"Well, the boat's white," Jena said. "What is it, about eighteen feet?"

Mac shook his head. "More like sixteen. Good size for alligators too; it can go in narrow channels."

Too bad there was no way to tell whether Ray had been the guy Cole had seen on the day the gators had been found. It would probably be too much to hope for that he'd open the door wearing a light-colored hoodie and holding a pair of binoculars. Besides, they were risking the wrath of the sheriff by even talking to him since the drug investigation was officially not their business.

They didn't make it to the front door before Ray walked out wearing a purple LSU T-shirt, raggedy jeans, and a smirk. "Why if it isn't my friends from Wildlife and Fisheries. Y'all still lookin' for pissed-off reptiles?"

"Actually, we're trying to account for all the nuisance gators sold this past year, just for monitoring purposes," Jena lied.

Mac had to respect a woman who could lie so convincingly on short notice. Unless, of course, she was lying to him.

Ray had been loading tape and zip ties and fishing rods into the back of the boat, but stopped short. "What the hell are you talking about, *Agent Sinclair*? I file paperwork with the state, so if you got questions, call your own department's nuisance program."

Mac sensed that Jena would arrest Ray for a bad attitude and send him directly to the Louisiana State Penitentiary if she got the chance. After what Ray had said to her the other night, Mac didn't blame her.

"Mind if we take a look at your unfiled paperwork?" Mac asked. "See if there are any that aren't on our list? I noticed you had a big stack of unfinished paperwork in your living room."

Mac stuck his hands in his pockets, an aw-shucks move. "And you said you'd been selling all your gators to Don Gateau, right?"

Mac watched Ray for any telltale body language, but the man was arrogant. Arrogant people didn't think they could be caught, and of course there was always the possibility that he had nothing to do with the drug scheme—if there even *was* a drug scheme. Couldn't arrest him for arrogance.

Plus, Ray Naquin had a good business; it was hard to imagine him getting pulled into this Black Diamond nightmare and risking everything. But why lie about his gator buyer?

Ray's kettle was boiling and about to blow. "Look, unless you two got a warrant to search my premises—and nobody's gonna issue one because you're on a bigger fishing expedition than the one I'm about to go on—get the hell out of here. You want to see paperwork, go look at your own."

"C'mon, Mac. Mr. Naquin's not going to be cooperative." Jena headed back to the truck and only paused slightly when Ray yelled, "So long, scarface."

Talk about boiling kettles. Mac was so angry, it was a miracle that steam wasn't blowing out his ears in a high-pitched whistle. He ended up inside the truck before Jena had fully climbed in.

Ray didn't give them the option of hanging around either. He stood beside his open pickup door, making shooing motions with his hands until Mac backed out of the drive and headed on down Shrimpers Row. He pulled into a tucked-away spot in the first parking lot they came to, and waited to see which way Ray went.

"There he goes, heading south." Mac's fingers gripped the steering wheel tightly enough to turn his knuckles white. "I'm sorry. You shouldn't have to hear shit like what he said."

"Oh, come on, Mac. You've got nothing to apologize for. He's just pissed because I wouldn't have pity sex with him the other night."

Mac ground his teeth. "Somebody needs to teach that jerk a lesson."

"Let's just drop it." Jena looked northward toward Ray's house. "Think we should take a look around his place while he's gone?"

"No way he's going to have anything incriminating left outside. He's an asshole but he isn't dumb. Well, yeah, he's dumb but not *that* dumb. Why don't we pay another visit to Amelia Patout?"

"Sounds good to me. I want nothing more to do with Raymond Naquin. Unless I run into him out in the field on a call, he doesn't exist to me."

Mac wasn't sure whether she was trying to convince him or herself. "Well, we're trampling all over the sheriff's territory anyway, so why not talk to Amelia? We just don't mention drugs. Good spur-of-the-moment lie back there, by the way."

Halfway to Houma, Jena's mobile phone pinged. "Just got an e-mail from Don Gateau." She punched the button. "Interesting. He says he hasn't bought a gator from Ray Naquin in a couple of years, but he heard Ray was sending all his business to Patout's since Amelia got sick, on account of his friendship with her late husband."

Mac made a noise that lay somewhere between a curse and a growl. "If Don Gateau's telling the truth, then both Amelia and Ray are lying. Let's look around and then let the sheriff know."

The Patout's Seafood van was still in the back lot, but the pickup and boat were gone. In their place sat a muddy black sedan—a recent-model Nissan Sentra. Jena took a photo of it with her phone and made note of its license plate.

"That was a white boat hitched to their pickup when we were here before, right?" Mac turned into the lot and parked near the front door. One other car sat nearby, so at least Amelia was doing some business today.

"It was—not too different from Ray's except older." Jena climbed out of the truck. "I guess Amelia's still driving, but I can't imagine she's out in a boat wrangling gators."

The tinkling bell that sounded when they opened the door caught the attention of Slade, who was behind the counter, wrapping up fish for an elderly couple whose clean white tennis shoes immediately marked them as tourists.

"Game wardens!" Slade said, smiling broadly. Jena pretended she didn't see the elderly woman raising her phone and turning to take a selfie-on-the-sly with real live game wardens, but Mac had no such reservations. "Hey, Sinclair, why don't you take a photo of me and these nice folks. Slade, you wanna be in the picture?"

The woman tittered, the man grinned, and Slade nodded vigorously. Jena couldn't refuse without looking like a bitch, which amused Mac. Besides, interacting in a friendly way with the public was a key component of their job. They wanted people to call them when they had a problem, not be afraid of them.

Way too many photos later, the couple left, heading down to Cocodrie for a commercial fishing tour.

The bell hadn't finished ringing from their departure when Jena asked Slade about Amelia. "Is your mom here today? We need to talk to her."

"Yeah, sure. Mom!" Slade didn't need an intercom system; nothing wrong with the kid's lungs. A few seconds later, Amelia came out of the back. She took one look at Mac and Jena and turned to her son. "Slade, honey, would you go and put away all that fish that was brought in yesterday?"

"Sure thing."

Mac waited until Slade went into the back before speaking. "We wanted to ask you some more questions about your business with Ray Naquin." He'd borrow Jena's story. "We're trying to account for all the nuisance gators that have been bought in the parish since the attacks started a couple of months ago. The nuisance-gator hunters are behind in their paperwork, so we thought the sellers might keep more up-to-date records." Damn, he was a good liar.

"That why you folks were asking about Raymond Naquin the other day, and I'll tell you again. He was a good friend of my late husband's, but he don't come around like he used to."

Amelia looked like shit. Her skin had a grayish cast and she was too thin. Today, she still wore a scarf around her head but she also pulled a portable oxygen tank on a wheeled backpack. Chemo had taken its toll.

"Ray told us the same thing—said he'd been selling over at Don Gateau's, but Don's been closed, so we thought maybe he'd gotten confused."

"No." Amelia didn't bother pulling out her laptop this time and, sick or not, Mac would describe her expression as stubborn. "I mean maybe he's confused, but no, he ain't been selling to me, not since the first of the year. Maybe check up in Bourg or over in Lafourche Parish. Or ask Ray again yourself."

Mac changed tactics; from the corner of his eye he could track Jena's movement as she wandered around the refrigeration cases. He had no doubt she was listening and watching, though. "Where are you in your treatment, if you don't mind my asking? My dad had cancer and it can turn around really quickly."

His dad had survived and been free of cancer for several years, but Mac didn't think the petite, dark-eyed Amelia Patout was going to have such a good outcome.

"My chances aren't too good." She spoke in a flat, emotionless voice. "It was all them damned cigarettes me and my husband both used to smoke like nobody's business. The cancer doctors up at the center in Houma done told me to get my affairs in order." She shook her head. "It ain't that easy, getting affairs in order. I got an eighteen-year-old who wants to run wild and a fifteen-year-old who's going to need some kind of care the rest of his life."

Her voice had gotten more shaky as she talked. "I'm sorry," she whispered, rubbing her eyes. "I didn't mean to go off like that. Is there anything else you need to know?"

"I hate to ask, but could you check your laptop again and find out the exact date when Ray brought in his last gator? Or any gators that have come in from other hunters since Christmas?"

"My computer's at home. I hadn't planned to stay here so long." As if to prove her point, Amelia pulled over a stool and sat down with a pained expression. "I been doing most of my bookkeeping at home since the chemo."

Mac wanted to get his hands on that computer, but they'd pushed it as far as they could.

"Well, that was not exactly illuminating," Mac said as soon as he'd pulled back onto the highway, headed for Thibodaux so Jena could give her presentation.

"Well, we know Ray or Amelia—or both—are lying," she said. "But we'll have to figure it out later. Now, I have to convince an arrogant DEA agent that his local drug mules have four legs, a tail, and seventy-two big white teeth."

CHAPTER 26

Friday morning dawned overcast, with gray clouds building to the southwest. Cole hadn't been fishing in a while, not to mention the law enforcement officers had pretty well laid waste to what was in his cooler.

He might have time to fish a little farther down the bayou before the rain moved in, though he wouldn't stray too far. Spring storms could be unpredictable. Might be a quick, hard rain that turned to nothing in an hour, or it could turn black as midnight and rain buckets for hours. In either event, he didn't want to be in a pirogue when a storm hit.

He optimistically packed a sandwich for lunch, gathered his bait and gear for channel catfish, and used the pole to push the pirogue away from the bank. Catfish were not picky eaters, so any bait would do. Cole had some raw chicken pieces and cheese and liver. He'd rather have gone farther south for red drum, but didn't want to risk the weather.

He set the pole aside and took up his oar, propelling himself southward on Bayou Pointe-aux-Chenes, stopping in different spots to fish for a while and keeping one eye on the clouds. He'd pulled in three good-sized fish before the sky turned the color of charcoal. Time to turn around and get home.

He spotted a boat just past the outlet to his house, and realized the guy was trying to pull in an alligator. Instinctively, he pulled out his pole and gently pushed himself closer to the bank, where he was camouflaged by the tall grass. He didn't think the guy had spotted him.

Was it the same man who'd been watching the day both Doris and Cole had found their alligators? Hard to tell. This guy had on a navy nylon jacket with the hood pulled up even though the rain hadn't yet started.

His gator was not happy, but the guy handled him like a pro. Cole waited for him to tape the jaws and zip tie the feet, then squinted through the first drops of light rain and saw the gator was already secured. The man was . . . what the hell?

He wasn't catching the gator; he was letting it go. First, he sat on the gator's back and cut the zip tie on his front legs, then the powerful back legs. The gator thrashed but, to give the man credit, he stayed on its back with one hand holding most of his weight on the back of the gator's neck. Reaching over, he cut the tape on both sides of the animal's powerful jaws and shoved it into the water.

Cole watched as the guy pulled out a second gator from the bottom of his boat and did the same thing, then a third. If Jena's theory was true, this might be the trafficker who'd picked up the gators near the Gulf and now was releasing them to be caught locally. He hoped the man had medical insurance. Releasing an angry gator would be tricky business. Sooner or later, the gator was going to spin and this guy was gonna lose an arm.

A fat dollop of rain hit Cole on top of his head, the precursor to the storm. Not a lot of rain yet, but the wind picked up. He decided to wait a few more minutes to see if the guy was going to call it a morning. Craning his neck, Cole thought he saw at least one or two more gators in that boat.

For the first time, Cole wished he had one of those fancy smartphones with the cameras in them. The guy pulled a black box and a crumpled sheet of paper from his pocket. After consulting the paper, he turned some dials on the black box and watched it for several seconds.

A gust of wind almost blew Cole into the middle of the bayou. He only stayed hidden by grabbing two handfuls of marsh grass and praying they had enough roots left to hold him secure.

They held, and Cole glanced up at the other boater. The wind was playing havoc with the guy's jacket, which was way too big for him. The hood finally blew back, and Cole got a look at the guy who might be one of the real drug traffickers of Terrebonne Parish.

Shit. It was a kid. Cole got a good look at his face, and spotted a vine tattoo on his neck. He was maybe seventeen or eighteen, skinny, with short white-blond hair that had probably gotten him called "towhead" a few times when he was younger. A kid dealing in dangerous drugs. It was a scenario that brought an eerie déjà vu over Cole, and sent a shiver down his back that had nothing to do with the dropping temperatures.

The rain was coming down harder now, and the boy seemed to have released his last gator. He pulled his hood back on, punched a number on his cell phone, and talked for maybe thirty seconds. Then he stuck the phone back in his pocket, started his outboard motor, and headed north. But not before Cole saw the prow of his boat. The white paint had been a recent job, he'd guess. Definitely a sloppy job. The boat's original name, "Gypsy," was still visible beneath its white topcoat.

Cole couldn't have kept up with him even if he'd wanted—not in a pirogue with a paddle. He made sure the guy was out of sight, then pushed himself away from the bank and rowed for home. By the time he reached the point where the inlet ran into his side yard, the rain was coming down so hard he ran the pirogue aground.

No time to waste, so he gathered up the catfish and threw them into the cooler, snatched his truck keys off the worktable, and managed to escape Sugarcane Lane before it turned into Sugarcane River, which could happen very fast.

Turning north on the state highway, he drove until he spotted a convenience store with pay phones. He dug out quarters, but each one slid straight through the machine and clinked back into the coin return. None of the damned things worked.

A young woman and her blond-haired child stood outside the door to the convenience store, watching the rain. Cole faltered for a moment, seeing Rachel and Alex, but shook the cobwebs loose. *Now's not the time, Ryan.*

"Excuse me." He approached the woman and hated the look of fear and doubt that crossed her face upon seeing him. "I hate to ask, but do you have a phone I could use? The pay phones aren't working. It's a local call."

Something about him must have sounded better than he looked because she nodded and handed him a phone.

He looked down at the screen, frozen. He had no idea how to use the damned thing. It didn't look anything like his old iPhone.

The woman laughed. "They can be complicated, can't they? Here, tell me your number and I'll punch it in for you."

Thanking God for kindhearted people and cursing himself for forgetting there *were* kindhearted people, Cole handed it back to her and dug into his pocket for Jena's number. This time, if she didn't answer the phone, he'd act like a normal person and leave a message.

But she answered with her brisk, "Sinclair."

"Jena, it's Cole. I just saw—"

"Where are you calling from?" Her voice sounded amused. "Caller ID says your name is Susan, and it sounds like you're in the rain forest."

"I saw him, Jena. One of the traffickers."

Any hint of joking left her tone, and he thought from the change in pitch and background noise that she'd put it on speaker, probably so Mac could hear.

Her voice was all business. "Okay, start from the beginning."

He gave her a truncated version of the gator releases. "His hood flew off in the storm and I got a good look at him."

"Describe him."

Cole could imagine her with her little notebook, writing furiously. Mac might have been taping it with his own phone. "Medium height, skinny kid. Just a kid, Jena. Maybe eighteen, with a vine tattoo on his neck. Short blond hair."

There was a long pause. "How blond?" she asked.

"Almost white. He was in a boat that had been painted white, but you could see its former name through the last coat of paint: Gypsy."

"Damn." That was Mac, but through the falling rain, all Cole could understand was "asswipe" and "Marty."

"Where are you, Cole?" Jena asked. "Whose phone is this?"

He told her. "I need to get back home while the road is still passable, unless I can help you with something."

"You helped a lot, more than you know," she said. "Go on home and I'll touch base with you as soon as I can."

Cole had a bad feeling as he handed the phone back to the woman and thanked her. "Where's the best place to buy one of those?" he asked.

"If you're not picky about it, you can buy a cheap one in the store here," she said. "Won't do much except make calls."

That was all he needed.

Cole went inside and came out with a brand-new cell phone. Now he just had to learn how to make the damned thing work.

CHAPTER 27

"No way is Marty Patout working alone on this; he's not that smart. Have you heard if the DEA has any idea where the supply is originating?" Jena sped down Highway 665 along Bayou Pointe-aux-Chenes. They'd picked up a patrol boat and hitched it to the back of her truck; since the rain had slackened, they'd nose around and see if Marty finished unloading his gators.

"Only that it's probably New Orleans or Houston," Mac said. "They've really clamped down in both cities, and O'Malley figures the supplier thinks Terrebonne is so isolated and scattered that it makes an easy entry point. So far, that's proven true. What did the guy think about our gator theory?"

Jena shrugged. "Well, he didn't laugh me out of the room."

"It's like looking for a needle in a haystack if you don't catch Marty Patout in the act of releasing a drugged gator," Warren had said after Jena called him with the newest information. "Rather than run up and down the bayous looking for him, stake out the area we know the gators were released this morning. Somebody's gonna come and pick them up. As soon as you see something, call it in. Don't get caught alone with any of these people."

"Marty Patout doesn't strike me as particularly dangerous," Mac said.

"Yeah, well, tell me that after he shoots your ass," Warren had said. "That kid spent his whole life on those bayous with his father before Martin got himself killed. There's a lot of money at stake, and money makes people do desperate things."

They launched from the Pointe-aux-Chenes landing and motored north along the bayou, with Mac steering and Jena handling the binoculars. They passed the inlet to Cole's house and went a few miles farther before conceding that Warren was right.

"Let's just turn around and watch the area where Marty released those gators." Jena shouted to be heard above the motor. "They've already lost two that we know of, Doris's and Cole's. I bet they won't risk letting them sit for long."

Mac nodded and maneuvered the patrol boat into a tight U-turn, navigating back south of the inlet to Sugarcane Lane. They chose a spot along the bank where the grass hanging over the side was thickest and took cover as best they could.

Then they waited, and Jena wondered how many hours of her life had been spent waiting. Waiting for lawbreakers, waiting for that indefinable thing that would make her feel whole and happy. Maybe no one ever found that thing, whatever it was. Maybe the happy-looking people were acting, playing the role.

She had a lot to be grateful for. She had a job she loved, and she was alive to enjoy it. She had colleagues she enjoyed working with, who were more family to her than her own family had ever been. She and Ceelie had formed a close friendship, so she had someone to do things with—at least when they could give Gentry the slip.

And then there was Cole Ryan, whose face had somehow slipped into her mental recounting of things for which she was grateful. They barely knew each other, yet her heart knew him. She understood him; he understood her. They were both coming out of really screwed-up places. Maybe something would come of it, at least after some plastic surgery. But she was still grateful for him. At the very least, she'd found another friend.

Three hours passed, then four, then five. They'd agreed to wait at least until dark set in, or maybe a little longer, but they'd both gotten fidgety from sitting too long. Jena kept stretching her legs out in front of her, then squatting, then tucking them underneath her, just to let one set of muscles rest while another set grew uncomfortable.

They were both in uniform, which increased the discomfort exponentially, especially with the humidity and their required life vests and duty belts. The vests were lightweight, but any extra layer added to the misery.

It was almost five thirty, and they agreed to give it another half hour before heading in to find something for dinner.

"Outboard coming from the north," Mac said, settling back onto his perch and pulling out his own binoculars.

The white bass boat looked very familiar, as did the man driving it. "Our old friend Ray," Jena murmured. "Let's see if he stops."

He did stop, and they watched—and Mac filmed with his camera phone—as Ray looked down at a black box and then maneuvered his boat slowly into place. He stuck a long pole in the mud and hung a line of chicken from it, positioned only a few inches above the waterline.

Then Ray waited, and they waited for Ray to make a move, careful to remain quiet. Jena texted Warren an update.

A gust of wind almost blew their cover away and even though they'd just gone on daylight saving time and should've had an extra hour of light, dark was setting in as another storm approached. It was supposed to be like this all weekend.

Mac touched her arm and pointed as an alligator, a beautiful animal with a nicely shaped head whose size would put it at about eight or nine feet, sprang vertically from the water and chomped down on the chicken.

Ray waited a few minutes until the gator got settled, then slowly began to pull the animal toward the surface using the other end of the line. The man was clearly adept at his job. He slowly hauled the gator up, wrestled with it a few seconds, and then delivered the kill shot in the quarter-sized soft spot at the back of the bony skull.

He pulled it into the boat and consulted the black box again.

But they'd seen enough. If the gator in Ray's boat had a belly full of Black Diamond, they had him and Martin Patout both. If it didn't, they at least could get him for poaching, a major offense that carried heavy fines, possible jail time, and suspension of Ray's nuisance-hunter license.

Plus, it was raining again, in earnest. Visibility was disappearing fast.

Mac pushed their boat away from the bank, and Jena's adrenaline surged as she stood up and pulled her SIG Sauer, yelling to be heard over the pounding of rain on water. "Stop there, Ray! We want to have a look at that gator you just pulled in. Put down the rifle slowly, and keep your hands where I can see them."

"Aw, honey, you still mad 'cause I didn't want to sleep with you?" Ray gave her a grin, and leaned down to set the rifle on the seat of the boat.

At the last second, he whipped it back up and fired. Mac cried out as he crumpled to the deck. There was no time to check on him. Jena returned fire immediately, but Ray had already started his outboard and was churning too much water for her to get a bead on him. All her shots went wide.

Ray was going to get away, damn it, and he'd be twice as hard to catch. Jena climbed over Mac and took over the navigation, circling to follow Ray. "Mac, can you shoot?"

"I think so." His right side was already soaked with blood, but he reached for the rifle sitting next to the console.

What the hell?

Ray was coming back, his engine on full throttle, heading straight for the smaller LDWF boat. He was going to ram them.

"Mac, get a shot off if you can. Otherwise, hang on!" Jena started firing and, next to her, Mac got off at least two rifle shots. But everything else became a sudden blur of water and chaos and blood at the impact of Ray's boat. She didn't know whether or not any of her shots hit home.

The patrol boat had been turned sideways and pushed toward the shore, dragging Jena underneath it. She held her breath and got her bearings with her feet—the water was too choppy and too much mud had been churned up for a visual, but the LDWF life vests inflated upon hitting the water and would pop her to the surface as soon as she pushed clear of the boat. *Stay calm. You know how to do this. Find shore first, then find Mac.*

Her lungs were on fire by the time she ran into the low bank and was pushed to the surface by her vest. She took in a few lungsful of air and turned enough to see Ray sitting a little ways up the bayou, watching. He raised his rifle, and Jena let go of the grass, loosening her vest so she could sink again toward the bayou's muddy bottom.

What was he thinking? That killing her and Mac would mean he was in the clear? Would he not realize they'd kept their supervisors informed? Then again, their portable radios and phones would probably be inoperable after being dunked in mud, so maybe he was gambling that they hadn't reported in yet.

Warren's words came back to her: *Money makes people do desperate things.*

She scrambled in the last direction that she'd seen her partner, and tripped over him. He was conscious and trying to reach a spot on the bank that would block them from Ray's view. He'd loosened his life jacket as well.

They managed to keep their heads above water, and Jena was glad to see a level bank. "You're hurt, so you're first," she gasped. "Move fast."

Mac belly-crawled over the bank and rolled into the tall marsh grass, disappearing from view. Jena was right behind him. She collapsed next to him in the mud with rain coming down so hard it stung.

Six months ago, Jena had had the option of standing and fighting, or running. That time, she'd chosen to turn and fight. And everyone had suffered for it.

Right now, Ray had the advantage, and she wasn't risking Mac's life.

Through the thick strands of marsh grass, she saw Ray Naquin raise his head above the edge of his boat. "Don't know if you're still out there, sweet thang," Ray called. She still couldn't get a shot at him, so she fired at his boat and heard him curse. "Go ahead and try, bitch. You can't lay in the grass all night, and the rain won't hide you forever."

Jena didn't plan to hide. She planned to run.

CHAPTER 28

Cole heard gunfire—or a backfiring motor—from the direction of the bayou. He stood on his porch and tried to see through the slanting sheets of cold rain, but everything was murky from where the inlet met the flooded water of his road. There would be no travel by truck anywhere else today.

He'd spent most of the day trying to figure out the cell phone and had finally thrown it out in disgust when it looked like he needed a landline phone in order to activate it. If he already had a phone he wouldn't need the damned thing. Finally, he picked it up and read the fine print. Reading instructions had never been one of his strong suits.

"Typical guy. Do first, read instructions later," Rachel used to say. To which he'd usually reply with something resentful like, "Some of us have to work for a living and don't have time to read the details."

Her insistence on being a stay-at-home wife had always been a sore point with him because, at least until Alex came along, she'd done little other than lounge by the condo pool and shop. It's how she'd been brought up, and Cole had spent five years chastising himself for letting resentment build up rather than talking it through.

Susannah Sandlin

Once Alex came, things had gotten better. Rachel was an attentive mother, and seeing Alex's happy little-girl version of himself when he came home from a long shift made it worthwhile.

Meeting Jena Sinclair had made him think a lot about Rachel the last few days. Before, he thought of "the loss" in unison, as if Alex and Rachel and his mom were a single entity. Jena had unknowingly helped him separate the three, and he had to admit something he'd been tamping down. He was angry at Rachel. It might not be reasonable, but it was how he felt.

There. He'd thought it, and on some level Cole waited for lightning to come blazing from the sky to punish him. Rachel had taken Alex out of day care to hit a sale at the mall. They shouldn't have been there. Alex should have been coloring dinosaurs or playing with her friends.

Part of him realized his anger was unfair, that Rachel would never have intentionally put Alex in harm's way. But another part of him realized the grief for his daughter had been so all consuming, it had covered up the fact that his grief for Rachel was not as fierce.

Was that true, or was he vilifying Rachel to make it okay for him to want Jena?

Another blast sounded from the direction of the bayou and, again, Cole went onto the porch. Then two more blasts. Damn it; that was no backfiring motor.

He ran to his bedroom, took out the black-hooded poncho he'd made from an old tarp, and slipped it over his head. He stuck a big flashlight in one pocket and his pistol in the other. He picked up his shotgun, then put it back and, instead, moved the pistol inside his shirtfront so it had a chance of staying dry. Even if it didn't, the pistol's ammo was more waterproof and a wet shotgun could be unreliable.

He hoped he wouldn't need either one.

Sloshing through knee-deep water on the way to his pirogue, which he'd tied to the edge of his porch, Cole paused and ran through different scenarios. This might be nothing, but the itch between his shoulder

196

blades said otherwise. He'd been thinking all morning, after seeing the kid with the gators, that today would be a make-or-break time in this drug case. He couldn't stand the thought of Jena on the losing end.

If he went paddling out into Bayou-Pointe-aux-Chenes, he could row himself right into a mess, depending on who was shooting at whom. Assuming anybody was shooting at all.

The spit of land next to his house—the one that formed the southern bank of the cut—was marshy and unreliable. It was crossable without a boat, however. He paddled into the blowing rain for what seemed like an hour before making it halfway down the length of the inlet from Bayou Pointe-aux-Chenes. At least the wind would be at his back on the return trip. And it was almost full dark now.

He secured the boat to a spindly, sad excuse for a tree that might have grown to be a thriving oak had too much salt water not been driven inland in the name of Big Oil. It was still sturdy enough to anchor a boat, however.

From there, he cut inland on foot for maybe an eighth of a mile, then turned east, toward the bayou. In places, he sank into cold water above his waist, keeping the pistol as dry as he could. He needed to figure out a way to turn a tarp into pants.

The rain slackened enough for him to gauge where he was—maybe three-quarters of the way to the bayou. It was too dark now to see if there were boats on the water, or even if there was water. Reaching inside his pocket, he pulled out his waterproof flashlight, an overpriced LED purchase he'd thought was a smart possession for someone who lived in an area that flooded so easily.

But it was bright, so he held it in his hand and only flicked it on occasionally to keep his bearings.

A light flashed ahead of him, sending a surge of adrenaline through his system. He slid his own flashlight into his pocket and took out his pistol, a sturdy .45. He made his way quietly toward the bobbing light, being careful not to make any unusual splashes, rounded behind the person, and saw a glint of light off red hair—very wet red hair.

"Jena?" He hissed as loud as he could for her to hear it but, he hoped, no one else would.

"Cole?" He found her then and pulled her into a tight hug.

"I thought I heard gunfire."

She pulled back and tried to scrub some of the water off her face. "You did. Mac's been shot, and our boat's disabled. We've gotta go back and get him."

"Are you hurt?" Cole liked Mac Griffin well enough, but the agent wasn't his top priority. "Let me get you to the house, then I'll find him."

"No, I only left him to get help. He comes first." She turned around and headed past Cole in the direction from which she had come. "Follow me."

"No." Cole grabbed her arm and pulled her toward him. "I'll go and find him while you go on to the house. You're headed the right way—just keep going toward the house—you can see the light a little through the rain. Tell me where Mac is."

She hesitated, then described the spot where she'd left her partner. As soon as she mentioned a tupelo tree, he knew the area. Trees weren't abundant in the southern parts of the parish. "It'll be easier if I go with you."

Jena wasn't going to change her mind, and Cole got it. He and Mike had been partners, so he understood that kind of bond. She must have been desperate to have left him at all.

"Okay," he said finally. "Let's go get your partner."

Mac was almost in shock by the time they found him, his eyes staring into nothing and his responses slow. Cole immediately hefted him up and made his way toward the house as quickly as he could go, Jena right behind him. Then he ran for the truck, yelling for Jena to take cover in the house. The road was too far gone, however, and the old pickup stalled halfway down the lane. Cole knew from experience that until the rain stopped and the road drained, they'd never get the truck out. He had to get Mac inside and put his rusty paramedic skills to the test.

Two hours later, with the wind and rain beating a steady rhythm on the roof, Cole finally stepped into the shower. He was freezing, and the hot water—well, tepid water was the best he could achieve—felt good after being in cold bayou mud for so long.

Mac had been lucky, although he probably didn't feel that way right now. The bullet had gone into his side below his body armor but didn't seem to have nicked any vital organs. The bullet hadn't gone straight through, though, so it was impossible to tell what kind of internal damage might have been done.

He'd lost a lot of blood, and it was going to be hard to keep the wound dry and uninfected until they could get help. Shock also was a concern.

Getting help anytime soon wouldn't be easy. Jena had speculated that as soon as this storm finished its way through, later this evening, Ray Naquin would come back to find his missing wildlife agents. Their trail would lead straight to Cole's house. Jena still had her mobile phone, but its supposedly waterproof case hadn't done its job. Mac's phone was somewhere in the bayou.

Cole figured they had two, maybe three, hours before they had to either run or defend themselves.

He'd given both Mac and Jena dry clothes to replace their uniforms and settled them next to his old wood-burning stove to get warm. The electricity had gone down not long after they returned to the house, but that was okay. Lights made the house a more solid target.

When he'd gotten home with Mac, Cole had tied the pirogue to the back rail of his house. If they had to make an escape, the water was probably the least practical because they'd be more exposed. But there it was, anyway, just in case.

After his shower, he tied back his hair, pulled on some warm clothes, and went into the utility area off the back porch. There, with the aid of his flashlight, he found his survival kit—a heavy backpack he kept ready for . . . whatever. The day a hurricane ran him out of his house and into his boat for who knew how long. The day a psycho drug-trafficking gator hunter came looking to kill people he cared about.

This might not be that day, or night, but there was no point in taking chances. Cole stripped off his sweater to keep it from getting soaked, took the emergency pack through knee-deep water to the workhouse, and set it in the back of the cooler, where he had constructed a back door.

It had seemed like paranoia at the time. Now, it seemed smart.

****

Mac had finally drifted off to sleep and Cole was in the shower, so Jena walked around his living room, trailing her fingers across all the things he'd made himself. Furniture, sturdy and comfortable. Tables, chairs, cabinets.

As much as Cole had thought he was running away from home, he had simply remade himself along with a new home. He'd shown up tonight, out in the marsh, just when she thought her feet couldn't slog through another inch of mud and water. She expected her partners to have her back, just as she'd always have theirs. But instinctively, she'd known Cole would be there for her even though it put him at risk.

She heard the back door open and close, and reached for her SIG Sauer. It had fired perfectly after its first submersion, and she'd cleaned it using oil and a chamois cloth Cole had given her, while he tended to Mac's wounds.

Holding the weapon to her side, she quietly eased through the hall and into the small kitchen, which was illuminated by a gas lantern that gave the room an extra warmth. The light of a flashlight bobbed through the windows of the workhouse, and in a few seconds, Cole stepped out and sloshed his way toward the back stoop.

By the time he reached the door, Jena had retrieved a towel from the bathroom and had it waiting for him. "You just got out of the shower—didn't get wet enough in there?"

He smiled and reached for the towel but took her hand instead, pulling it—and the towel—toward his chest. "Help me?"

She dried off his chest, trying not to pant over the smooth skin over muscle, the lightest dusting of hair. "Turn around," she whispered, and he did, pulling his long hair around his shoulder while she dried the taut muscles of his back.

Don't start what you can't finish, Sinclair. And you can't finish this.

When he turned around, Cole cupped long fingers around her face and leaned in to kiss her. "You scared the hell out of me tonight. Don't do that again."

"I'm sorry I brought trouble to your door."

He nodded. "Even if this Naquin guy doesn't know you and I have . . ." He paused, as unsure of what they had as she was, and they both laughed. "Even if he doesn't know we're connected, this is the only occupied house around here. Wouldn't take a mental giant to figure out where you'd go."

"Believe me, Ray's no mental giant," Jena muttered.

"You sound like you have firsthand knowledge. You've been involved with him? I mean, it's none of my business."

"No! God, no. Ugh. He has the manners of a gorilla, not to mention the worst pickup line ever."

Cole grinned, and Jena realized she'd seen him cry but never really laugh. How warped was that? "Okay, you opened the door," he said, and his laugh was infectious. "What's the worst pickup line ever?"

Jena's smile faded.

"Hey." Cole put a hand on her shoulder and slid it down to wrap his fingers around hers. "Did I say something wrong?"

"No." Jena shrugged. "Let's just say he indicated being with me wouldn't be too bad in the dark. Can't see scars in the dark, right?"

Cole's blue eyes blazed. "Any chance you shot that asshole today?"

"I wish." Maybe she had winged him but there was no way to know. "I think we need to change the subject."

Jena looked at him, suddenly aware of the heat coming off his body, of his closeness, of the finger he ran along her jawline before he kissed her. She wanted him so badly, his warmth, his desire, and his ability to make her forget the world.

She gave in to it for a few moments, just let herself taste and feel and smell. Every sense was engaged except her brain, and she shut it out as their tongues tangled, his skin both silky and hard beneath her fingers.

Until he slid a hand to cup her left breast. She felt him hesitate, and it was as if the roof had blown off and the rain had come in. Her brain reengaged and reality came with it.

Jena took a step back. "I better check on Mac." And have a good cry.

"No you don't." Cole grasped her wrists and pulled her into his bedroom, taking the lantern with them.

"Cole, don't feel obligated." God, that sounded harsh, but she wanted a pity fuck from Cole Ryan even less than one from Ray Naquin, from whom she expected no better.

He pulled her to the bed and sat. She had no choice but to do the same. He didn't speak for a few moments, as if collecting his words. Great, now he was going to treat her like a china doll.

"I have two things to say. Which do you want first—hard and practical or soft and practical?"

"Do I have a choice? What if I don't want to hear either one?"

"Neither was not an option."

She sighed. "Fine. Hard and practical."

"Okay then. I'm a paramedic, or I used to be. I've seen a lot of gunshot wounds. I know what bullets do when they go into soft tissue, and

I know how it looks when they come out. That has no bearing, positive or negative, for me in wanting to be with you. There are millions of women with perfect bodies, and I'm betting yours was one of them until six months ago. But the one you have now is the one I want—not the one you had before I knew you."

She stared at him. "Forgive me if all I can say to that is, Why? Why would you choose deformity over beauty?"

He smiled, and it was the smile she'd first seen from him. Fragile and gentle and broken. Like her.

"Because we're alike, Jena. Everybody has scars; some are more visible than others, that's all. But anyone without a scar is someone I don't want to know because it's someone who doesn't feel things deeply. You have to understand loss to recognize a gift when you see it."

He leaned over and kissed her again. "You are my gift. I want to be yours, if you'll let me."

She gave him a small, halting nod that seemed to take every ounce of energy she had.

Jena gave herself over to him, relishing the feel of his hands as they slipped beneath the sweater he'd given her to wear, but reality had another interruption, this time in the form of Mac's voice.

"Hey, guys, stop whatever you're doing. We've got company!"

CHAPTER 29

Damn it. Cole gave Jena a final smile and quick kiss, then pulled on his sweater, extinguished the lantern, and led her to the living room, all in a few seconds. Mac was still propped near the wood-burning stove, but had pulled himself into a seated position.

"I saw lights outside but couldn't even crawl over there to assess the situation." A state about which he was clearly unhappy.

Cole and Jena peered out either side of the front windows. "Two boats pretty close to the front porch," Jena whispered. "One's Ray Naquin's."

"The other one's the Patout kid," Cole said, squinting. "He's holding . . ." Damn it, a bottle, into the neck of which he was stuffing a rag. "Molotov cocktails, I'm guessing. They're gonna try and burn us down, and probably think they'll shoot us like ducks in a gallery when we run out."

Cole turned to Mac. "Can you walk, with my help?"

"Walk where?"

"We're all going to the workhouse." Cole tracked the progress of the Molotov cocktail. Make that cocktails, plural. The Patout kid was making a line of them. He was going to lose everything he'd worked so hard to build. Those thoughts had to stay in the background for now, though, or they wouldn't survive long enough for him to mourn. Their best hope was getting the hell out before the fire started flying.

"Okay, guys. Here's my only suggestion. I have an escape into the swamps out the back of the workhouse cooler and a pack of emergency supplies I've already stashed near the exit in case they tried something like this. But we need to move now. The outside of the house will take a while to burn because it's wet, but if they get a Molotov cocktail through one of these front windows, the interior will burn fast. We don't have much time."

Jena spoke up, and Cole recognized her agent voice. "Get Mac out there now. Fast. I'll keep them occupied for thirty seconds to give you a head start, then I'll follow you."

Cole didn't like it, but he saw the determination on her face and knew he could help Mac better than she. Her training was inarguable, but she was still recovering herself, and he was strong. "Okay. You ready to go, big guy?"

Mac muttered something Cole thought it was best he didn't hear.

"I'm going to break out the window and shoot Naquin if I can, so don't stop if you hear gunfire," Jena said. "The kid might run if he's on his own."

"Got it." Cole helped Mac to his feet, slung the agent's right arm over his shoulders, and they headed toward the back. Before they walked out the back door into a slackening rain, Cole heard breaking glass and then a blast as Jena knocked out one of his windowpanes and took a shot with no hesitation.

He didn't know if she hit anyone, but she got their attention. Everything in him wanted to run back inside when he heard return gunfire, but he couldn't. Mac was really hobbling, though, so when they finally got to the back steps, he said, "Sorry about this, Mac."

"Wha—"

Before the agent could finish his question, Cole picked him up in a fireman's carry and sloshed through the water to the workhouse, praying he didn't reopen that wound. At least it wasn't on the side rubbing against Cole's back and neck.

"You're a load," he said, noting with approval that Mac had put on his shoulder holster and had his weapon. Also, that once he'd gotten over the shock of being picked up, he'd gone limp and hadn't fought.

"Yeah, well, warn me next time you're gonna do something like that, okay?"

Cole edged inside the workhouse, set Mac down, and gave him a grim smile. "Agreed. Try to get to the cooler in the back of the room. There's a panel in the rear that pops out and we can exit there—it was a safety measure to keep anyone from getting locked inside the cooler. I'm going back for Jena."

By the time he reached the door of the workhouse, though, she was halfway across the backyard. Beyond her, he saw flames and heard the crackle of something small exploding. A window maybe.

Rage filled him, the rage he'd spent five years tamping down so it wouldn't destroy him. Yet it wasn't the same kind of rage. This time, his rage had a legitimate target that he could either fight or outwit.

This time, he had a chance to save the people he cared about. If his house burned, big fucking deal. Houses could be replaced. People couldn't.

"Come on." Jena tugged at his sleeve. "It won't take them long to figure out we exited the back way."

Cole shook away the cobwebs, closed the workhouse door, and turned the deadbolt. Every few extra seconds offered an advantage. "To the cooler."

Mac stood on one leg in the back of the refrigerated unit, the surroundings eerily lit by his flashlight. He'd removed the panel, but the activity had taken a toll. He looked pasty, and his situation was not going to get easier.

Cole closed the cooler door behind them and nodded at Jena to open the back door. As they stepped out into thigh-deep cold water, the sound of a single shot and splintering wood sounded from behind them. "They're in the workhouse," he whispered. "Go straight ahead, as fast as you can. Don't use your lights any more than necessary. I'm right behind you."

The going was brutal, with mud sucking at each step as if reluctant to let the foot go. Mac didn't make it far before he was breathing heavily.

"Jena, think you can carry this pack?" Cole slung the emergency rations backpack from around his shoulders and held it up, illuminating it very briefly.

"Slip it on me." With a little fumbling, he managed to get her arms through the pack, and heard the click of her fastening it around her waist. "I've got it. Help Mac."

Exactly what he had in mind. He moved ahead of her until he almost fell over Mac. "Buddy, we're gonna have to do this again so we can make some time, okay?"

"Yeah." The strain in Mac's voice and his lack of argument spoke volumes about the pain he was in.

It took some help from Jena, but he finally got Mac out of the mud and settled onto his shoulders. Cole looked around to get his bearings, and ducked instinctively at the sound of a rifle shot. "Let's move," he whispered. "Jena, can you keep one hand on me to make sure we don't get separated? I've got my pirogue stashed about halfway up the inlet, and we're gonna try to reach it using the light as little as possible."

"Right behind you." She paused and whispered, "I might not want to know the answer to this, but what do I feel brushing past my legs every once in a while?"

Snake. Gator. So many options. "Probably a fish, but don't think about it too hard." He was trying not to.

They needed to find people, someone with a phone, or at least a dry spot to hole up in until daylight. Which meant they needed to get to the highway that skirted Bayou Pointe-aux-Chenes.

They trekked on silently but for the sucking mud and slosh of water. In some places it was only up to their ankles, then it would gradually deepen to Cole's waist before the mud beneath it tapered up again. He was glad Jena was a tall woman, and he was glad that, so far, the land had tapered and not dropped off suddenly. A broken ankle or leg, and their chances of getting out of this would dwindle. They'd drown if they didn't get shot.

Every five or ten minutes, he'd stop and listen. So far he'd heard gators, owls, frogs. A couple of times something else slithered past his leg and he tried not to flinch where Jena might notice. She'd kept fingers under his poncho and cinched through the belt loops on his jeans the whole way.

What he didn't hear was other people, though, even ones trying to move quietly.

Cole had been trying to count steps to give him an approximation of where to make a northward turn to reach the outlet and, he hoped, find the pirogue. They'd kept a steady eastern pace for what he estimated to be an eighth of a mile—it just seemed like longer because their pace was so slow.

"Jena, I'm making a sharp left now. We're going toward the outlet and see if we can find the boat."

"Gotcha." The words came out breathy, but then again Cole was sucking wind himself. Mac wasn't a tall man—maybe five ten or five eleven—but judging by his weight, he was all muscle. Plus, when they'd started their trek, he'd been holding part of his weight up with his arms to relieve the pressure on Cole's back. Now, not so much.

"Mac, you doing okay?" Cole whispered.

No answer.

"Hold up and let me look at him," Jena said. Cole stopped and, behind him, Jena softly shook Mac and tapped on his face a couple of times. "He's out."

"That's probably a blessing, at least until we can get somewhere dry and stop moving. You ready?"

"Ready."

They slogged on for another half hour, give or take an hour in this dark night. Cole stopped abruptly when something poked him in the cheek, causing Jena to run into his back.

"What is it?" she whispered.

"I don't know; I need both hands to hang on to Mac. Step around me and see what I've run into. I don't want to use the flashlights."

He felt her moving to his right. "It's a tree," she said, her voice barely a whisper. "And listen."

Faint voices reached them from the direction of the bayou inlet, which was a lot closer than Cole had thought. This had to be the tree to which he'd tethered his pirogue. It wasn't like there were dozens out here from which to choose.

He kept his voice as soft as possible. "There should be a rope tied to the tree about waist high. See if you can find it."

She stepped forward again. "Got it."

Okay, good news: he knew exactly where they were. Potentially bad news: the fact that there were audible voices meant someone was nearby. At this time of night, unless Wildlife and Fisheries had realized Jena and Mac had been off radar too long and put out a search, it might not be anyone they wanted to meet up with.

"One of us needs to keep Mac out of the water," he whispered. "The other needs to follow the rope to the outlet without breaking cover and assess. You want rope duty?"

"Yes," Jena said. "Since you've been carrying him so long, I might have fresher legs and can get to the water faster. Plus, I weigh less, so I can move more quietly."

It had been a long time since Cole had been willing to put his fate in someone else's hands, but Jena knew what she was doing. Probably better than his DIY Swamp Man macho badass self. Might as well admit it.

"Agree. Take Mac's gun—it's been in the water less than yours. And drop the pack next to my foot—it's waterproof and you can move faster without it." With their modern pistols and watertight ammo, switching pistols probably didn't matter, but she needed every advantage.

"Okay." She slipped behind him and fumbled until he heard her unsnap the strap on Mac's holster and pull out the gun. She found Cole's right hand, slung over Mac's legs so tightly he wasn't sure he'd ever be able to straighten it out, and wrapped his fingers around cold metal until he had it in firing position. "That's my pistol, just in case. Don't move or I'll never find you again. I'm going to follow the rope now."

He felt a gentle press of her lips against his and then she was gone. Forget the past five years; he'd never felt so alone.

CHAPTER 30

Jena was so sick of being waterlogged, she didn't care if she ever had so much as a shower again. She sure didn't want to slog through the wetlands in the pitch dark any longer.

She didn't like the way the rope played out in her hand, though. If it was attached to the pirogue, and the pirogue was partially on marsh grass, it should have more tautness than what she felt.

If the pirogue was compromised, she wasn't sure what Plan B might be, but she had a feeling Cole probably had Plans B and C already lined up. Ironically, after tonight, she thought The Hermit of Sugarcane Lane might've made one fine LDWF enforcement agent.

Moving methodically and displacing as little mud and water as possible, Jena followed the rope but didn't pull on it. If someone was watching the pirogue, any movement of rope or boat could give them away. They'd been smarter than Ray and Marty so far, not that a couple of cane toads couldn't outwit those two on a normal day, but she didn't want to reverse their record.

Plus, today was far from normal. Ray was mean and he was desperate; he had to know his only hope at keeping up his Black Diamond shipping operation and keeping himself out of federal prison would be to get rid of her and Mac—and now Cole—in some way that didn't implicate him. Mean plus desperate equaled dangerous.

Because things had happened so fast when she and Mac had lost control of the situation, she couldn't remember the last message she'd sent to Warren. She thought it had simply been a terse sentence or two to let him know they were staking out where someone fitting Marty Patout's description had been seen dumping gators back into the bayou.

Unless Mac had sent a text later, it could be sometime tomorrow before anyone began looking for them, and they'd probably start looking at Marty, not Ray. Marty was up to his scrawny neck in this, but Ray was older and smarter.

Was he smart enough to figure this out on his own? The more Jena thought about it, the more she knew there had to be another player. Someone able to order the stuff and coordinate the deliveries. No, make that two other players. Someone to order the stuff and someone to order the stuff from, whether in New Orleans or Houston or Timbuktu.

Marty Patout would know how to order stuff on the Internet. Ray Naquin? Maybe.

The person who had plenty of time, a desperate need for money, and maybe the savvy to pull it all together was not Marty Patout, however, but his mother. She was fighting an illness she had little hope of beating, a business that was probably mortgaged to the hilt to cover medical bills unless her late husband had a hefty life insurance policy, and a young son who would need some degree of care the rest of his life.

Jena tried to put herself in Amelia Patout's situation and she could understand. To a degree she could sympathize.

Everyone ended up in their own deep, black pit at some time. It was how they climbed out that separated them. Jena had tried to kill herself out of guilt and a feeling of inadequacy, but had been blessed enough to have someone intervene in time for her to realize how much she had that was good. Cole had withdrawn from the world in pain and distrust but, when pushed between right and wrong, he had chosen right.

Maybe Amelia Patout had taken the only road she could see to provide for her sons when she was gone, and greedy old Ray had been happy to play along. Hell, he probably thought he was doing charity work.

Charity work that had already destroyed a lot of lives.

Jena saw lights gleaming on the water, and decided to crawl the rest of the way, or as far as she could. The water was about knee-deep, so she tucked Mac's pistol in the back of the pair of jeans borrowed from Cole, which she had belted with cord.

Crawling was easier than walking upright, except the part about the front of Cole's sweater soaking up brackish water like a sponge.

When she got close enough to see through the grass to clear water, she belly-crawled the rest of the way to the edge, very slowly so as to move the tall grass as little as possible. Finally, she reached a point at which she could see through the grass across the inlet. Ray's boat sat directly across the water. He perched in a chair on one end with a rifle propped beside him, binoculars trained toward Cole's house. On the back end of the boat sat Marty Patout, his hair glowing white, watching the pirogue.

That would be the half-submerged pirogue, Jena saw with a sinking stomach.

And—wait—why was visibility so good all of a sudden?

At first, she thought maybe sunrise had arrived, except the light was coming from the west. From her hiding spot in the grass, Jena looked left and saw flames licking into the sky not only from Cole's house but the house the Benoits had occupied. Maybe the other house on the lane too. They were burning every option they thought their prey had to hide in. Even the cane fields looked to be on fire. Everything would burn slowly because it was wet, but eventually, it would all burn.

Moving with exaggerated slowness, Jena made a one eighty, felt for the rope, and pulled herself back toward the oak tree, still on all fours. If she could see better, Ray and Marty had improved visibility as well, so quiet and slow had to be their marching orders. Or slogging orders, assuming there was anywhere else to slog.

If she had to find a positive in the situation, it was that Ray and Marty seemed sure they'd show up either on Sugarcane Lane or at the pirogue. They were sitting back and waiting to pick them off, not actively pursuing them.

As the water deepened enough to hit Jena's chin, she pulled herself to her feet with difficulty and tried to wring out as much water from the sweater as she could. It probably weighed as much as Mac now.

The grass was taller here, more than head high, so she felt safer walking. She tugged on the rope to help propel her back toward the tree. No way would her tugs move that tree, which she could see outlined well before she reached it, as the night sky was lit with the flames from Cole's burning world.

Cole turned and watched her approach, Mac still slung across his shoulders and unconscious.

Her blank, professional-law-enforcement face had apparently been left back on the sinking pirogue because he could tell by looking at her. "Boat's gone?"

She nodded. "About half submerged." She looked at the flames licking into the sky, glad the height of the grass at least kept them from seeing his house burning in detail. "It's not just your house, Cole. It's the one the Benoits lived in too, and the cane fields. I'm not sure about the other house at the far end of the lane. Ray and Marty are sitting on his boat, watching both places, rifles ready."

"They're probably burning everything." His voice was steady and matter-of-fact. "They want to drive us out like rats, or run us from place to place until they can catch us or we simply don't have anywhere else to go."

"*Do* we have anywhere else to go?" Jena looked around at an endless, shadowy vista of flat marshland broken up by an occasional tree. And it was not solid ground but spots of land interspersed with floating islands too unstable to hold an adult's weight.

"Our best bet, given Mac's condition and ours, is an old fishing camp hidden back in the marshes so deep, I'm not sure anybody's been there in years other than me. It might give us a safe place to stay until daylight." He studied her face. "Question is: Do we have it in us? It's an hour due south of here, and no easier than the marsh we just crossed. At least, thanks to Ray's bonfire, we can see."

He turned to watch the fire. "Our second option is to try circling behind the burning houses and slip through the cane fields to reach the highway. It's shorter, but there isn't much cover, even less if the fire speeds up. We'd be exposed for at least an hour—dangerous, considering Ray's bonfires would backlight us and make us easy targets."

"Is there a third option?" She'd been right about him meticulously creating Plans A, B, and C.

"Our third option is to stay where we are, hunker down under the blanket that's in the pack, and wait for daylight. That's dangerous for Mac, though. I want that wound out of this water as soon as possible, and he has to be bleeding again from being hauled around like this. I'm worried about infection setting in."

He was still watching the flames. Jena wanted to cry on his behalf since he'd gone stoic and practical on her. "Cole, I'm sorry. I know that *bonfire*, as you call it, is your whole life."

The look he gave her brought to mind some ancient Viking prince, with his long braids and lowered brows. She'd been wrong about the lack of emotion. He had plenty; it just wasn't what she'd expected. Not anger or anguish, but steel.

"That's not my life, Jena. It's just a house. Our lives aren't where we live; it's who is in them with us." His gaze returned to the flames, but not before she caught the small quirk of a smile. "I had a lot of time to get all philosophical while you were crawling through the mud like a jungle warrior."

Jena looked down at the front of her sweater. Yeah, that's exactly what she had done. She found the rations pack, shoved her arms through the straps, and fastened it in place. "We better get going before Ray and Marty decide to get off their asses and look for us. I vote for the cabin."

He nodded and shifted Mac on his shoulders, earning a groan from Jena's partner.

She was glad Mac was out, but it worried her. Now that they had some light, she could see the blood soaking his bandaged side. It had spread into the shoulder and back of Cole's sweater as well. Mac had lost way too much blood.

"Okay, let's do it." Cole turned and began the slog again, moving at a steady pace but slower than before. He had to be exhausted, shoulder muscles screaming, from carrying Mac so long. Jena caught up with him and they walked side by side now that they could see. The light wouldn't last long, though. Either the flames would die down or they'd get too far away to see them.

"Cole, why don't you let me carry Mac for a while and give your shoulders a rest? I promise you, I can manage it."

"It's not a matter of whether or not you could do it—I know you could." He grimaced. "But I think my arms are frozen in this position. Better for me to just keep him in place as long as I can go, and easier on him not to change position too much."

"Okay then." Jena checked her wristwatch. "It's almost two a.m. and at least three hours until sunrise, or at least enough daylight to see.

At that point, they'll start looking for us again. I can't imagine either of them slogging through this marsh, but is there a way for them to get to that cabin by water?"

"I'm not sure." Cole stopped for a moment and shifted Mac slightly. "Can you pull a bottle of water from your backpack? I need to rehydrate."

She dug for a bottle among medicines, protein bars, and small assorted tools. "Here you go." She unscrewed the top and held it up for him to drink without having to put Mac down. He guzzled about half the bottle before he stepped back and jerked his head toward Mac. "You should finish it, unless you can get some down his throat."

She couldn't, though, and ended up putting the almost-empty plastic bottle back into the pack.

They'd been on the move no more than five minutes when a gunshot sounded behind them, followed by the sound of Ray's voice.

"Hey out there! I know you're there. Thought I spotted you earlier. How 'bout we meet you at the old Conner house about sunrise? I'd like my favorite redhead to spend her last sunrise giving me a good blow job before I blow her head off."

"Whatever I'm biting on will die with me," Jena muttered, then to Cole: "I assume that's where we're going? The old Conner house?"

Cole sighed with the exhausted expression of a man who'd been wandering through a boggy marsh for hours carrying another full-grown man on his shoulders. "I've never heard it called that, but it's the only place around here so it must be. I should've known he'd be aware of it. A nuisance-gator hunter has to know his territory pretty well."

"The light's almost gone, and we're going to be in pitch black again soon." Jena reasoned it out as she talked. "If we continue to the cabin, we can get Mac in a dry spot and be waiting for them at sunrise."

She waited for Cole to argue, or at least make a countersuggestion, but he just nodded. "I'm spent. Our only other option is to wait it out here and hope they pass by us, but we'd have to put Mac in the water. I don't have the legs to circle all the way back to the house now, and I don't think you do either."

Jena closed her eyes. "We'll take a stand, then. Let's keep going."

She could tell when they approached the old cabin because the land beneath them rose gradually and became more solid. What also was solid: the blackness of the air around them. Clouds obscured any moonlight or stars, and they'd lost all view of the fire.

"I'm gonna do this from memory, so hold on to me," said Cole, whose belt loops she'd grasped again. From his movements, Jena could tell he was kicking ahead with each foot before taking a step. Finally, his foot kicked something solid.

"I think there are three steps that lead onto a porch," he said. "Let's get out of this muck."

Jena followed him, grateful for that first step that still squished liquid between the toes of the overtopped waterproof boots, but at least the step took place on a solid surface.

"Okay, I'm setting Mac down and then you can pull off your pack. Feel around in there and see if you can find a small-wicked candle about the size of a votive. We'll just burn the candle long enough to get our bearings."

Mac groaned again when Cole lowered him to the porch and covered him with the poncho. By the time Jena found the small candle, Cole had come up with a dry match from a plastic bag in his shirt pocket.

Jena lit it quickly, spotted the front door, and walked into the cabin. They needed to limit the exposure of even that tiny spark from eyes that could already be approaching. Cole grunted as he lifted Mac again and brought him inside.

"Can you clean off that table a little? I want to put him up there."

Jena used a cloth from the pack to wipe off as much dust and grime as she could from a rickety wooden table in the center of the otherwise-empty cabin. "I'm surprised there isn't more dirt in here, or trash, or dead animals."

The cabin wasn't exactly clean, but it wasn't unoccupied-for-twenty-years dirty either.

"I stay here every once in a while when I'm trekking around the parish." Cole set Mac gently on the table, took one look at the agent's side, and pulled out a knife from its sheath.

"How's it look?" Jena knew how it looked—it looked like a bloody mess. "He's lost an awful lot of blood."

Cole used the knife to cut off Mac's shirt around the wound—or his shirt he'd given to the agent—peeled the fabric away, and then cut through the blood-soaked bandages he'd wrapped around it at the house.

Riffling through a small first aid kit from the pack, he used sterile wipes to clean the wound again. "I don't like how much swelling he's got around the entry point." Cole gently probed around the circular hole of blood on Mac's right side above his rib cage. It was a swollen mass of angry red skin stretched so tightly it looked like an overstuffed sausage about to split its casing.

He cleaned and rebandaged it loosely, then went to set up a make-shift resting spot in the corner with a couple of blankets, water, food, and guns.

The perfect ingredients for a family picnic. Not that Jena had ever been on a family picnic. *Why would one ever wish to dine outdoors?* she could hear her mother ask. *There might be insects.*

Or murderous drug traffickers.

They settled Mac on the blanket next to the wall so they could shield him if Ray and Marty arrived early, maybe even with backup. "Ray must know a shortcut, a way to get here by boat." Jena stretched out on the blanket between Cole and Mac, and helped spread the second blanket over them to help warm them. They both munched on protein bars. "He's not going to slog through the marsh the way we did."

"Won't take him that long," Cole said. "He knows where he's going and he'll be able to see."

"We need to get busy, then." Jena craned her neck and surveyed the room not as a shelter but a potential fort. "There's no reason Ray won't set the damned thing on fire and try to force us out again, so we have to put ourselves in a position to make the first strike. You got a hammer in that pack—do you have nails?"

Cole sat up and dragged the pack over. "Enough to brace the table in front of the door, but probably not enough to nail stuff over all the windows."

He paced around the room while Jena tried to think of a way to get the jump on Ray. "We could board it up as if we're in here . . . but not be in here," Jena said.

Cole looked back at her from the front window. He'd ripped a rickety kitchen cabinet door off its hinges and was seeing how much of the door it would cover.

"So, what, we settle in the marsh somewhere in sight of the front of the house and wait for them?"

"Only problem is, we'd have to put Mac in the water," Jena said. "And I already don't like the look of that wound."

"Leave me."

She spun around at the hoarse whisper behind her. Babyface had cracked open those pretty brown eyes, thank God. Jena had been swallowing down her fear that she'd never see them again. They looked too bright, though, and she reached out and felt his forehead. "'Leave me,' says the man who is feverish. You think Cole hauled your butt all over this corner of the parish just to leave you?"

"I got a bad feeling about this, Jena." Mac struggled up on one elbow, pulled back the blanket, and took a look at his side. "Holy shit, that's probably the end of my dance career." He flopped onto his back. "I'm serious. I'll just pretend I'm dead. It won't be too big a stretch."

"There's no way in hell I'm leaving you here, Griffin. You're my partner. I even take back what I said about you not being my friend. Forget it." Maybe he was being noble. Maybe he was feeling sorry for himself. Or maybe he truly thought he was going to die.

But if he thought Jena was leaving him here as potential roadkill—or marsh kill—for Ray Naquin, her partner might as well think again.

Cole came to stand beside them, looking down and frowning. "I think Mac's right."

CHAPTER 31

Damn, but that woman was stubborn. It had taken Cole and Mac both to bring her around, but she had finally agreed to the plan.

Cole had helped a shaky Mac to a standing position where he could lean against one of the old kitchen counters, then Cole and Jena had moved the blankets to create a makeshift cocoon for Mac against the kitchen cabinet baseboards. He was out of sight of all the windows and the front door.

While Jena stayed busy moving water and ibuprofen within Mac's reach in case he was alone for very long, Cole turned the kitchen table on its side and nailed it across the front door, along with the cabinet door. Then he was out of nails.

The back door, they planned to leave unlocked. Marty Patout apparently had a skill with Molotov cocktails, so if the little SOB tried that again, whoever was closest would enter through the back and get Mac out as quickly as possible.

If one of them had a rifle trained on the back door? Cole didn't have an answer for that one, so as he nailed, he tried praying, finding that maybe his faith wasn't as dead as he'd thought. Jena had given him hope, and its friend faith had come along. Everything had seemed to be rolling toward this morning at ever-increasing speed, from finding Big Bull to meeting Jena to telling her the truth about himself to realizing that he wanted to live around people again, wanted them in his life.

Wanted Jena in his life.

He had to have faith that all this snowballing of events meant something bigger, that they couldn't be random.

So he prayed they weren't random.

Now the hardest part. "Jena, c'mon, we need to talk, over here where Mac can hear."

They sat cross-legged on the floor, and Cole had to figure out how to use words that would help Jena override the instincts of her training, if that was even possible. "Here's how it needs to go down."

"We agreed that—" Jena halted abruptly at Cole's upraised brows. "Okay, what, but make it snappy because we need to get in position."

"I agree," Cole said. "As we decided before, I'm going to take cover on the west side of the cabin, you on the east. We have about an hour before sunrise. If Ray or Marty shows up before then, I'm not going to ask you to take Ray out in an ambush. I know that goes against everything you've pledged to do."

Cole leaned forward. "But I've pledged *nothing*. These men have burned my home and everything I've spent the past five years building. Worse, they've tried to kill two people I care about, and that is not something I take lightly. If I get a chance, I will kill Ray Naquin; I won't wait until he takes the first shot so I can claim self-defense. I'll take him out. I'll only shoot Marty in self-defense, but Ray doesn't get that luxury.

"If you have to arrest me afterwards, well, that's your job and I understand. Are we clear?"

Jena nodded. "It would be within your rights anyway because they're coming here to kill us. No charges would stick. And if you think I won't shoot the son of a bitch, you've forgotten who and what I am."

Cole smiled. "There's one other slight change of plans."

"Then what was the point of us making the damned plans in the first place?" she snapped. Cole suppressed the urge to smile, not only because he didn't think she'd be pleased to know he was baiting her, wanting her angry instead of sad, but because he thought she might clock him.

"Here's the deal." This was the part he had to make her buy into. "As soon as there's enough daylight to see, whether Ray's anywhere around or not, you need to go due east, as fast as you can, straight to Bayou Pointe-aux-Chenes and the main highway. Flag down a car or a boat. If there's nobody to flag, stay along the road and move south until you find someone. Then call in the troops."

She crossed her arms over her chest, prompting a cough or a chuckle or a groan from Mac—maybe all three. Cole couldn't look away from her fierce glare. "And what will you be doing while I'm busy running away like a girl?"

Cole gave an exasperated squint at the ceiling. She was playing the gender card? "Jena, you aren't running away—you're our best bet for getting help fast. You said it last night. You're lighter. You can move faster. You have a badge."

Jena still looked pissed, but not quite as pissed.

He softened his tone. "And yeah, let's talk gender. If you show up asking for help from a stranger, looking like you've been dragged through the mud, I'm pretty damned sure you're gonna get help. If I show up with this hair, covered in mud, asking for help, I might get help or I might get run over. We don't have time to wonder which it'll be."

He leaned over, cupped her face in his hands, and kissed her, not caring that Mac was watching. "I'm staying with Mac. He can't go through that marsh again, and this area's trickier than what we went through last night—lots of flotons, lots of drop-offs. It has to be you that gets us out of this."

The depth of her sigh told him he'd convinced her. Jena was practical, and he'd spoken the truth.

She looked at Mac. "What say you, Junior?"

His smile was weak but sincere. "I say Cole's right."

Cole looked at him and laughed. "I think that's the first time you've ever called me by my first name, Agent Griffin."

Mac snorted. "After falling asleep in your arms several times recently, I figure we might as well be on a first-name basis."

"And what is your first name?" Cole didn't remember Jena referring to him in any way other than Mac.

"McKenzie."

"Ah. I think I'll call you Mac."

"Good move."

He looked at Jena. "You ready?"

She shook her head. "No, but that doesn't really matter, does it?"

CHAPTER 32

Jena had agreed to Cole's sudden change of plans because they made perfect sense to her head. Her heart did not like them. It went against everything she held inside her to leave her partner injured while she made a safe escape. It was wrong to leave a civilian in charge of dealing with the criminals while she took the easy way out.

Still, her head argued, the only way Mac and Cole—and she—could survive was if Cole was forced to commit murder or if she made a safe escape.

For that reason as much as any other, she'd agreed to go.

Cole thought he was comfortable shooting Ray Naquin, and he might be okay with it today or tomorrow or for the next month. But one day, eventually, it would haunt him. He'd been haunted enough.

So she agreed.

"*Please* be careful," she said.

"You think you need to tell me that? We have unfinished personal business, I do believe." He smiled. "And I do love to make you blush."

"It clashes with my hair."

He kissed her long and deep, promising what might be—if she made a safe escape.

"There's one more thing," he said.

Damned overplanning type-A male. He had to ruin a perfect kiss by adding stipulations.

"What?"

"Once you start going, Jena, and it should be now, because it's light enough to see, do not come back here alone. Remember what you told me last night at the house? If you hear gunshots, don't turn around. Keep going as fast as you can."

Was he insane? "But if—"

"I'm serious. It might be me shooting Ray, in which case you don't need to know right away. It might be Ray shooting me, and you don't need to know that either. I'm not saying you *will* hear gunshots. Those idiots might not even show up. But for my sake, and for Mac's, don't turn around no matter what. Request medical help if you hear shots fired, but don't turn back. I want a promise on that."

Damn him. She gritted her teeth and nodded because, again, he was right. "I promise."

They kissed again, and she tried to memorize every movement of his lips and sweep of his tongue before he stepped back, gave her a long look with those deep-blue eyes, and ducked into the tall grass, headed to the cabin's west side.

It wasn't yet dawn, but Jena could see. So she sent up prayers for both Cole and Mac, and set off as fast as she could. This time, she could look for possible deep spots where a broken ankle would surely ruin all of Cole's plans.

Cole's plans.

Damn it, Jena, you're an idiot. She hadn't been mad because Cole had to talk her into being the one to go for help. She was mad because it should've been her idea. She was the senior agent here, not to mention the only uninjured one.

So she gave herself a good talking-to as she instinctively followed the dawn. She'd read an article once about how women were more apt to be people pleasers than men. They learned to play dumb so they wouldn't show up their male colleagues. They learned to giggle because people thought it was cute. They learned to play up their looks because prettiness earned praise. Take the cultural bias and add it to her own childhood, which she'd spent constantly trying to please a mother whose MO was displeasure, and she'd been wired to distrust herself and step to the background by instinct.

She didn't entirely blame her mother. That was too easy a cop-out. It accounted for a lot when Jena was six or even sixteen, but not at thirty. She had to own her reluctance to take a leadership role. Maybe she hadn't started the pattern of being a follower, but she'd perpetuated it. No more.

She spotted the early light glinting on the water of Bayou Pointe-aux-Chenes while still a quarter mile away. It was choppy from last night's storm, and it looked like she'd be emerging in one of its wider areas, which meant the chance of finding a boat was good. She hadn't seen traffic on the highway, but it was the only north-south route in the area, so somebody would be on it soon.

Jena tripped and fell to her hands and knees by instinct at the sound of a gunshot behind her. Chills ran up her spine and spread around the back of her neck. Every facet of her training told her to run as fast as she could back toward that cabin.

Instead, when two more shots rang out—one a rifle, she thought, and the second a .45—she ran toward the bayou as fast as she could. She didn't care how much noise she made, or how hard she splashed, or whether she stepped into an abyss, or if mud sucked the sturdy boots off her feet. She had to reach the water.

When she got to the road, the bayou alongside it was wide, brown, and choppy, and there were no boats to be seen. Cole was right, though—if she ran farther south, she'd run into boats or cars, even if it took her all the way to the lands occupied by the indigenous people of

Pointe-aux-Chenes, a band of Native Americans that continued to live in the disappearing marshes of the lower bayou.

She didn't have to go nearly that far. In less than five minutes, she came across a trailer on stilts and a dark-skinned woman watering the profusion of blooms spilling out of the boxes on her deck.

She turned in alarm at the sight of Jena running up her stairs and stood there with an open mouth—but not an ounce of fear. Had it been Cole, the woman might have beaten him over the head or run inside.

The woman met her at the top of the stairs. "What's wrong wit' you, sha?"

"Please, I have an emergency. Do you have a phone I could use?"

$$****$$

Within fifteen minutes, Mille Ardoin had quite an entourage of neighbors gathered around to see the tall, muddy redhead who'd shown up on her doorstep, but Jena didn't mind. What mattered was that Warren had quickly assessed her rambling account of the evening and told her to stay put. He was sending help, both to her and to the old cabin.

Meanwhile, Jena had been taken care of by Mille, who'd shooed her inside without her boots and given her a chance to clean the mud off her face. Cole's sweater was a goner. By the time she'd returned to the deck, there was a plate of diced potatoes and andouille, cooked up together in a skillet, that Jena felt guilty eating, but she managed to get down a little to make sure Mille knew how grateful she was.

"Are you really a game warden, sha?" Mille asked. She was broad, bronze-skinned, and black-haired, and had been joined by her best friend, Beatriz, from next door.

Jena was saved from having to answer by the arrival of an LDWF truck coming fast down the highway and lurching to a stop in front of

Mille's house. Thank God, now there was somebody more exciting than her for them to focus on.

Jena had been trying to act cool, but she was worried. Her hands shook so badly she'd been forced to eat the few bites of food with her fingers because she couldn't hold the fork still.

She hauled herself to her feet, looked over the edge of the balcony, and smiled. Part of her had hoped for Gentry to get here first, but the sight of Paul came as a relief. Paul wasn't one for chatter. He'd get in and get out, and things would happen.

By the time he got out of the truck, Mille and Beatriz were trying to make a fuss over him, but his gaze latched onto Jena as she hobbled down the steps.

"You okay, Sinclair?" He pulled her into a hug, which was surprising, not only because Paul wasn't a hugger, but because she was filthy and if she'd ever seen a man who'd fidget over filth, it was Paul Billiot.

He hung back a few seconds, talking to the women in their own patois—Paul himself was descended from another of the indigenous tribes in the area and active in their communities.

But only for a few seconds. They were headed north again before Jena had her seat belt fastened. "Here's what I know," he said, pulling the truck out onto the highway, running lights without sirens and moving fast. "Broussard and Knight—the new guy—are on their way to the old Connor cabin in a boat. Is there any way for us to get there in the truck?"

Jena shook her head. "No way. It's by boat or on foot."

Paul's jaw clenched. "We'll head back toward Ray Naquin's place, then. Warren has called in the troops—SO, state police, whoever's available—to start an all-out manhunt in the span between Chauvin and that cabin. They should have APBs out for both Naquin and the Patout kid."

"They need to be looking for Amelia too." Jena went through her rationale about neither Ray nor Marty having the brains to run this kind of operation. "I mean, the woman had to be pretty sharp to keep that processing business open year-round on her own after she lost her husband. And she's dying, Paul. Her older son doesn't want to process seafood, probably because it's hard work and he's just a kid himself, and the younger son will need care. She might be desperate enough to do something like this."

Paul shook his head. "That situation sucks any way you look at it, but there have to be other ways. And desperate or not, you think she knows how deep into this her older son is?" He glanced over at her. "You remember any details about when her husband was killed?"

"Only that it was a murder and one of our agents found the body." Jena frowned at Paul. "I don't think it was ever solved. Why?"

"There were rumors in the community—nothing anybody could substantiate, mind you—that Martin Sr. was moving drugs through their processing plant. They do as good a business as anybody during gator season and have their retail store, but that's a big operation to keep up year-round. And they always seemed to have money."

Jena processed that information. "So you think maybe Amelia or Ray picked up the business after Martin Sr. was killed?"

Paul shrugged. "Maybe Amelia. I knew her when she was younger, and she was a smart woman—everybody up around Theriot, where she's from, thought she could do better than Martin Patout. So she's smart enough. Not Ray Naquin, though. He could follow orders, but he isn't smart enough to run the show."

Jena watched the flat marshland fly past her window. "I can't see her letting her son get involved."

"Maybe Ray brought him in and not her. Who knows?"

Jena sure didn't know. All she knew was that Marty had been the one to set Cole's house on fire. She'd seen him lighting the Molotov cocktails. She might cut him some slack for being young and stupid, but was he innocent? No.

"We need to get to Patout's."

"That's where we're headed then. I'll call Warren to send Houma PD their way too. We'll come down on them like a Cat Five."

Jena nodded. That was good. She felt really sorry for Amelia Patout, but if her suspicions were true, the woman had a lot to answer for.

"Warren gave me a bare-bones account of the past twenty-four hours, so fill in the blanks," Paul said.

She gave him the rundown, to which his general response was a deepening frown. Finally, when she got to the part about leaving Cole and Mac, and Ray's promise to attack at dawn, he shocked her with a "fucking asshole," which she assumed was aimed at Ray.

She stared at him open-mouthed for a few seconds. Paul rarely cursed—she'd heard rumors of it happening once during the manhunt after Ceelie Savoie had been kidnapped, but this was her second personal experience this week.

She didn't smile, though, because she had to ask a question that was already haunting her.

"Did I do the right thing, Paul? What would you have done in that situation? Would you have left your partner behind and in danger? Would you have left him with a civilian and kept yourself safe?" She didn't share Cole's rationale, or her agreement with it, because she wanted no excuses.

She considered Paul Billiot the consummate professional enforcement agent. What would he have done?

Paul and Gentry were the only ones she'd ask that question of. They wouldn't sugarcoat it if she'd made the wrong call. Gentry would be honest but kind. Paul? He'd tell the blunt truth even if it stung.

He thought about it a while before answering, and she imagined the scenarios playing out in his head.

Finally, he nodded, his Native American features—dark hair, black eyes, strong jaw—emanating confidence and competence.

"You did exactly what I'd have done in your situation. You wanna know why?"

Relief washed through her, seeking out the guilt and stomping it flat. "Yes, please."

"Well, I figure Ryan's a smart guy. He'd made a nice little place for himself out there all alone. That takes a mental fortitude I admire. He also has to be physically strong and able to take care of himself. That's the only kind of person I'd trust my partner with."

Paul thought a moment longer. "Plus, I have to look at logistics, which I assume you did. I am smaller than Ryan, and faster. I have the authority to enforce the law if I have to force somebody to stop and help me."

Jena shrugged. "Cole also said someone would be more likely to help a woman than a big muddy dude with waist-length hair."

Paul laughed, earning another stare from Jena. She'd seen him smile a little but didn't know he laughed. Ever.

"Your Cole sounds like a smart guy."

"He's not *my* Cole." Where would he get such an idea? Mac hadn't had a chance to talk, and if Gentry Broussard had been gossiping, she was going to wipe those dimples right off his cheeks, even if he was her best friend.

"Sinclair, this ain't a big parish and there ain't that many tall female redheads who are enforcement agents. Actually, there's only one. So when she hangs around the jail in Houma till midnight so she can take a witness home with her . . . well." Paul laughed again, but sobered quickly. "I just hope they're okay. I told Gentry to call or text when they found the cabin."

"There were three gunshots back there after I left," she said, looking out the window and trying to embrace her professional calm. "One rifle, one pistol. The first shot took me by surprise so I'm not sure what fired it."

"Mac has his SIG Sauer?"

Jena nodded. "And Cole has mine. Ray was using a rifle last night."

A generic ringtone sounded from the dash, and Paul grabbed his mobile phone. He put Gentry on speaker.

"Billiot here, and Sinclair. Where are you?"

"At the old Connor place," Gentry said. "Looks like quite a fight went on here, but no sign of anybody now."

Jena sat up straight. "What? Mac's not there? Cole Ryan's not there?"

"Nobody. Spent casings, lots of blood on the interior and the porch of the cabin. One area of the cabin near a window where it looked like a Molotov cocktail went off course and ended up in the water. Just singed one spot and didn't catch.

"We can tell by the foliage there was a boat in here recently, so we have to assume Ray Naquin and Marty Patout are on the water. Jena, give me a description of Ray's boat."

She told him everything she could. She'd lost the notebook where she'd written it down, but Gentry could easily look up the license plates.

Paul ended the call, with Gentry and EZ headed for Patout's. They'd have to pass Ray Naquin's house along the way.

Paul glanced at her. "What do you think?"

She thought she might die. She thought about how much she'd come to respect Mac Griffin and how she'd given him such a hard time at first. She thought about how much she cared about Cole Ryan. She didn't know if she loved him. Theirs was the ultimate foxhole relationship between two wounded people under stress both from the outside and from their own pasts. But she wanted to find out if it was as real as it felt.

She couldn't lose either one of them.

Jena rubbed her temples and tried to put herself in Ray Naquin's head, which wasn't a pretty place to be. Ever.

"If I'm Ray, I know people are onto me now because one of the wildlife agents who knows about me has escaped"—namely, one Jena Sinclair—"so I'm desperate. If I were smarter, I'd get the hell out of

Dodge and sail to some Caribbean outpost and spend all my hard-earned drug money. But because I'm a dumb, arrogant jerk, that doesn't occur to me."

She ignored Paul's chuckle. The man had turned into a laughing fool all of a sudden. "So I'm desperate and I want leverage. What's a better bargaining chip than an injured wildlife agent?"

Paul glanced over at her. "What about the civilian?"

Jena refused to get in her own head; she had to stay inside Ray's. "He's not worth as much. He's a loner. Nobody's gonna pay to get him back, except that cops never like to see civilians hurt. So maybe I shoot Ryan, just injure him enough to put him out of commission, and take both of them with me as hostages."

"Where do you go?" Paul was driving faster now.

"I don't go home because that'll be the first place everybody looks. Patout's is iffy because they're looking for Marty now too. But nobody knows Marty's mama is involved, and she'll hide them out or give them enough money to disappear."

"I agree," Paul said. "We continue to Patout's."

CHAPTER 33

Cold. Blood is everywhere. It coats the floor. It coats his arms. The blood, vibrant and red, should be warm and still pulsing out of her body, but it isn't and everything's cold and she's dead. They're all dead.

Ryan! Cole! Wake up!

He brushed the nagging, faint voice away, and saw red again. But he had been wrong; the red wasn't blood. It was red hair, so dark and rich it was almost burgundy. It flashed in the sunlight, and flames reflected over it in the dark. It fell in a silky sweep against a long, graceful neck.

She wasn't dead. Jena was alive. Jena was safe.

Ryan! Damn it, you big, antisocial, agent-seducing, long-haired son of a bitch, wake up!

Cole opened his eyes with a jolt as something sharp jabbed in his back. He blinked a couple of times trying to figure out where he was, but he had no clue, nor any idea of how he got there.

"Ryan, I know you're awake. I saw your shoulders tense. Roll onto your back. It's Mac. Can you hear me?"

Lord, that man never shuts up. And now he was poking Cole in the back again.

Cole was lying on his right side on a tile floor that reeked of fish. That, more than anything, got his face moving, and he tried rolling to his back. His right arm wouldn't work, though.

"Can't," he finally said.

A hand grabbed Cole's left shoulder and pulled him to his back. Now he had a view of stained acoustical ceiling tiles.

"Where are we?" Damn, but he was cold. Had a front moved in?

"We're in a goddamned freezer, that's where we are. You got shot in the arm. We've gotta find a way to stay awake and keep from freezing to death before somebody cuts us into fillets and sells us to a tourist for dinner."

Slowly, it all came back. Maybe twenty minutes after Jena had left, Ray and Marty had come toward the cabin from the rear in Ray's bass boat. Hiding in the tall marsh grass west of the cabin, Cole hadn't been able to get a clean shot at Ray and didn't want to shoot Marty cold. It was too hard for him to not think of Marty as a screwed-up kid surrounded by bad role models.

But then Marty began preparing his specialty, the Molotov cocktail—so simple. A bottle, some gasoline, a rag, and a match.

Cole didn't have a choice. He'd been so damned smart and nailed the front door too tightly to bust open. He had to run for the back door and hope he could dodge a bullet. If he could get inside, he might be able to get Mac out a window before the whole place burned down on their heads. Or get a clear shot at Ray.

But he didn't make it. Ray had shot him in the right arm as he made the race for the stairs with Jena's gun in his hand.

The force of it spun him counterclockwise, and he instinctively raised Jena's SIG Sauer and fired at Ray as he turned. Cole had stumbled into the house and slammed the door behind him, but not before he saw the front of Ray's T-shirt bloom red. He'd hit his target.

The rest got fuzzy, though.

He tried to sit up, and gasped at the sharp pain that shot through his gut. He had no choice but to flop to his back again. The gunshot wound was a gnat bite compared to the pain in his gut.

"What happened after I was shot? It's a blur. No, it's not even a blur."

"Marty Patout happened. We didn't give him enough credit for the number of mean-bastard lessons he learned from Ray, I guess. You were out of it, so he came in and knifed you. If we weren't hurt and in a freezer I'd fry your balls for dinner. Why didn't you shoot him?"

He remembered then. "I hesitated. I thought with Ray gone we could talk him down. He's just a—"

Mac grunted. "Cole, he's eighteen, and kids do a lot of bad shit. Plus, he had a knife. Maybe a gun, for all I know. Now he has my gun. It would've been self-defense."

"I couldn't do it." He didn't know why, exactly. Maybe because he'd done such dumb stuff when he was a teenager—nothing criminal, but dumb. Stuff that probably should've gotten him killed. And then there was the kid on the drawbridge. The broken neck on the kid who'd shot up the mall and hanged himself in his jail cell. "I just couldn't do it."

"I know, man. Ignore me. You're so good at this stuff I forget sometimes that you're not one of our agents."

"No way. The work's too dangerous."

"Tell me about it. Hey, are you cold?"

"Not as much as I was. Sleepy." He just wanted to doze off, and it would all go away. Mac needed to shut the hell up. First the man was unconscious forever and now he kept running his mouth.

"That's it. We've gotta get moving."

Cole was dreaming of the soft fall of red hair again when a whack to the face woke him up. Mac leaned over him and had his hand raised for another slap.

"What the hell do you think you're doing?" Cole raised his good arm and batted the agent's hand away.

"Waking you up. If you think I'm going to tell Jena I let her man freeze to death without a fight, you're nuts. She'd eat me alive, and I don't mean that in a good way."

The slap had reengaged his brain, at least. "I know we're in a freezer, but where? How'd that scrawny kid handle both of us?" He sort of remembered being thrown in a van or truck of some kind, but it was so vague he might've imagined it.

Okay, he'd been shot in the right arm. The stab wound, he needed to see since he didn't remember it.

Mac had managed to sit up, and his wound actually looked better. The cold of the freezer would help the swelling if it didn't kill him from hypothermia.

"Can you help raise my left shoulder? I'm going to try and prop on that arm long enough to look at the stab wound."

Mac grabbed his shoulder and lifted as Cole maneuvered his left hand underneath him and straightened his arm. Blowing out a breath of pain, he gasped, "Pull up the sweater."

Once Mac had uncovered the wound, Cole studied the knife's entry point—a surprisingly smooth thoracic slice right between his ribs. He couldn't tell what internal damage had been done, only that he'd lost a lot of blood given how long he'd been out of it and how bloody he was. It hurt like hell. The stab wound was like a more benign version of Mac's gunshot wound, almost in the same spot.

Except, wait. "What kind of blade did he have?"

Mac eyed him. "You really want to ask that question, given we're in the freezer of a fish processor?"

Oh hell. He'd be lucky if he didn't end up with a nasty infection; he doubted that *Sterilize fillet knife before stabbing human with it* had been on Marty Patout's to-do list. Ironically, the cold of the freezer would also help ward that off and stanch the bleeding. If he, also, didn't freeze to death.

"Okay, you're right. We've gotta move."

"That's more like it."

By sliding to a counter and pulling himself up, Mac was able to get to his feet before Cole. He found a mop and broom in the corner and, turned upside down, found both worked as makeshift crutches.

He hobbled his way over to Cole and leaned down, extending his arm. "It's going to hurt, but you've gotta get up."

Cole gritted his teeth and took hold of Mac's arm. He used as much leg muscle as he could, but the pain took his breath away. It probably hurt Mac worse.

With the agent's help—and the mop's—he made his way to a big aluminum cutting table and began easing his way around it, following Mac's example. Every step was excruciating.

"So what did you mean by me being Jena's man? Am I Jena's man?"

Mac's breath came out in short, sharp puffs of condensation. He was getting winded too. "I dunno. You kissed. More than once. Never heard of her kissing anybody else."

Cole seriously doubted a woman that striking had gone her entire life without kissing anyone but, still, it was good to know she was as unattached as he'd assumed. He liked the idea of being her man, although it still kind of freaked him out.

Before, he'd been a self-reliant man living off the grid. Now, he was going to be involved as a witness in a criminal case, for sure. He was going to have hospital bills—maybe a lot of them—for which he had no insurance. Even the money from his family's life insurance policies wouldn't cover it all. And he was homeless but for some literally scorched earth.

Jena should run like hell from being involved with him, and probably would.

CHAPTER 34

The drive from lower Pointe-aux-Chenes to the western side of Houma was never fast, but Jena didn't think it had ever been this slow, even with speed demon Paul Billiot behind the wheel.

Since Paul wasn't a big conversationalist—he was the anti-Mac, in other words, and today had been the longest she'd ever heard him speak in consecutive sentences—Jena watched the scenery for a while. Then she decided to study the inside of Paul's truck to see what she could learn about him and take her mind off Mac and Cole.

Technically, it was exactly like hers and Gentry's. It had a black exterior with a blue light bar across the top and the Louisiana Department of Wildlife and Fisheries Enforcement Division logo on the doors.

It was tech heavy on the front dash, just like theirs, with LDWF, Terrebonne Parish Sheriff's Office, and Louisiana State Police Troop C radios, a laptop, a GPS unit, and a weather unit.

In her truck and in Gentry's, the cords and wires were a colorful tangle of plastic and metal, usually with extra plugs dangling around like vines. Paul's cords were all black, and he had them woven in pairs and tucked underneath the dash, where they neatly disappeared.

She leaned over to see how he'd achieved such a thing, and noticed identical zip ties holding them in place.

"Sinclair, I hate to ask, but what are you doing?"

He sounded more bemused than annoyed, so she said, "I'm psychoanalyzing you based on the interior of your truck."

He almost ran off the road. "Why?"

"Your scintillating conversation was putting me to sleep."

His dark brows knit together but he seemed to have no answer to that.

She turned around in her seat, as much as the seat belt allowed, and continued her study. Paul had a 12-gauge shotgun and a .223 carbine mounted right behind the driver's seat, same as in her own truck. The mounts had hidden release buttons so the agents could get the guns out one-handed and quickly.

But where her truck had a catch-all supply of stuff, from paper towels to zip ties to evidence bags to fast-food wrappers stuffed in the back, Paul's backseat was empty but for a zippered storage container normal people used for shoes. Each space held different stuff, all neatly arranged. Jena spotted evidence bags in one. Zip ties in another. Notebooks. Citation books. Paperwork. A spare uniform hung over one window, with a dry-cleaner's tag dangling from the shirt's top button.

Good Lord. She turned back around.

"What did you learn?" Paul finally asked.

"You're an obsessive-compulsive neat freak," she said. "Accent on *freak*."

He shrugged. "And this surprises you?"

"Not at all. Only that you didn't alphabetize the items in your storage bag."

"That's a great idea."

Before she could tell whether or not he was joking—the man did have a sly sense of humor—his phone rang again. "It's Warren," he said, putting it on speaker.

Jena's tension rose. She'd hoped it was Gentry, saying they'd found Cole and Mac.

Instead, Warren's voice was terse. "This might be good news. A fisherman on Bayou Pointe-aux-Chenes called in a body found about a quarter mile from that little inlet that leads to the back of the old Connor place. It was Ray Naquin, dead from what looks like a .45 to the chest."

Jena closed her eyes in relief, then felt ashamed that she was glad for anyone's death, even a snake like Ray. But it told her that maybe Mac or Cole had shot him, which increased their chances of still being alive.

But where were they?

"Sinclair's got a theory about who's really behind this whole thing and you need to hear it," Paul said. "I think she's right."

His words reminded Jena of her moment of clarity in the marsh on the way to the bayou that morning. She was a leader. She was smart and strong. Other people saw her that way, so it was time she believed it.

"Okay, let's hear it, Sinclair. Who's the mastermind?"

"Amelia Patout," she said, shooing away a gnat of self-doubt. It was ingrained.

There was a long pause, until Warren said, "Damn. I hate to think it was her, but it sure as hell makes sense. She needs the money and she and Ray have worked together legitimately for years. He and her husband were good friends. You're still on your way to Houma? What's your ETA?"

"Maybe fifteen minutes," Paul said. "We're caught in rush hour."

"Go in with lights and sirens and see if you can move the traffic out of your way. I'll call Houma PD and the sheriff. And maybe Agent O'Malley." Jena thought maybe the last was added a little grudgingly.

Adrenaline coursed through her when Paul flipped on the siren, and startled drivers began the chaos of trying to move out of the way.

A few minutes later, with Patout's in sight, Jena leaned forward to get a better look out the window. The white boat with "Gypsy" visible under the bad paint job sat in the back lot, hitched to the pickup.

The van, however, was crossing the lot and heading for the exit.

"We need to stop the van!" Jena shouted.

Paul cursed at a driver and, at the last second, was able to angle across two lanes and block the exit, forcing the van to lurch to a stop.

Paul was out of the truck with his gun drawn before Jena had finished unbuckling her seat belt, but she caught up with him.

Amelia Patout rolled down her window. "What's the trouble, agents?"

Jena spotted Marty, hoodie raised, slouched in the passenger seat. She didn't see Slade, and hoped he wasn't here to witness this. She looked at Amelia just as the woman's gaze slid to the left. Jena realized Amelia was going to try going around Paul's truck and jumping the curb.

Well, she'd have to run over Jena to do it. Jena ran to block the middle of the front parking lot just as Amelia stomped on the gas and turned in her direction. As soon as she saw Jena, she slammed on the brakes again.

With Paul's spare SIG Sauer drawn, Jena crossed to Amelia's side of the van as soon as it stopped. "Show me your hands!" she shouted. "Show me your hands! I want to see them!"

Houma PD came in a few seconds later. Within a few minutes, law enforcement of every stripe had descended on Patout's Seafood, along with a TV news crew. Great. Cole and Mac weren't in the back of the van, but officers were combing the building.

Paul had finished reading Amelia her rights and was leading her away in handcuffs when Jena stopped them. "I want to talk to her for a minute."

"Okay with me," Paul said. "Maybe she'll tell you where Mac and Cole are. Hasn't said anything yet."

Warren and Paul stepped back to talk to the Houma officers, leaving Jena with Amelia. Jena patted the woman on the shoulder. Amelia had done all the wrong things, really bad things, but Jena thought it had to be from an honest worry for her children.

"Is Slade in a safe place?" she asked. "Do we need to send anyone to take care of him?"

"He's at home by himself." The woman began to cry. "This was for him. Doesn't that make it okay? It was all for Slade."

Jena sympathized with the woman's plight, but too many people had been killed or injured. It was all such a waste. "Where are the others? The agent and the other man?"

At Amelia's hesitation, Jena added, "Please. Don't let anyone else die."

"They're in the back freezer," Amelia whispered, the fight gone out of her as she watched her older son being stuck in the back of a Houma PD cruiser. "The key is hanging by the cash register. I'm sorry; they've been in there a long time."

Paul, who'd been listening more closely than Jena thought, was already halfway to the building before Amelia finished her sentence, but Jena and Warren weren't far behind as a couple of Houma PD officers led Amelia toward a squad car.

Paul snatched a key chain off the wall behind the counter and ran into the back.

They waited, Jena almost jumping out of her skin each time he tried a key and failed. Finally, the lock clicked and Paul opened the heavy doors.

Cold air and condensation spilled out, and the first thing Jena saw was a broom and a mop in the middle of the floor, then a lot of blood.

"Here they are," Paul called from the back. "We need paramedics and two stretchers."

Jena slid around the corner. Oh God. Mac looked still and cold, but he didn't have more injuries that she could see. Cole was covered in blood. Neither of them was moving. "Are they . . ." She couldn't say the words.

Paul had two fingers pressed against Cole's carotid; he'd already checked Mac. "Their body temps are really low, but they're both still alive."

Jena stayed to watch the paramedics, promising Warren she'd come in to give a statement as soon as she knew they were okay.

An ambulance had been pulled into the back lot, so it was a short walk to roll the men into a more controlled environment, first Mac and then Cole. Jena flashed a badge at the head paramedic. "These are our guys. I'm riding with you."

He nodded. "Sure. It's gonna be crowded, but I might need the extra hands."

Inside the back of the ambulance, the heat blasted while the paramedics cut off clothes and covered both men with heating blankets and heat packs. The ambulance had room for only one stretcher, on which Mac rested. Cole had been strapped onto a backboard on a bench that ran the length of the treatment bay. As soon as both patients were secured, one paramedic exited to drive them to the hospital, leaving room for Jena to climb inside.

She knew heart attacks were always a danger for hypothermic patients, but these guys were strong.

"What do you think?" she asked, making sure to stay out of the paramedic's way.

"They're pretty stable," he said as the vehicle pulled into traffic, headed toward Houma and the regional hospital. "They aren't as cold as I would've expected. I'd say they've been able to stay active to some degree until recently."

"Hey, Red." A raspy voice drew Jena to Mac's stretcher. She got on her knees and took his hand.

"Hey, Motormouth. Feel like you're back in Maine, eh?"

He managed a weak smile. "Yeah, but Cole's hockey skills suck. How's he doing?"

Jena looked over at the bench and broke into a smile at the sight of two slightly unfocused but still bright-blue eyes looking back at her. Cole returned her smile.

"I think he's gonna be okay."

EPILOGUE

May might bring spring flowers in most places, but in Terrebonne Parish it brought the first taste of summer heat, high humidity, and mosquitoes.

Jena stepped back to look at her handiwork. The ridiculous foyer of the White Rhino was now a deep teal color, with royal-purple accents and cream trim. She'd have to send a photo to her mom.

She might be growing older, but it didn't mean maturity followed. She suspected she'd never outgrow the need to poke the beast.

This was the next-to-last room of her big painting project. Every day since she'd figured out the drug case, she'd begun making the White Rhino her own. When she second-guessed her own decisions—which she also might never outgrow—she was learning to second-guess her second-guessing.

So when her gut told her royal-purple made a great trim color for teal, she ran with it and it looked amazing.

The only room on which she waffled was her bedroom. She'd chosen a color called Calypso Blue and was jazzed about it until she realized why she'd picked it. Cole's eyes were almost the exact shade.

She hadn't seen him in almost a month. He'd recuperated fast from the wounds he'd suffered, and the department had helped collect money to pay his hospital bills since he'd been instrumental in solving the drug case. Rumor had it the DEA chipped in a chunk of change, but Warren wouldn't confirm or deny it.

Mac would be back at work next week and paired with his original partner, Paul Billiot. To Jena, Mac had bitched about the change, but she thought it probably would be good for both of them—as long as neither made the other's brain implode.

Jena was back with Gentry as her partner and it felt good to be on regular patrol again, without the "light" attached to her assignments.

All in all, things had turned out well except for the Patout family. Marty was going to be in jail for a long time unless some fancy legal work took place, and Slade was in a Department of Children and Family Services group home while they looked for someone to take him in. She'd been told that he rarely spoke, and that broke Jena's heart.

Amelia had died two weeks ago, leaving behind two damaged sons and a community still reeling from the influx of Black Diamond. At least the flood of drugs had been stopped for now, and on her deathbed Amelia had admitted running the operation with the late Ray Naquin, although she blamed him for getting Marty involved. She also never gave up the identity of the drug supplier—only that it was someone in New Orleans. That had sent DEA agent O'Malley slithering off to NOLA to make the NOPD's life miserable for a while.

Everything had been wrapped up quickly . . . except for Cole. A month ago, he'd gone off the grid again, simply telling her he'd be back. Nothing more. She hoped he would but wasn't putting anything on hold—and wasn't painting her bedroom the color of his eyes. Talk about pathetic.

She decided to take a break, and put the painting supplies away before opening the front door to check the mail.

Weird. A torn sheet of paper lay on the welcome mat and atop it, still in its packaging, lay a wrench.

Jena couldn't wipe the grin off her face.

In black marker, the note read:

Have info that might help painting case. Will drop by today abt 5.

Will only talk to you. No other officers. Please.

—Coleman Ryan

P.S. I lied before. I am very dangerous.

Jena looked at her watch and it was only 1:00 p.m., so she took a leisurely shower and stood before the mirror afterward, staring at her wounds. A puckered, misshapen channel of a scar on the underside of her left breast. The small, pink, round scar in her lower abdomen.

Cole would have a couple of new scars too, and she didn't care. It didn't make a difference as to how she felt about him and, yeah, she admitted it, how much she wanted him, whether it was for a day or forever. So maybe he had meant it when he said he didn't mind her scars. She was going to play things by ear, and trust her gut.

Her new motto.

Somehow, she ate up three hours trying to decide what to wear. Cole was a casual guy. Then again, he'd had to start over again. He'd accepted his past, so maybe he was returning to his old life.

Maybe he's moving back to Mississippi, her inner doubter taunted. *Maybe that's what he's coming here to tell you.*

No, that note wasn't saying good-bye. It was a seduction, pure and simple.

Susannah Sandlin

Her gut told her a seduction with this particular man had to be casual and spontaneous. If he'd changed enough to require a little black dress, he wasn't the guy she'd grown to care about.

By five, she'd donned jeans that made her legs look insanely long, a deep-green curve-hugging top, and wore her hair down because she knew he liked it. Then she paced. He was late—again.

Finally, through the window, she saw a faded-red pickup turn in from the main road and come rumbling up the drive. She moved to stand with her back to the door, trying to calm her racing heart and adopt some of Mac's chill attitude toward the opposite sex.

Oh hell, she was a geek thinking about having sex for the first time since she'd moved to the parish. Who was she kidding?

She turned and opened the door before he rang the bell and they both stopped and stared. He looked different. He'd cut his hair. It was still long, but shoulder length and no braids. He wore jeans and boots and a black T-shirt just tight enough to show the muscles shifting underneath it when he moved. He still had the clearest, bluest eyes she'd ever seen.

He smiled. "You look great."

"You too. Come on in."

"Not yet. I believe I promised you some intel on a painting case."

Okay, they were going to flirt. She could flirt. Maybe. "Yes, I think you did. Should I take notes and record your statement?"

"Why don't you listen first, and then I can repeat it." He returned to the truck and came back with a box, which he handed to her. "Pick out a color, and I'll come by on my weekends off and paint this house for you. And remember, white is not a color."

She led him into the living room and put the box on the table. It was full of paint chips. As in, spilling over. "Did you hit every hardware store in the parish and—wait—what do you mean weekends off?"

"Well, I've been doing some little projects for the last month, in addition to healing, of course. I'm not ready to go back to Yazoo City

250

for a visit, but I did talk to my friend Mike and my uncles who still live there to let them know I was okay and planned to stay here in Terrebonne Parish permanently."

"Permanently?" Jenna caught her breath and tried to keep at least a semi-dignified expression on her face. *He's not leaving.* "I was afraid you had moved back and I might be the one getting that call."

He smiled. "No way, Jena. This is my home now, and we have unfinished business. There was just something else I had to get taken care of first that required me to spend some time in Baton Rouge."

Her mind spun around *unfinished business* a few moments before the rest sunk in. "What's in Baton Rouge?"

"Even with everything your department did—which was huge—I still have a lot of medical bills and no insurance. The damage was gonna blow through all I had left of the insurance money. There was an opening with one of the big ambulance companies in Houma that works hospital ER calls in Terrebonne and Lafourche, so we made a trade. I retrained and got licensed as a paramedic in Louisiana, so now I work for them and half my pay goes toward my bills."

"When do you start? Where are you living? Are you hungry?"

Oh, she was such a dork. Might as well embrace it.

He laughed. "Next week. A fleabag in Chauvin for now, but I'll start rebuilding my house down on good old Sugarcane Lane as soon as I can. Mac's gonna help. And I might be hungry a little later." He paused. "Very hungry."

Oh God, here she went. Her face had heated up to at least 103 degrees.

"I always did like to make you blush, Agent Sinclair."

"Yeah, you seem to have a skill for it, and it still clashes with my hair," she muttered, suddenly feeling nervous. "Want to see the new interior house colors? My brother and I had named the place the White Rhino, but I don't think it quite fits anymore."

They walked from room to room. "It's the opposite of the White Rhino, that's for sure," he said. "I can't seem to find a pattern to the color choices."

"The pattern is that I like them," Jena said, flipping on the light to a pale-pink-and-gray room that had *nursery* written all over it. "My brother, Jackson, and his girlfriend . . . well, his sometimes girlfriend . . . are having a baby. I'm hoping at least Jacks can bring the baby to visit. I'm less excited about Brenna."

Jena and Jackson had reconciled, although things were still a little strained between them. He had apologized, and so had she. She'd helped him find a place near UNO, out from under their parents' roof, and he was back in school.

As far as she could tell, he was clean.

"What about this last room?" Cole walked into her stark white bedroom with its white furniture and bedding. Even the freaking ceiling fan was white. "Isn't this your room? You haven't decided on a color?" He waggled his eyebrows. "'Cause I know a man with a whole box full of paint chips."

"I have a color in mind, but I'm still struggling with the decision."

The look he gave her went straight to her core. "What are you trying to decide, Jena? Can I help you make a commitment?"

She swallowed hard. "*Commitment* is a scary word. Cole, you've lost so much already, so much more than I have, that—"

"Hush." He turned to face her, slowly reached out, and pulled her to him. He was the perfect height for her to feel his hardness pressing against her, and it took all her willpower to stop her knees from buckling. She had wanted him for so long and had thought he might have run away again. But here he was. With her.

"We've run from commitment for too long." He tangled his fingers through her hair and pulled her toward him. She wanted fire. She wanted him to take control. Instead his kiss was heated, but short. "You want to hear about my commitment?"

She nodded, not trusting her mouth to work and afraid she'd stick her foot in it if she opened it.

He brushed kisses along the curve of her neck, and his breath was warm against her throat when he spoke. "I'm committed to staying in Terrebonne and making it my home."

Her voice came out in a croak. "I'm glad."

His hands, which had been resting on her waist, slid underneath her sweater to cup her breasts, and she couldn't help but flinch when he ran his fingertips along the underside of her left breast, feeling the scar. She closed her eyes, not to increase the sensation but to avoid the pity that probably marked his face.

"Look at me, Jena." Cole's voice was soft against her ear as he tugged her sweater and bra up, exposing her breasts. She gasped when his mouth took over for his fingers, and finally she did look down.

He was . . . not feeling pity. In fact, he stopped the work of his mouth and smiled up at her. "You're as beautiful as I knew you'd be—at least what I can see. Take off the sweater."

All the air had left the room, or at least she had trouble breathing. "You first."

"No problem." He stripped off the black T-shirt, and he was just as beautiful as she remembered. She grabbed the hem of her sweater and pulled it off, tossing it on the floor next to his shirt. Then she paused, tugging her bra back down to cover herself.

"See this?" He pointed at his abdomen, where a long pink slash crossed his rib cage. "And this?" A round hole, a darker red, scarred the inside of his upper arm.

"I've shown you mine; you show me yours."

Jena nodded, sucking in a breath and reaching behind her to unhook her bra. He slipped his fingers under the straps and pulled it off, kneeling to kiss one breast, then the other—the ruined one. "I'll have plastic surg—"

"Don't." His voice was ragged with need, and his kiss this time—his lips hard against hers, his tongue tangling with hers in a language without words—made her head spin.

They fell backward onto her immaculate white bedspread, but Jena didn't have long to think about it because Cole was wrestling with her jeans and not doing too well. "Damn, woman, I know I'm out of practice and you look hot as hell in these things but did you paint them on while you were doing the rest of the house?"

She laughed—no, God help her, she giggled—and shimmied out of the jeans. "I picked them out for you . . . and now you're overdressed."

"I can take care of that."

****

Cole shed the rest of his clothes and lay beside Jena, stroking and kissing, sliding his fingers to keep her hot and distracted. He didn't want her getting too far inside her head even if she wanted to. He didn't care about the scars. She was the one he wanted. Only her, and the scars went into making her the person she was. So did his, both the internal and external scars. Without those scars, they'd have never met.

Their losses were serious, but so was what they had found buried beneath the ashes of their pain.

When he rolled on top of her and slid a strong thigh between hers, he could tell how ready she was for him—as much as he was for her. He rocked his hips, and her body took over by instinct, rocking upward to meet him.

"I think we can do better." He reached down and lifted her leg to his waist so that he was pressed against her more directly, rocking gently until she closed her eyes and moaned. He thought it might be the sexiest sound he'd ever heard.

"I'm gonna arrest you if you don't move faster," she panted. "And don't think I can't do it, by God. I ran through a marsh to get to this point."

"Yeah, you did." His gentle thrust was meant to ease himself inside her, but she clamped her thighs around his hips, and his control was gone. Her hair spread across the white pillow like crimson silk as they moved together, and watching her come—to lose control and then send him into an unfurling spiral of heat and mindless pleasure—Cole knew he was where he was meant to be.

He'd spent so much time and energy pushing people away that he hadn't realized what he'd given up for his so-called independence. Home. Love. Belonging.

Later, they held each other beneath the white bedspread, and Cole thought Jena was sleeping. Until she propped up on one elbow and looked at his face. Their gazes locked, and he felt the heat building in his groin again.

"I've made a commitment," she said.

Yeah, well, so had his body, although he wasn't sure that was what she meant. "What's that?"

"This room." She looked around at the white walls, white furniture, white—and very rumpled—bedspread. "I'm painting it Calypso Blue. Want to see the paint chip?"

Oh hell no.

He pulled her on top of him, and she gasped when she felt him pressed against her. "Does that feel like I want to look at a paint chip?"

ACKNOWLEDGMENTS

I have been blessed with hard work on my behalf by agent Marlene Stringer and editors Chris Werner and Melody Guy—all of you make my writing infinitely better. Thanks to the whole team at Montlake for believing in me and getting my work out there. Huge thanks always to the ultimate first reader, Dianne Ludlam, who can spot a plot hole at a thousand paces (Pensacola or bust!), and to Deborah Brooks, who is always ready to read and offer sound advice. Special thanks to longtime law enforcement officer, author, and consultant Wesley Harris at Write Crime Right, for steering me through the world of law enforcement procedure and terminology (as always, any errors are purely a result of my own stubbornness). Finally, thanks to the support of the Southern Magic RWA chapter in Birmingham and to my Auburn Writing Circle crew Larry Williamson, Shawn Jacobsen, Robin Governo, Matt Kearley, and Julia Thompson—especially Matt and Shawn and their firsthand knowledge of snakes and gators and the speed at which things will be dissolved by alligator stomach acids. Which proves one never knows when one's expertise will come in handy.

ABOUT THE AUTHOR

Susannah Sandlin is most widely known for her two award-winning series, The Penton Vampire Legacy (paranormal romance) and The Collectors (romantic suspense). She is a three-time winner of the Holt Medallion and a finalist for an RT Reviewers' Choice Award in both 2014 and 2015. As Suzanne Johnson, she has also written the Sentinels of New Orleans urban-fantasy series and several urban-fantasy novellas. *Black Diamond* is the second book in her Wilds of the Bayou series.

A longtime New Orleanian, Susannah lives in Auburn, Alabama, which explains her love of SEC football, gators, and cheap Mardi Gras trinkets. To learn more about her and her work, visit www.suzannejohnsonauthor.com.

11/16